PETER ALFRED
SCHNEIDER

THE ADJUSTER

novum pro

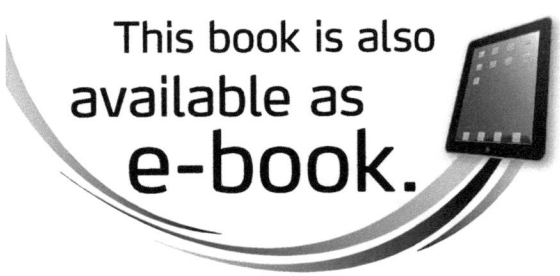

This book is also available as e-book.

www.novum-publishing.co.uk

© 2023 novum publishing

ISBN 978-3-99131-987-0
Editing: Yarach Atarah
Cover photos: Bowie15, Martingraf, Rudi1976, Bjorn Hovdal, Skrypko Ievgen, Tomas1111 I Dreamstime.com
Cover design, layout & typesetting: novum publishing

www.novum-publishing.co.uk

Climate neutral
Print product
ClimatePartner.com/16547-2201-1002

TO MARLON

THE ADJUSTER STARTS.

A Novel by Peter A. Schneider.

CHAPTER 1

Paul Winter sat in his favourite chair, a coffee brown leather swivel chair, doing what he liked most: watching out of the window.

He looked out and enjoyed the panoramic view from the large bifold windows. They faced northeast, towards the tall buildings and trees, which were now almost leafless. It was early September, around nine o'clock, and the temperature was already at 30°C. It was a desert climate, and he hated that sort of heat. It made breathing and sleeping difficult. As a matter of fact, almost everything was made difficult.

Next year, in February, it would be 20 years since his arrival in Brazil. It felt like an eternity. He would also be turning 60 in February, although most people said he looked closer to 50. He was tall, standing at 1.80 m without any boots, and weighed 79 kilos, with little fat but a rather muscular body – not like a security guard, more like a runner. His face was well defined: a good nose; thin lips; dark blond hair, with streaks of grey beginning to show; blue-greenish eyes, that started to fade a bit. Things had gone reasonably well in those 20 years; raising a family, doing lucrative business...

He had arrived at the airport with two large suitcases and $5,000 in cash. In one of the suitcases, he had brought a drill, a German model. He liked that one and would not leave it behind. The customs officer had mistaken it for a gun . drew his pistol, told him to back off, while he examined it. That was his first impression of the new land: nervous people with a big imagination, something that could come in handy later when dealing with the locals.

Helen, his second wife, had picked him up at the airport.

They stayed a night in Sao Paulo, and on the next day, took a bus to Curitiba, the Capital of the State of Paraná, to the south. He had read that the climate there was more European-like, with clearly defined seasons and acceptable, not too high temperatures.

However, upon arriving it was raining hard, with the temperature at around 14°C, staying that way for a whole ten days. "Too cold, too wet," he thought, "for that kind of climate, I could just as well have stayed in my home country." So, he asked his wife to pack the bags, and they made it to Goiania, Capital of Goiás, which was to the north, much closer to the equator, with a hot climate throughout the year.

Thinking back now, sitting in his chair, he made the correct decision. Goiania, in the early 2000s, was a so-called developing state, with a strongly growing economy, mainly based on agriculture. The prices for food, land, apartments, and services were still low and very attractive. When he had left Switzerland, in the early 2000s, he was exactly 40, with a solid 24-year banking career to show for it. He had started out at 16 as an apprentice, and they had taught him most of the tasks a bank would perform in the mid-70s. He completed his training and education with the second best score of his year. For this achievement, his employer gave him an extra Fr. 50 per month, bringing his initial salary to Fr. 1,950 – not bad for a young fellow of just 19, with ambitions and good looks, and a very keen interest in girls.

He started to work right away, in the letters of credit department – an activity that would later open the doors to international finance, travel, substantially more money, and women, he hoped. He worked hard and fucked any female that crossed paths with him in the department. He even had an affair with the personal secretary of Director Brunner Elisabeth, Beth, as he called her. She would phone him from her internal phone, just across a few other desks, in the very department, in plain sight of everybody else, telling him to visit her tonight, after work. She would cook dinner, and do everything he and, most importantly, she had in mind.

This charade went on for a few months until he got tired of her. It also became more complicated and dangerous to hide their affair from their other colleagues in the department, let alone Brunner, who started to look ever more suspiciously at his personal secretary, who arrived in the morning with black circles under her eyes, making ever more mistakes in the letters he dictated to her.

Then, on the verge of his 20th birthday, Paul was drafted into the Army.

CHAPTER 2

Paul never took any women too seriously, at least in the beginning, and he also did not take his drafting into the army too seriously. Besides, he knew it was coming; it was scheduled long ago; so he went to the medical military examiner's test, passed with flying colours, and was assigned to the 37th Regiment of Infantry Mountaineers, based in Chur, capital of the state of Graubünden.

He packed a bag, said goodbye to Beth and all the others, and took the train to Chur. The bank, though, was obliged to pay him his full salary during army service. In addition, the military service would render SFr. 3.50 a day to begin with.

Arriving in Chur shortly after 1 p.m. the shouting began. On that day, some 20,000 young men arrived at more or less the same hour. It was chaotic to run to that barrack, wait, then go to yet another barrack, and so on and so on. He learned on that first day that shouting was more important than thinking, and that it was better to follow instructions than have an opinion, at least officially. By midnight, all the new soldiers had been given three different sets of uniforms, two pairs of walking boots, a backpack, tools, gasmask, and helmet, etc. The weapons would only be handed out the next day. So his first day in the army ended. Exhausted, he dropped into his bunk and fell asleep immediately.

The 37th regiment was a Zürich based regiment, so the bulk of his fellow soldiers were from that region. There was, though, one battalion from the canton of Tessin in the south of the country. They spoke Italian, rather than German, and some of these recruits were allocated to his company, which was Company C. One of those recruits was even an Italian native, who somehow made it into the Swiss Army. He must have been given citizenship, so he was drafted.

The next day, everybody was handed his weapon over the flag of the Swiss Confederation, at the time a 59 SIG semi-automatic assault rifle. This was a very heavy weapon, weighing over 8 kilos, with a large 7.8 mm calibre, perfect for battle and long range, precise shooting, but heavy to carry and difficult to service.

So the days went by, shooting, running, fighting, marching, theoretical enemy reconnaissance – it was unclear who the enemy in the eyes of the Swiss army was, so the high command created some fictitious army name from the east to concentrate on.

Paul was not too bothered with all of that army business; he was strong, healthy, fast, and a good observer. The endurance marches of 40 km plus did not give him any trouble. He liked the shooting exercises, and always scored high, a quality that would later in life become useful to him.

The weeks and months went on, and his superiors became ever more aware of him, until, during the 3. last week of his basic army training, came the proposal. The proposal was a letter signed by the regiment's colonel and his captain, proposing that Paul become a Swiss Army officer, a lieutenant. None of his friends in the company had received the proposal; in fact, nobody knew he had received it. The proposal suggested that he underwent the two-and-a-half-year officer's course, beginning next year, here in Chur. They gave him 24 hours to accept or, very unlikely in his superiors' minds, decline.

Now, for Paul, the fun was gone. He considered it carefully, had a sleepless night, and early the next morning walked into the captains and higher officers' card room and politely declined the offer, alleging that he was being sent abroad to London by his employer to study international trade – a brave lie. What Paul wanted was to get back to normal civilian life as quickly as possible, making money and a career and, most of all, being with the ladies. He could not see himself wasting two and a half of his best years in that dreadful old casern of Chur, learning how to soldier professionally. His captain looked at him and the written, signed denial of the proposal, very awkwardly and angrily, if not disappointedly, and dismissed him. From that moment on, for the last three weeks of his service, his superiors looked at him with disgust and ignored him. He had become the odd bird.

Two weeks later, he got his discharge papers – 20,000 hip hip hurrahs, and off he went, together with his pal Morelli, to Grauboden. It was a 15-minute walk away from the barracks, towards the car park, with a full backpack, his rifle, and his army bag containing his personal belongings. Paul walked fast, almost running, trying to avoid the massive traffic jam that would no doubt build up with all these men and their cars more than keen to leave the place as fast as possible.

Opening the boot of his dark blue '73 Alfa Romeo 1750 GTV, Morelli put all their belongs in there, while Paul started the powerful engine. It came to life immediately with a loud roar. Morelli got into the passenger seat with a jump. His main task was to provide the ice cold Hürlimann beers and Marlboro reds, which he did. Paul headed north through the suburbs and took the A1 east and then north. The Alfa Romeo would easily go over 200 km/hour, so it would take Paul about 70 minutes to get to Zürich and civilian life. On this cold Saturday morning, traffic was light. They made it to Zürich just before 11 o'clock and said goodbye.

Paul and Morelli would stay friends over the next 12 years; the yearly one-month army repetition course and their common interest in girls and hanging out would tie them together.

CHAPTER 3

Half an hour later, Paul arrived at his good-sized, one-bedroom apartment. It had a balcony, a dining area, a living room with two good windows, and one bathroom. He had rented it just before being drafted, so Paul had looked forward to enjoying his home. It was situated in a good neighbourhood, a bit up from the city centre, on the slopes of the local mountain. He took a shower, stored his army items, and phoned Susi, his current girlfriend, to advise her that he would be arriving to pick her up. It was a sheer delight; dinner, a few bars, and then they went to Paul's flat to do what they liked best – fucking. Susi was an easy-going girl, with brown hair, big tits, a round arse, and not too bright or ambitious. She was very happy that they were finally together again. The eight months of separation due to Paul's army service had driven her crazy. More than once, when Paul was on guard duty during the weekend, she had driven down to Chur to see him while he was making his guard rounds outside the casern. They would sneak into some abandoned barn and do it right there. In this regard, Susi was a no-nonsense girl, with no time to waste.

Lying in bed with him now, she was hoping that he would stay now, for a good time, if not forever. She loved him and had plans for the two of them.

Paul, though, had quite different plans. These did not include Susi.

On Monday morning, he shaved, put on one of his better suits, a white shirt and dark blue tie, and went off to work in his old department at the bank after more than eight months. Throughout these months, his employer had deposited his full salary, and by law they were obliged to guarantee his job on his return.

His old desk was almost the way he had left it. The colleagues were all there to greet him, the men more reservedly, and the women more warmly. Beth had, in the meantime been sacked by her boss Brunner. Rumour had it that the old bastard had made advances, which she refused; so she was sacked and had to go.

He settled in to work, read all the new information and instructions, and had lunch in the intern canteen with his colleagues.

After work, he went for a beer or two, in one of his favourite bars downtown. After a few rounds, Daniel, one of his old pals from the bank, walked into the bar. They hugged each other and sat down at a small round table in the far corner from the bar, starting to talk.

They had not seen each other in almost a year, so there was lots of ground to cover. Daniel told him all the latest gossip, rumours, internal intrigues, undeserved promotions, and so on. He was a good seven years older than Paul and knew the internal machinations of the bank better than anybody else. Although it was interesting news, somehow it left Paul strangely detached, unimpressed and not really interested.

Somehow, after Daniel had left, Paul felt that maybe it was time for him to move on to more exciting jobs. A smaller outfit, foreign perhaps; more challenging, faster promotion, more cash. He paid for the beers and walked out of the bar. By now it was almost midnight, raining hard, and utterly cold. He had brought no overcoat, so he hurried to the tram station nearby, took one of the last connections, and arrived home, going straight to bed. Tomorrow was another day, but still he was thinking; leaving his present employer now was out of the question. He had to stay at least a year, but nothing could prevent him from starting to look around.

14

CHAPTER 4

The High Life was a night club, ducked under a 20-metre-high express motorway built right above the river, with its immense concrete pillars standing right in the water of the river. Every time Paul looked at this marvellous piece of Swiss engineering he was stunned. Why pay for and buy expensive land, or dis-appropriate landowners if you could build the expressway right above the river, following its natural course?

The club was in an old residential building, built some 80 years ago. There were no neighbouring buildings, and nobody would ever go near the club if it was not for dog walkers during the day. One reached the building by a service road, no cars allowed, so Paul had parked his car some 300 metres away and walked at a leisurely pace, up to the bouncer at the entrance. A tall, bald Serbian with shoulders as broad as a garage door, and arms as thick as a car tyre. When he spotted Paul, he waved. Paul approached him, ignoring the queue that had already built, gave Tito a tenner when they shook hands, and in he was. He went straight to the cashier's booth, where a woman in her forties with short bleach blonde hair and glasses accepted his SFr. 20 note and gave him a rubber stamp on his right wrist. Tonight's stamp was a blue dragon in a green circle.

The club consisted of three different set-ups. The ground floor housed the dance floor, with the DJ and his equipment in the right corner. It was huge, with a state-of-the-art sound system and strobe lights shining from the ceiling. The windows were blacked out with thick black paint and could not be opened. There were four doors leading to the toilets. Walking up the narrow staircase, fitted with dark red carpet and golden hand railings, there was the first floor, with the main bar. A huge counter, with at least 30 chairs in front of it.

There were three barmen working nonstop. Scattered around the bar were round, black wooden tables with either two or four chairs. He ordered a gin and tonic, sat down at the bar, and relaxed. Saturday night was the best night of the week, with money in his pocket, and him keen to have a good time.

Shortly after 12:30 am, Martin Affolter walked in. They had agreed earlier to meet in the club. Paul waved to Martin, who sat next to him at the bar.

"You look like a man with pussy on his mind. See anything interesting?" Paul greeted him. Martin said nothing, just grinned. In any case, he was not much of a talker. He was slightly taller than Paul, maybe 1.82 metres tall, with dark, full hair, sad brown eyes, and a thin moustache. Paul liked his quiet ways. They had met downtown shortly before he went off to the Army, and had stayed in touch ever since. Martin ordered his usual vodka on ice. He said vodka would smell less on his breath if the police stopped him to look at his registration papers, and his old, worn down Toyota Corolla.

They sat down on the smaller round chairs, starting to look around. By now, the high life night club was already packed, the action in full swing.

The music pumped loud from downstairs. Lots of girls were at the bar by now, working hard to have fun. Tall, short, fat, slim, beautiful, acceptable, and straight out ugly, with the assorted guys around them, like flies on dog shit. A mixed bag of young people from all walks of life; employees, waitresses, bus drivers, clerks, salesmen, public service assholes, hookers and whores, and the local dealer, a short, skinny man by the name of Mouse. He was accepted by the club owner, as long as he was discreet. His role was an additional feature to the club. Paul looked at the girls, and saw one that interested him: a medium-sized dark brunette in a short red skirt, a yellow blouse with no bra and very open in the front, and high heels. She had a good-sized, round arse. He would try to talk to her later, but right now he gestured to Mouse to follow him. They finished their drinks, heading upstairs to the second floor, Mouse following right behind. Paul gave Tin a 100 Franc note and told him to get 1g of blow. Tin entered the male bathroom, Mouse following. After two minutes they both came out, deal done. They were to have a good time tonight; coke was for strictly recreational purposes, never during the week. The second floor also had a bar, a smaller one though, with round tables. Its main feature was the large comfortable sofas and couches where one could chill out and relax, have a private conversation, and become more friendly with your chosen one for the night. Paul ordered another round of drinks, the usual. The room was very dark, dimly lit by small lights set into the walls; cosy and relaxing, you could barely see your hand in front of your face. They did a few rounds of coke, good stuff, and chatted about nothing in particular: football, places to go, maybe a trip together to Frankfurt, and so on and so forth. Then the brunette, out of nowhere, sat down on one of the bar chairs. She ordered a whisky on ice and lit a cigarette.

"Here we go," thought Paul, a man who wouldn't waste time if he could avoid it. He told Tin to sit tight and approached the brunette. Paul was wearing a light blue shirt, open in the front, and a lightweight, dark blue Italian suit, despite the cold weather of January. He sat down next to her and introduced himself.

She said her name was Tania, and by her accent he could immediately tell that she was Yugoslavian. He liked that, and always took what he could get. She had a lovely face, brown eyes, full lips; she was also slightly drunk. By that time, Tin had chatted up some blonde, probably a whore judging by the loud, too-short dress she was wearing, but he was occupied, so Paul could concentrate on Tania.

Tania said she was a waitress in one of the large restaurants in the city centre. He thought he had heard of it, but he wasn't too sure. She said she had a younger brother and a sister almost her age, and that she was here with a female friend who was drinking downstairs. She then asked Paul if he wanted to go down to dance. Paul told the waiter, Bruno, to keep their drinks, and off they went to shake their bodies.

It was good American disco music, the latest hits. They had danced two songs, starting to sweat, when the DJ put on a slow Scorpions song. Paul liked that song. He pulled Tania tight to his chest. She was a good dancer, smooth. They kissed long and intensely, and he touched her arse, which she did not mind. When the music stopped, they went back upstairs for a few more drinks and two lines of coke, which Tania gladly accepted. She said she didn't do drugs, that this was her first time, but watching her snort the lines up like a vacuum cleaner it was clear to Paul that she was no beginner.

By now, Tin and the whore were nowhere in sight – they had probably already gone to some sleazy fleabag place to get down to it. No problem, Paul would call tomorrow night. By now, it was almost 6 a.m. and the club was about to close. They left, walking, if not stumbling towards the car, entering it immediately. They started kissing again, Paul caressing her breasts. She was squeezing his dick, which was hard by now, eager for action. The Alfa Romeo was a two-seater sports car, no way to fuck in there, not enough room, and it was too cold and risky to fuck her outside the car, with the sun coming up already. She pulled her skirt up to her belly, showing a full black bush, no panties. She blew him right then, and he came in her mouth. Opening the door, she spat the cum out and took a Kleenex from her purse to wipe the excess cum off her lips. They held each other for a while, then drove off to the outskirts of town where Tania lived. Tania said she wanted to see Paul again and gave him her telephone number, written on one of her tissues. Paul said yes, he wanted to, took her number, and kissed her goodbye. She stood there in the cold morning light and waved. Paul accelerated the car, turned round a bend and, out of her sight, threw the Kleenex with her telephone number out of the window.

Tomorrow would be another day. He drove home, took a shower, and went straight to bed.

CHAPTER 5

Paul Winter sat at his desk in the office, analysing the letters of credit in front of him.

Mueller, his direct supervisor, had dumped them on his desk early this morning, saying it had to be concluded by 4 p.m. today. Arrogant, shitfaced asshole, this Mueller, but Paul had to play ball. He wanted to impress Director Brunner, so he would sign the authorisation papers to send Paul on a four-month intensive course at the University of Cambridge, England, fully paid by the Bank, in order for him to get his proficiency certificate in English. The first certificate in English was already his. He needed that certificate if he was to work for a foreign institution, which he intended to be able to achieve in the next seven months. The LC papers and the freight documents in front of him on his desk were written in some Creole French and poor English, dealing with an export of high value timber from Mozambique to the importer in Germany. The German company paid a very good fee to the Swiss bank for them to check and make sure all the papers were in order. It was a nightmare, but Paul had almost concluded his analysis and was ready to sign them off when his phone rang. It was Martin Affolter.

"What's up, man?" Paul asked.

Tin mumbled, "I'm gone, gone."

He wasn't making sense. "Talk straight, and speak into the phone set," Paul said. Tin's voice was strangely muffled, as if he was talking through a piece of cloth. "Talk, and tell me what's going on."

"They sacked me this morning, gave me 30 minutes to clear my desk and take my shit. No compensation, nothing, just fuck off. I'm done, finished."

"Why would these fuckers do that? What happened, Tin?"

"I felt down this morning, hungover, needed a drink, so I took one of those big brown internal envelopes for distributing mail, stuffed it with some newspaper cuttings, said I had to deliver this, and left the building by the service lift. I went straight to Joe's Bar and Restaurant, had a few beers, I swear nothing more, and after roughly an hour and a half, left the bar and went back to the bank."

"An hour and a half?" Paul asked.

"Yes, not more, but I was perhaps a little bit tipsy. When I was about to enter the service lift, who stood there was Selig, my supervisor. He took me straight to Bemmer, the department head, and on the way up he said, 'Beers any good?' Bemmer sat me down in front of him, opened the envelope, seeing it contained shit, and said, 'Affolter, you are fired with immediate effect. Leaving the premises during duty is unacceptable. Don't expect any recommendation letter. You don't want to know what I have to say about you, you lousy, lazy, cheating drunk. Get out of here now.' And that was that. Now I'm back at Joe's," Tin said.

Paul thought long and hard, letting Tin hang on the line. Finally, he said, "Pay and go home straight away – and stay home. I will call in two days, see what I can set up for you. Don't get your hopes up too high. You fucked up real good this time," and hung up.

Paul finished the LC docs, signed them off, handed them to Mueller without a word, not even looking at the slimy shitter, and called it a day. He walked to his car, smoking a cigarette. Shit. He had to help Tin, the guy would go under, no chance.

It would not be easy, though. Tin had no credits or referrals to speak of. "All he has is his loyalty," Paul thought, entering the car. He already had an idea of how to sort his friend out. He drove off, heading straight to his flat. No drinking tonight, he had some thinking to do.

After two days, he called Tin, giving him a telephone number, name, and address, and told him to present himself the next day at nine o'clock sharp. If he didn't act too dumb, he might get himself a new job. He also said to call after the meeting. On Friday morning at 10:15, Tin called, saying they had given him the job. He would like to thank Paul and buy the drinks and food. Paul said good, and that was that. Paul felt that Tin would remain very grateful to him for a long time to come, and continue to do what he always did; distributing and despatching the mail to the various internal departments of his new employer.

After he called Paul, he was not keen on going home to his shitty little one-bedroom apartment in the working-class suburb of Urdorf. He had parked his car in the public garage at Sihlstrasse. It was a beautiful late summer day. Later today they would have drinks and dinner, so he had a few hours to walk around, getting his feelings and thoughts organised. When he reached a public phone booth, he entered and called his mother. When he went home on the dreadful day he was sacked, he had stopped at his mother's house. She lived in the same small town, a few blocks down the road. She had cried and almost collapsed; her only child without a job, and her being over seventy, in poor health, living off the small social benefits the city council would pay her. She was a frail woman suffering from a bad heart, with grey hair combed back into a tight knot, always in that greyish long dress and sandals. She would rarely go out, only to do the groceries.

She spent most of her time cleaning that small social project flat and waiting for Tin to pay her a visit. When he called, giving her the good news, she started crying again, this time for joy, and said to invite Paul to visit, as she knew what they both liked to eat.

Tin said OK, hung up and stepped out of the telephone booth. Gripping an envelope under his arm, this time containing his new job contract, he walked up Bahnhofstrasse just to ease his mind, looking at the expensive shop windows; Rolex, Tissot, Omega, Breitling, and the like, some of those costing more than he earned in a full year. He also watched the high-class ladies with their expensive Chanel and Gucci dresses, sunglasses and pearls, golden necklaces and designer shoes. A beautiful sight, way out of his league, though. Walking up the beautiful, tree-lined street, he had arrived at the upper end, where the street ended in a large square just before the lake, shimmering in the sun, a light blue, reflective mass of light. He had a beer and a sausage in one of the stalls in front of the lake. The next boat would leave in 25 minutes, doing the grand lake tour of four hours. That sounded just right. It would bring him back in time to meet Paul later in the afternoon. He paid for his ticket and stepped onboard. He chose a seat outside, at the edge of the great ship's hull, giving him a good position to watch the lake and the villages they would pass on their journey. For the first time in many days, he felt at ease, looking more positively to the future, and being very grateful to Paul.

After he had had lunch, the daily special, he sat outside again on one of the many wooden chairs, this time at the rear end of the vessel. They were by now already approaching Rapperswil, the city that lay on the far south side of the lake, where the long bridge connecting the west and east sides divided the main lake from its smaller section, the Obersee. Some ten thousand years ago, all this water had been a huge glacier coming right down from the Alps, brushing aside all the earth and stones, forming the two hilly slopes facing each other that now housed some of the best and most expensive villas, overlooking the lake from their respective sides.

Contemplating the view and the big Swiss flag fluttering on its mast at the starboard, he thought of his poor mother and his father. He had few memories of his father, a steel worker at Brown

Boveri who had died when Tin was just ten. He also thought of Anton Meier, Hunchback Tony, as he was known, due to his curved back. Tony and Tin had grown up together and had attended the same elementary school. He had bumped into Tony on the main street the day after he was sacked. They went for a coffee, and Tin told him about his misfortune, having no job and no money. As a matter of fact, he said he was broke. Tony listened to his friend's litany, and then said money was short for a lot of people, but not for Migros, the largest supermarket in the country. Tony worked for them, not in one of their many branches, but in the huge distribution centre, right here in Urdorf.

Tin asked, "Why do you say money isn't short for Migros?"

Tony bragged, "I myself see lots of cash every month, since it is me who delivers it to the personnel department at the distribution centre."

Tin tried not to look surprised, although he almost fell off his chair, hearing that piece of information. He only said, "Some people have it, and most don't," and said goodbye, though not without mentioning, that he would like to see Tony for a beer next week, talking about old times.

The hunchback said "Great," and walked out, happy and cheerful about meeting his friend soon again.

The vessel now approached Buerkliplatz, where it had started out, ending the grand tour. Tin was still deep in thought about the hunchback's info, but he could not piece it together. It was almost six now, time to meet Paul. If Tin knew one thing about Paul, it was that he indeed understood money. He would tell him everything he had learned straight away.

Stepping off the boat, Tin would slowly walk over the bridge that led to Bellevue Square, still clinching the envelope tightly under his arm. They had agreed to meet at Kronenhalle Bar, an elegant, trendy place Tin had chosen to thank Paul. He had borrowed SFr. 200 from his mother, who had reluctantly given it to him when Tin explained what he needed it for.

He walked into the bar, which had begun to fill up already. The headwaiter of the bar, in his immaculate white apron, greeted him. The room was fitted with dark wood panels on the walls, going way up to the high ceiling with its huge golden chandelier. Golden rails were fitted around the walls, the small tables being covered with white tablecloths. The huge bar itself was one big piece of blue Brazilian marble, with small lamps on it and dark wooden bar chairs scattered around it; a classy place. Paul had not arrived yet, so Tin choose a table to the far end of the bar, enabling them to talk while watching the sexy female secretaries chatting to each other.

Paul entered ten minutes later in one of his black Italian business suits, a white shirt, and a grey and black tie, carrying a leather briefcase, looking like a thousand Francs. An elegant figure indeed; tall, with his full blond hair combed back in a leisurely fashion, looking like nothing could bother him, and he would care for nothing. Tin had a feeling that what he was going to tell him would bother him a lot.

They ordered the drinks; the waiter bringing them in no time, along with some almonds, peanuts, and pretzels.

Tin showed him the new contract, taking it out from the now-crumpled envelope. Paul read it and said, "Good, well done," and changed the subject. After a while, talking about the girls chatting away at the bar in front of them, Tin could not control himself any longer, and started to tell the hunchback's story.

At first Paul did not pay too much attention, until the part about the cash delivery. All of a sudden, Tin had his full attention.

Paul squinted, saying, "Are you sure he does the delivery by himself? No one else riding with him?"

Tin said, "Yes."

After a long silence, Paul looked at him again, this time hard, no fun in his eyes, and said, "I want you to meet Tony next week, invent something. I need the date he delivers. You get that, maybe I can work something out." Tin agreed to work on the hunchback to get the date. "Work on him. It costs what it costs. Anything else?" Paul responded.

"No, nothing, that's all for the time being. Let's get out of here. I'm hungry."

Tin settled the bill, paying with his mother's cash, and they walked to Paul's car, parked a few blocks away. They entered it, and Paul started the engine. They shot off, roaring down the street north. They had agreed to have dinner at La Rocca. Paul turned on the radio, which played some silly sentimental music. They drove in silence until they reached the restaurant.

Paul parked nearby. It was by now eight o'clock, perfect timing. Salvatore, the owner, stood at the door, greeting them both warmly and showing them to a good-sized table. He said fresh vongole clams had been delivered this morning. Paul loved that; Tin wasn't too sure about it. He would go along with Paul's choice.

The waitress, a good-looking brunette in her early twenties, brought them two chilled glasses of Prosecco to kick it off.

They looked at the menu. La Rocca specialised in northern Italy's regional cuisine, so for starters they ordered a mixed primo piatto of ham, cheese, and two types of salami. The segundo dish would be the spaghetti alle vongole. They choose ossobuco with polenta and assorted vegetables for their main dish, and to drink, a nice cold bottle of white Pinot Grigio from the Veneto. For the main course, Paul also chose a Brunello de Montalcino. After all, they had something to celebrate.

When the waitress brought the spaghetti, the whole restaurant seemed to smell of garlic, parsley, olive oil, and white wine; delicious. They dug in and drank the wine. Paul could not help looking at the waitress. Good body, medium height, nice face, and long straight hair. When they left the restaurant, Paul slipped his phone number into her hand, whispering he had something to show her. Once again, Tin settled the bill, and they drove off to the public parking garage where Tin had left his car early that morning. What a day! When they hugged each other goodbye, Paul asked Tin to call him as soon as he got the information requested. Tin said he would call immediately.

Paul drove off, his mind going at a 100 km per hour. This Sunday morning, all being quiet, he would go on a recon tour to Urdorf, alone. He knew more or less where the distribution centre was, but he needed to check the surrounding roads, buildings, and the vegetation along the road, for size and distance. He was getting excited.

CHAPTER 6

At 8:30 on Sunday morning, Paul drove the Alfa Romeo to Urdorf. On the motorway, heading southwest, it would take 14 minutes to reach the village. Everybody asleep, no sound but the church bells ringing, he drove down the main street, where the banks were.

One of these banks would hand the money out to the hunchback.

He then drove towards the intersection on the outskirts, where the town's roads connected to the motorway in both directions. Somewhere before the intersection must be the road that connected to the distribution centre. When he slowly approached the intersection, he saw it, about 40 metres off the crossing. It was not prohibited to drive down that road, there not being a no entry sign, but there was a sign saying dead end road. Few cars would take a road leading to nowhere and a dead end. Paul, however, did. It was narrow, just barely allowing a big lorry to pass through. On the left side was the motorway, going north, fenced off by a steel fence. To the right were fields with fruit trees and grass. No buildings. Good.

Paul put the car in second gear, driving slowly. The road was lined on both sides with big trees, with small bushes, about 1.20 metres high, between the trees. Good again.

As Paul reached a curve, he slowed down even more. After the curve, the distribution centre came into sight. A huge, low-lying greyish building, with big ramps for the lorries to make deliveries.

It had to be done just before the curve. No other spot possible. Slowly, a plan began to take shape in his head. He turned the car around and headed back, at normal speed now, took the highway and sped off. He had to wait for the call.

Wednesday morning, nine o'clock, the phone rang. It was Tin, alright. "I met with Tony last night." Tin said.

"Not a word on the phone," Paul snapped, "meet me at the Zeughauskeller at noon today," and hung up.

Paul had arrived 15 minutes early. He wanted a quiet table, almost impossible in that huge room that must hold more than 200 tables. The place was already busy. Zeughauskeller, or Arsenal Cave, had been operating at the same place for over 150 years straight. It was one of the oldest and most traditional places. The walls were adorned with weapons dating back to the 15th century and through to the present day. Spears and lances, full armours, Hellebarden. The spiked lead balls on metal chains, to smash the skull of the enemy. Swords, daggers of all sizes and shapes. A cannon hung from the high ceiling; suspended in mid-air were the Swiss regiments' original banners and colours, all of them; the more modern weaponry, a complete heavy machine gun, up to assault rifles, from the early versions to the one Paul kept in his wardrobe at his flat, like any other Swiss army member did. The sight of all this weaponry brought him into just the right combat mood.

He saw his pal Tin entering one of the heavy wooden doors and waved. They shook hands.

Tin said, "I met the hunchback last night for beers. He will ride alone in the truck, definitely. Only when he's sick or on leave would Martin, his substitute, come in ... never together."

"What about the date of delivery?" Paul asked.

"Well, I had to get him quite a few drinks, but in the end he said cash delivery, always on the 22nd of the month. No exceptions.

If the 22nd falls on a weekend or holiday, they move it up one day, but never after."

"Good," said Paul. "Let's have lunch."

They both ordered the roasted sausage with potato salad house special and two large beers. When they finished, Paul consulted the small calendar he had brought along. The 22nd fell on a Thursday, today being the fifth of the month. That would give them about three weeks to plan the heist. He would call it the Migros job.

"Did he say how much is in the case?" Paul asked.

"No, he does not know, but says it s heavy," Tin replied.

"OK," Paul said. "I don't want you to go near the distribution centre. Stay away. They know you in Urdor.I check out the flow of lorries, their timetables. What I need from you is your bicycle. From today on, leave it outside your house, near the garbage bins, under that tree, unlocked. I will use it. I can't drive around in the Alfa Romeo, draws too much attention. You will have to hire a car, I will tell you one day before. Pay cash and get it in a different town, not Urdorf – most probably Spreitenbach. I will check and let you know. You will have to stay low. Just get a piece of sewer pipe about 40cm long and 5cm thick. The rest I will provide. And Tin, not a word to anyone, I mean anyone, not even your mother's dog. I will call."

Paul paid the bill, and they said goodbye and walked off in different directions. Paul headed back to work, and Tin to the nearby quarter of Niederdorf, just to wash the excitement down a bit.

On Saturday morning at nine o'clock, Paul, having had his first coffee, was sitting at his dining table and thinking hard. He knew that the distribution centre operated 24/6, the only day off being Sunday. They operated three shifts, each eight hours long. When Tin had asked Tony about the workers, he said they were mostly Yugoslavians and Albanians. The workers loaded and unloaded the heavy crates and packages on the lorries. It was unskilled work but demanded good physical condition. Hunchback had said each shift had roughly 50 workers, because the bus that collected them at the train station had a maximum seating capacity of 52, including the driver, giving a total of 150 workers, plus three foremen.

Paul knew that most of the Yugoslavs and Albanians did not speak proper German, even after many years in Switzerland. Many of them could not read and could only write their own names. They were not well educated, and highly suspicious of anything official, like governments and banks. Most of them did not even have a bank account. If at least half of them had no bank account, that would make about 75 people getting cash. An average of SFr. 2,000 a month per head meant that in the hunchback's delivery bag was, in any given month, a clean SFr. 150,000, Paul figured. Not bad, and very tempting.

Yesterday he had told that asshole Mueller that he would take a week off. That would give him six full days to check the road movement – the times of the comings and goings and the number of cars. Thinking now, he decided he was going to buy two black ski masks. The plan was taking shape. Timing was of the essence. They had to watch the banks, making sure the hunchback came out with the bag, speed ahead, set up the trap and wait. They could not be early and wait too long – they would risk being seen by somebody walking his dog – or arrive late, with Tony having passed already. It was tricky, all depending on time and a bit of luck. He would start early Monday morning, around 3:30 a.m., when it was still dark. He had to get this right. He also hoped Tin had left the bicycle where he needed it to be. That was all for today; any further action had to wait until Monday morning.

The weather was still good and warm. He would go to one of the lidos on the lake, take a swim, and watch the bikini girls – check whether there was anything worth grabbing.

Monday morning, 2:40 a.m., the alarm rang. Paul put on some dark-coloured jeans, boots, and an AC/DC world tour '80 T-shirt. He poured his hot coffee into a thermos, then wrapped the sandwich he had prepared in tin foil. All this went into his backpack, together with a pair of binoculars, a bottle of water, and a book. He closed the door, locked it, and went down the stairs and out into the fresh cool night.

Strolling around the block to where he had parked the car, he got in, put the backpack behind his seat, and turned the ignition key. The engine did not start. "Shit, don't let me down now," Paul thought, and turned the key again. On the third try, the engine sputtered to life.

Once the job was done, he would change cars, buy the newer model, the Alfa GTV 2 litre engine. He would also rent a bigger, better apartment in one of the classy Zürichberg locations overlooking the lake. Yes, that was a thought, but first he had to get this heist done. He drove through the dark streets, heading to Escher-Wyss-Platz, where he'd take the motorway, strictly sticking to the speed limit. He did not want to get stopped and searched by a police patrol.

He entered the motorway with almost no traffic. It was 3:40 now; he would hit Urdorf around 4 a.m.

He parked the car in a public car park about two blocks from Tin's apartment, far away from the entrance behind a large black Buick. The Alfa tucked away, out of sight behind the big car. Paul took his backpack and walked quickly towards Tin's place; he could only pray that the bicycle was where it should be.

There it was. He mounted it and pedalled away, first through smaller streets and then to the main road leading to the intersection roundabout. He reached it in 20 minutes and took the road that led to the distribution centre. Just after the curve, he ditched the bike in a bush and crept up the slope leading to the open field. He chose a big apple tree to lay down under in the soft grass. It was 4:30 now, still dark, with orange light coming up on the eastern horizon. He lay very still, took out his notebook and binoculars, and started watching the centre.

Nothing. Not a sound. Then, at exactly 5 a.m., four of the big ramp doors opened almost simultaneously. Out came the first lorry, the Migros sign on both sides, headlights on, slowly heading towards his hideaway post. Minutes later the second lorry came into sight, and a few minutes later the third and finally the fourth. All of them in one unique procession, surely a routine they would not break.

It was by now 5:29 a.m., with the early morning sun already up. The four ramps were closed. Paul noted the time in his notebook and opened the thermos, pouring a hot, steamy cup of coffee. He drank it in silence with his binoculars aimed at the centre, while also observing the road in the other direction. Ten minutes later, a lorry approached from the other side of the road, heading towards the centre. A few minutes later another one came, then a third... a fourth... and a fifth. They all disappeared on the other side of the logistics centre, which must be the delivery side, bringing in fresh supplies. At 6:20 a.m. all action seemed to stop, and it was quiet again. No movement on the road, no early dog walkers, nothing, just utter silence. At 7:25, the company bus came into sight, delivering the 50-plus workers to start their shift. At 7:50 a private car drove down to the centre, followed by another two, in short intervals. "These cars must belong to the manager and the foremen," Paul thought. After that, nothing, no incoming and no outgoing traffic. At

8:10, a grey VW van was heading towards the centre. That must be Tony Meier, the hunchback, starting his workday. Half an hour later, the hunchback's van was exiting again, probably delivering some documents and paperwork to the administration centre Migros had in Altstetten. That was the hunchback's job, driving around all day delivering stuff. Paul had no interest in that, though; it was not yet day 22.

He kept lying down, sipping some coffee, drinking some water, watching and observing the road and surroundings. Nothing. At 10:15, a woman with a black dog came into view, but they were very far away, at least some 600 metres. He could barely make them out with the binoculars – they could never see him. Paul stayed in his observation post until shortly after noon, then put everything back in his sack and slowly walked to the bicycle, took it, and pedalled away from the centre. He left the bike in the same spot and headed back to his car.

The banks opened at 8:30, so the hunchback would get the money bag between 9 and 9:30, counting the cash twice, and signing the forms. A pattern began to form in Paul's mind. It was possible and feasible, but risky. There were elements he could not control, timing was crucial, and it had to be done fast, flawlessly, and efficiently – but it could be done.

For the following three days, Paul repeated the observation routine, until he was sure he had the pattern down as accurately as possible. He would also have to find a place to ditch the case and everything else they would use in the heist. He would search for a dense stretch of wood and prepare a hole in the ground, ready for a quick hide after the heist was done.

The hole had to be marked. He would also hide his car near the hole, so the whole switch would take less than four minutes, give or take.

He opened the door and drove off, back to Zürich. He would call Tin later to organise a meeting, but first he wanted to buy the two ski masks and two pairs of gloves. Having that done, he would go home and do some serious planning, getting his thoughts in order. He was excited, but at the same time worried, feeling a little bit guilty. They would not kill anybody, just knock him unconscious; he guessed he could live with that.

Having completed his four days of observation, Paul knew the routine. There was no change in the operational pattern of the centre during all these days, he was sure of it. What he now needed was to find a stretch of wood a reasonable distance away. He left the bike, took the car, and passed the motorway, driving towards the outskirts of town, searching for a secondary road connecting the villages. After driving around for a while, he found an ideal spot. A narrow service road led towards the woods, marked with a no entry sign. He took it, and drove some 200 metres until the road opened a bit, giving room to turn a car. That was the spot. Not a sound, not a soul in sight. He took out the shovel he had brought along, walked a good 30 metres into the dense forest, and started digging. When he was finished, the hole was about 60 x 40cm with a depth of around 40cm; perfect to ditch the case and everything and cover it with earth. Nobody would ever find that one. He marked the spot with a wooden stick, ramming it deep into the hard ground, walked back to the car and drove off.

Earlier that morning he had called Tin and asked him to come around his place at around 9 p.m. Shortly after 9 p.m. Tin arrived, Paul opened two cans of beer, and they sat down at the dining table. Paul explained the plan in detail, leaving nothing out. Tin nodded along, now and then asking a question. Paul had a feeling Tin liked the plan, even more so when he heard about the amount of money he was to make. Again, Paul asked for no communication whatsoever; no meeting, no talking, no nothing. Lying low, going out of the flat only when it was unavoidable, but keeping the routine up with his mother. Strictly no contact with the hunchback, either. Paul then handed Tin the cash for the car rental. He said he wanted the cheapest, most common model, nothing flashy – something grey or beige, etc. The most boring colour he could find. He also told him to rent it in Spreitenbach, at that big rental place near the bridge. He should go there one day before the job, shortly before they were closing, when the clerk, after a full day's work, would just want to get out, not paying attention to yet another customer. They would use that car for the heist, with Tin returning it late the next day, throwing the keys into the return key box fixed on the inner wall near the entry gate. Before that, he would wipe the car clean as a precaution.

Paul asked whether he had any questions, if everything was clear. He should ask now, since they would not meet again before the job. All Tin said was, "Can I have another beer?" They drank their beers in silence, and then Tin left.

CHAPTER 7

At exactly 8 o'clock in the morning on day 22, they met at the spot in the forest. Paul had already turned his car to face the outgoing direction, and was leaning against it, smoking a cigarette, when Tin arrived in an old Opel Kadett, a very common, simple car.

"At least it's got wheels," Paul said, as Tin stepped out of the car. He opened the boot of the Opel and checked it – the sewer pipe was there. He then brought the masks and gloves and put them into the Opel. The blue sports bag he left in the Alfa's boot. "All set," Paul said, pointing out the hole in the woods where they would dump their gear later.

Tin said, "I'm nervous."

"Cool down, have a cigarette," Paul responded, and handed him one.

They got into the Opel, Tin driving, out of their hiding place and back into town. They parked their car 50 metres down the road from the three banks. They watched the exits, waiting and smoking. The hunchback would come out of one of those doors, carrying a full bag of cash.

The main road was busy by now, lots of people doing their errands. The sky was blue, and the sun was beating down on the Opel. They had opened the windows just a bit, to get the smoke out, but –not enough for anybody to see their faces. At exactly 9:50, they spotted Tony coming out of the bank, carrying the case – but he had an escort, probably a bank clerk. "Shit," Paul thought. But no, hunchback entered the car alone, with the bank security guy closing the van's door. He didn't start the van yet. What was he doing? The Opel's engine was already running, ready to leave the curb and speed off to the trap.

Finally, the van started to move. The Opel sped ahead; they had only about four minutes to set the trap and wait for the van. Shortly before they reached the bend leading to the distribution centre, Paul turned the Opel, blocking the road. This way, the hunchback would be unable to see the number plates.

Tin put the ski mask on, while Paul put his in the pocket of his trousers. Paul put on the large pair of sunglasses and the sports hat. He then laid down on the side of the car, facing away from incoming traffic, the left car door open. All the hunchback would see was a man lying by the side of the car, in the middle of the road. Tin was hiding behind the bushes, ski mask on, lying flat. No traffic, no sound…they waited about three minutes before the van arrived. The van came to a stop some two metres away from the car. When the hunchback got out and approached Paul, leaning over to check on him, Tin hit him hard on the left temple of his head. He cried out loud and fell next to Paul.

Paul stood up and yelled, "Get the case," opened the boot of the Opel ,put on the mask, and with the boot open, started the engine and turned the car in the other direction, motor running. "Get the case, damn it!"

"The case is attached to the base of the passenger seat, heavy chain," Tin shouted.

"Stay there!" Running to the back of the van, Paul opened the rear door, searching for the tool box, a piece of metal, anything. He found the box, and beside it, wrapped in old dirty cloth, a crowbar. He threw it to Tin. "Yank it off!" Four precious minutes had passed already. It was getting very tight now.

Finally, it came off with a loud bang, the chain still attached to the case, the other end loose. Paul took the case and the metal bar and threw them into the boot. Tin was already getting into the passenger side. Paul slammed the boot shut and sped off as fast as the little car would go, both now without glove and mask.

Just as they entered the roundabout, driving in the midst of other cars, a lorry took the road to the centre. That was very close; it would take the police no more than 12 minutes to hit the scene. Tin's hand was trembling, blood dripping from it. He had cut himself hitting the metal base of the van's chair at full force. It was not the only blood Paul saw that day. When he looked back at the hunchback, a small pool of dark blood had already formed on the asphalt beneath his head. There was also a larger pool of a more transparent liquid around Tony's knees. The hunchback had pissed himself.

Paul drove their small car at normal speed out of town, towards the forest. He entered the narrow dirt road. The Alfa was there where he had left it. He stopped the engine, and they both got out of the car. Paul opened the boot, took out everything, and headed to the hole he had dug. He found it immediately, the wooden stick still there to mark it. He had given the Alfa's key to Tin, who had already opened it, and brought over the large blue sports bag.

He threw the sewer pipe, the metal bar, the gloves, and the ski masks into the hole, but not before wiping the metal off with the cloth from the van. He then opened the grey Samsonite briefcase. It was heavy, containing nothing other than neat stacks of SFr. 500, 100, and 50 notes, to a total of SFr. 150,000, Paul figured.

All the notes were wrapped in plastic, with the logo of Kreditanstalt, his very employer, stamped on them. Paul could not help but to smile at the irony of it. But there was no time to waste. He would count the cash at home. He took out the bundles of bank notes, put them into the sports bag, then put the Samsonite case in the hole. It fit nicely there. He then took the shovel he had brought along and started to fill the hole until it was fully covered, no sign of the case any more. He then trampled over it a few times to pack down the dirt and mud. Lastly, he took a branch of a tree and scratched and whipped the ground with it, making it look just like the rest of the earth around it. Finally, he threw a few branches and leaves and dirty pieces of wood over it. Nobody could find this one. He stepped out of the underbrush with the bag under his arm, and put it behind the driver's seat in the Alfa, throwing his jacket over it for good measure.

He walked towards the Opel, Tin already at the steering wheel. His hand was bandaged with a piece of cloth. Looking at Tin, both grinning, Paul said, "We did it."

"Yes, we did," Tin replied.

"Drive straight to your place, park the car a good few blocks away, and wash your hand, get it disinfected. Then, after six, when the rent-a-car company has already closed for the day, return the car," Paul said to Tin. "I will call you tomorrow, arrange a meeting."

"OK, great," Tin said, trusting his friend. They both drove off, Tin in the direction of Urdorf and Paul away from the village. He would take the motorway back to Zürich; he did not want to go near Urdorf again.

Opening the door of his flat, he took off his dirty shoes and washed his hands. He opened the bag and put the cash on the dining table, having already closed the curtains. He stared at the pile of bank notes, and then, slowly and carefully, began to open the sealed plastic covers, putting the notes on the table. When all the notes were out, he slowly began to count them. A first time, then a second, and then a third time, just to make sure.

The number he came up with was always the same: SFr. 162,500. Holy shit. Even better than his estimate. A cool SFr. 81,250 for each of them. That kind of cash would get him right on track. He stashed the cash back into the bag and took a shower.

Next morning, waking up early, he shaved and put his grey suit on, with a pale blue shirt and a dark blue tie with white and red sections, pure silk. He felt great. He locked the door and walked out into the bright, sunny morning. Today he did not take the car, but walked to the nearest tram station and took the number 7, which brought him straight to Paradeplatz, the iconic square on the last third of the Bahnhofstrasse. He sat down at Spruengli Cafe, today's newspaper in hand. Its headline screamed: "BRUTAL AUSSAULT ON MIGROS VAN IN URDORF."

He ordered a double expresso and a croissant, and carefully started to read the paper.

Police reported that Anton Meier, the Migros driver, was in hospital with a significant injury on his forehead, but in no life-threatening condition. He would probably be released by the next day. Preliminary enquiries had revealed nothing so far. Mr. Maier did not see any of the assailants; did not know how many were involved, male or female; and did not recognise the make of the car, nor the registration plate. When asked about the colour of the car, Meier said he could not remember – he knew, though, it was not white. Nothing. Police were to make further enquiries, preliminary checks having revealed nothing. No witnesses, nobody. Police reported that it might have been an inside job. Further investigations pending. The amount of the theft was not revealed.

Paul leaned back in his chair, sipping his coffee, and smiled to himself. They had shit, and that was it. Tony would never be of any help, simply because the poor bastard really did not remember anything. In two or three months the case would blow over, police concerned with more pressing matters. Still, he would only give Tin 5,000 today, and the same amount again for the next three months. Things had to cool down in Urdorf, first; he did not want Tin to make waves there, flashing cash around. He paid for his coffee and walked to the bank, starting his workday. At nine he called Tin, and suggested to meet at Sonne Bar at six tonight for beers, to kick it off. Paul was eager to celebrate, and hopefully, get laid. He needed to get his rocks off, cool down, savour their success, and be happy.

Paul walked into the Sonne Bar just after six. Tin was already sitting at one of the tables, outside. He smiled at Paul, and they hugged.

"Well done old sport," Paul said, then ordered their first drinks , two pints of cool Huerlimann beer. They gulped it down, almost emptying half at once, then started to look around.

A few girls were chatting amongst themselves, cheaply dressed, with skirts too tight and short, heels too high, and way too much makeup. Their faces glittered in the evening sun, revealing years of abuse and bad food. The two heisters ordered another round of beers, and then Paul told Tin to go to the gents and stay there; he would follow in about two minutes.

When he entered the bathroom, Tin was washing his hands. Paul handed him a white envelope; he took it and entered one of the stalls, closing the door. Paul took a piss, washed his hands, and returned to their table. The Filipino band was now getting on stage in their glittery black and red suits, and turning on the amplifiers. Music would soon start. He had seen them perform before; now and then they missed a tone, but they were fun to listen to, and alcohol consumption increased to record levels when they were on.

When Tin came back to the table, he made a face at Paul, not too happy. "There is 77,000 plus missing," he said.

"1 know," Paul replied. "You will get 5k every 30 days until you've got 20k and three months have passed , then the rest. It's a precaution. I don't want you walking around flashing cash, trust me. No sweat. You'll get your share. You have my word." They shook hands to seal the agreement, Tin now beginning to smile again.

After the third round, they went into the bar. The Filipinos were playing Mamma Mia, girls already on the little dance floor trying to draw attention, but it was way too early in the night and they both felt hungry. They paid the bill and walked over to the nearby Metzger Halle. They ordered pork chops with baked potatoes and beers. A healthy meal of epic proportions, they would not have to eat again for the next two days!

By now it was 11 p.m., the streets bustling with people of all kinds. Whores, transvestites, drunks, junkies; black, yellow, brown, and white people; young and old, well-dressed and shabby; police sitting in their patrol cars, anti-drug squads walking with their big dogs on the leash; ordinary people seeking some fun, endless rows of them desperate not to miss any action, if there was any to have. They were walking down Langstrasse, in the red-light district of town. They entered Lugano Bar, but movement was slow – only three rather old, ugly whores with bad teeth smiling at them in desperate hope, bending over to show their tits. They ignored them, leaving the bar. Paul suggested the Olé Olé bar. When they got in, there was a good crowd. Sitting down at the bar, Paul ordered his gin and tonic and Tin had his customary vodka on ice. Music was playing loud through the speakers, good rock and roll: the Stones, Deep Purple, Creedence Clearwater Revival, etc.

They stayed on for about an hour; it was now 1 a.m. When they could not chat up any women, they went to Kreis 4 Bar and Disco. For the late hour, that was the place. After having to wait for about ten minutes in the queue that had formed at the entrance, it was their turn to enter. The place was packed. Heavy smoke mixed with cheap perfume, alcohol and sweat filled the almost unbreathable air, but there were lots of women.

They fought their way to the bar. There were no chairs, just cramped standing room. It was fun. A brunette with generous curves, her tits almost hanging out of her blouse, caught Paul's eye. He approached her, introduced himself, and walked her back to his place at the bar.

"My name's Nicole."

Paul doubted it, but said nothing. "Are you on your own?"

"No, I'm with a friend, Paula." At that moment Nicole spotted her and waved her over.

When she said hello – strong accent there – he introduced her to Tin. He took a liking immediately. The state he was in by now, he would have liked Paul's grandmother. They had more drinks and danced, Paul grabbing Nicole's arse. She didn't mind. Tin had spotted a table for four, and they ran over to take it. Sitting was much better for what he had in mind: fondling the girls' thighs under the table while they caressed the men's cocks, the music pounding away. At 3:30 the bar would close, which gave them 30 minutes to organise things with the girls. Paul had not brought his car; Tin had, but was way too drunk to drive. That left them with the option to walk or take a cab. Paul remembered a flea-bag, shithole place nearby. He did not recall the name of the street, but was sure he could find the place, a rundown building of greenish colour.

They stumbled entangled out of the bar, supporting each other. After seven minutes, he found it. Ringing the bell, it was now shortly before 4 a.m. After two minutes, an old Thai woman dressed in a night gown opened the door. Paul recognised her immediately. After negotiating the price for the room, her in half bad English, half German, Paul mumbling about, they agreed on SFr. 120. Paul put the money in her leathery brown hand,

and she smiled, opened the door, and waved them through and down the corridor, to door number 4.

The room held two single beds, a dirty, smelly bathroom, and one chair. The four of them undressed immediately and began to fuck like there was no tomorrow, each couple in one of the shaky beds. It was not Paul's best performance, but he came with a loud grunt. So did Tin, a little later; they all fell asleep, too tired and drunk to stand up and wash.

At 9:30 the leathery old Thai whorehouse watchdog and janitor, began to pound on the door, yelling about how they had to go immediately, their money only lasting until just now. Paul told her to fuck off and give them five minutes. They took a shower as best they could, money changed hands – little money though, the girls too tired and worn out to argue – and each one went his own way. No phone numbers were exchanged; if they wanted to see the women again, Paul knew where to find them.

They waved goodbye, Tin saying he would call, and Paul walked off to the nearest tram station. The streets had already been cleansed of last night's filth and rubbish. He bought the papers, stepped onboard the tram, and headed to his flat. He took a better shower and slept for the next 12 hours.

On Sunday morning he would check the advertising section, see whether he could find an apartment that interested him, one of those new terrace flats overlooking the lake. He could afford it now, after all.

CHAPTER 8

On Monday morning, arriving at his desk, he started work right away. Mueller had dumped three letters of credit cases on his desk. He quickly scanned them. "Not too complicated. OK." At noon, he had his lunch at the internal canteen. Afterwards, he went for a stroll, bought today's daily, and sat down on one of the chairs on the patio in front of the main entrance of the bank's administration centre. The sun was up, the sky blue, with only a few white clouds. Birds were chirping away in the trees, work colleagues chatting, sipping their coffees, or eating their sandwiches. Paul was not in the mood to join them.

He scanned the pages of the newspaper. Nothing on the front page, nothing on the following pages, either...then, on page nine, he found it. Under local miscellaneous: "On the assault on the Migros delivery van last Thursday in Urdorf, police report that Tony Meier has been released from hospital and given ten days' leave before he was expected to be able to get back to work. There is no remaining damage as a result of his injury. Police continue to investigate; no new leads."

Paul knew it would remain that way. He felt relieved, his mind clear and sharp. He tossed the papers in the trash bin and went back to his desk. By 5:20 p.m. he had completed the three cases and was cleaning up his desk when his internal phone rang. Director Brunner's new private secretary, Hilda, an ordinary fortyish looking woman with strange hair, was on the line.

"Hi there, Paul. Director Brunner is requesting you meet him in his office tomorrow morning at 8:30 sharp. There are urgent matters to discuss. Be punctual," and she hung up.

"Stuck-up bitch," Paul thought, intrigued by the call. He cleared up his desk, put the three LC cases, resolved and signed, on Mueller's desk, and walked out of the building. He ignored the tram station and kept on walking. The weather still being fair, he needed a walk in the fresh air, thinking about the call. Brunner calling and summoning him could mean any one of three things: 1. he would sack him – unlikely, as Paul had put in some good constant work; 2. he would get a raise – also unlikely, since he had only spent ten months in the job; or 3. his request for the bank sponsoring his proficiency course in English at the University of Cambridge had been approved. That must be it. The question was, would Brunner put any conditions on this? Paul was not interested in signing anything tying him down to his present employer. He had other, quite different plans. But first, he had to listen to the Director, talk him up, showing respect and being grateful.

Next morning at 8:15, Paul sat in one of the waiting chairs in the anteroom, staring at Hilda and waiting to be summoned. He had put on his black Italian suit, white shirt, and green and black striped tie, as well as his black leather shoes and his briefcase. At 8:23, Hilda answered the phone, nodded, and waved him in.

He entered Director Brunner's big office decorated with all kinds of certificates showing Brunner's achievements. There was also a regiment's coat of arms; no doubt Brunner, being a military man, ran the regiment as commanding Colonel.

Brunner waved Paul into one of the chairs in front of his massive dark mahogany desk, shook his hand and started, "Good morning my dear Paul, how are you today?" clearly not expecting any answer. "Good news for you, old sport," Brunner continued, "I have approved your request for a four-month intensive study programme at the University of Cambridge, all costs paid by this reputable organisation, including course costs, flights, accommodation and meals. What do you have to say to that, Paul?"

Paul had prepared himself for this moment. "I can only express my deepest gratitude to you, Director, and to all of the staff and supervisors of the department. I thank you very much indeed for giving me this opportunity, and I will strive to compensate the bank with my enduring efforts and commitment to this fine institution." With that, Paul stood up and shook Brunner's hand.

Brunner, visibly flattered by Paul, said, "You start university in a week from Monday. Flight vouchers and documents, etc., will be handed out by Hilda. And Paul, there are no commitment papers for you to sign when you come back, but I expect you to show your gratitude and continue to work hard for this department and the bank. Doing so, you have fine career prospects here, under my guidance and direction." Standing up, Brunner shook his hand again and waved him out. When Paul opened the door, he said. "Don't chase no girls in old England. This is no vacation trip. Study 24/7, nothing else, and everything will turn out just fine for us."

Hilda gave Paul some documents and asked him to bring his passport tomorrow so she could confirm and book flights, accommodation, university, etc. He said thanks and promised to bring it first thing tomorrow morning. Hilda then asked him to sign some course documents. They said goodbye, and Paul walked out of the anteroom.

He went straight to the gents and smoked a cigarette. "What the hell," he thought, "great, first the heist last week, and now this, a four-month fully paid course at university, with, according to old dog Brunner, no strings attached." He felt very good indeed, intending to call Tin later that day to give him the news and have a few beers together. He finished his cigarette and went back to his desk.

Everybody was staring at him when he crossed the main room of the department. John, a young chap with whom Paul sometimes lunched, asked what that was all about. Paul only said, with a big grin on his face, that Brunner had sent him on a trip overseas,.

Later, Paul called Tin, arranging to meet at the Bauschanze Restaurant and Bar at Bürkliplatz at six.

Having finished his workday, he walked to the Bürkliplatz. It took him more than 40 minutes, but he needed the walk, enjoying the view, his head light, and his steps determined. "What a day!" He now had five days to organise himself before the trip. The new apartment would have to wait.

He would have to buy a new, bigger suitcase, and a new raincoat. England was known for its lousy weather, but what the hell – he'd come back with the diploma in his briefcase. With that, nothing could stop him any more. He was now in for the big ride, in a foreign outfit – no more Swiss employers for the rest of his life, hopefully! He had gotten tired of them, although he had definitely liked the girls.

At the Bauschanze Bar, he gave Tin the news. Tin was happy for him, knowing that Paul wanted this diploma badly. They had their beers and said goodbye, promising to meet once again before Paul's trip, when he would hand over another ten grand. That would have to suffice until he was back.

The next Sunday night at 7:40 p.m., he took a Swissair flight from Zürich Airport to Heathrow. Arriving at Heathrow, he went through immigration, no problem, took a train to King's Cross Station, and from there, the next coach available straight to Cambridge. He arrived at Cambridge Central Station. It was by then 11:30. Passing his address to the cab driver, off they went into the dark rainy night, windy and chilly, being late October now. It took 14 minutes to get there. He paid the driver, took his suitcase and briefcase and walked to the main entrance, ring the night bell. The building was a large, brown brick construction, with three storeys and annexing smaller buildings. After a long three minutes standing in the rain, he heard some noise coming from inside, and a light went on. Shortly after, he saw a shadow behind the door, and a woman with red hair, wearing a dark blue suit with the University of Cambridge coat of arms on the front, opened the door. She introduced herself as Sally McGuire, course coordinator, and waved him in. Paul gave his name, showed his student number, and Sally ticked his name off a list she had brought along with her. She led the way, chatting with Paul about the weather, until they arrived at door number 217 on the second floor.

Sally unlocked it and let him in, handing him the keys. "The washroom and toilet are down the hall," she waved her hand in their direction, "and the refectory is at ground level, just to the left of where you came in. The kitchen opens at 7 a.m. Sit where you please. At 9 a.m., I'll meet you and your fellow students in the auditorium, also at ground level, where you will meet your colleagues, be introduced to the tutorial staff, and the class groups will be organised. See you tomorrow, and goodnight." With that, she turned and was gone.

Paul looked at the tiny room, which consisted of a small bed and tiny desk with a lamp, a chair, and a window overlooking the internal patio, with its banks and trees. "Well," Paul thought, "not exactly the five-star Hilton, but manageable and sufficient." He was here to study. No distractions, no luxury. He needed that diploma.

He washed his face in the sink, brushed his teeth, and went to bed, having set the alarm for 6:00 a.m. He slept like a stone that first night, never woke up once.

The next morning, he had his first breakfast, which consisted of a watery, weak coffee, scrambled eggs, and toast. After having finished, he walked around the building; the patio, the backside, the adjoining roads, getting his bearings. It was a big place, built some 40 years ago. In the distance, he could just make out the ancient building of the university, with its tower standing out.

Punctually, at 8:40, he went to the auditorium and chose a seat with good visibility of the stage. The large room began to fill up. All kinds of people from all over the world walked in and took seats. Indians, the girls with their bright yellow, orange and blue dresses, some wearing scarves; Germans; a group of Austrians; Czechs; Swedes; Italians; Spanish... He recognised some of the languages they spoke, but not others. What a mix.

At 8:55, the staff entered, and they all took a seat in front of them. Sally opened the meeting, greeting them all. She then introduced the teachers, a good 20 of them. After that the headmaster, Mr. John Appleby, made a speech explaining rules and procedures. Sally took the mic again, switching on the overhead projector. There were nine groups, each containing 45 students. The projector showed the assigned groups with the respective two main teachers' names, students' names, class identification, and room numbers. She asked for everybody to write down their respective group and class numbers and proceed to their respective classrooms. Paul was in EPC 6, room number 3B, on the third floor.

He stood up, and went straight up to the third floor and, looking around, he found the room and sat down in the centre of the second row. Again the room began to fill: lots of guys – too bad – but, luckily, some girls too. Three Indians, and two rather good-looking girls, friends perhaps, definitely northern looking – tall with blonde hair. He looked again. One of them was very pretty. He would try to talk to her later.

The teachers entered the room and sat in front of them at their desks. When everybody had found a chair and settled down, they introduced themselves. One was Ian Cunningham, a skinny man of middling height with spectacles, and the other Brian Maker, who had a rosy complexion and no spectacles but a big pot belly. No doubt this guy liked his beer. They explained the class rules, proceedings, and timetables, and handed out four books to each of the students. They explained there was a third teacher, Miss Anne Bancroft, who would join the class tomorrow. She would teach English culture and literature. Cunningham explained that every Friday morning there was the weekly test, with a mid-term exam in early January, and the final test scheduled for the third of March. If everything worked out and they studied hard, they would get their diplomas, no doubt. In 30 minutes, they would start a tour of the university, visiting the main building and the library, the old classrooms, the church, and the auditoriums, all built in the 13th century, with 1209 being the founding year. The university's motto was, "Hinc lucem et popula sacra."

Paul took the tour with great interest. After over two hours, when it had finished, they all went to the refectory for lunch.

"Class will start at 1 p.m," Ian informed them.

When lunch was over, Paul went over to where the two Scandinavian girls had just stood up. He introduced himself and helped the pretty one with her tray. She said her name was Ingrid Gustavson, from Bergen, Norway. Paul asked if she liked beer; she said yes. He then invited Ingrid for a beer after class. She accepted. Good. No time to waste. They then walked together back to the classroom.

The next weeks flew by. It was a haze of hard work, hard study, weekly exams, and lots of reading. Teaching was almost eight hours long per day, with Saturday and Sundays off. All the teachers were professionals and knew what they were doing. It was a machine, no bullshit, no wasted time; they had a reputation to uphold. Paul was in his element. He loved the English language, always had. He made steady progress, studying hard; he also made progress with Ingrid. After about two weeks they had become friendly, and then lovers, Paul always wearing his social, buddy-like, non-aggressive hat. All the free time they had they spent together. Their love making was tender, sometimes urgent, but nothing too kinky. They had found each other a perfect match.

They walked Cambridge's narrow streets hand in hand; explored the local pubs; took the punt tour on the river, with the guide using his long wooden stick to navigate the small boat; and had lunch in one of the many parks, with lush vegetation, their green lawns immaculate. They walked the small bridges over the river, rented bicycles, and rode the ancient stone cobbled pavements, admiring the richly decorated facades of the ancient houses. It seemed Cambridge was one big university, everything in town gravitating around it, with over 100 colleges in the town alone. There were locals, yes, but the main population seemed to be students, and students only. Ingrid and Paul would only speak English, although Ingrid spoke a bit of German, but no way. This was England. Saturdays and Sundays they would have lunch at their favourite pub, the Fox and Rabbit, and more than once they took a coach to London and spent the weekend there. Paul showed her around as best as he could; Trafalgar Square, Piccadilly, Regent Street, Soho, the River Thames and the Banks, and the East End with its expensive new flats facing the river. Ingrid loved it, and in the night reciprocated with everything she had, in her earthly Norwegian way. She was fun, and he started to see her differently, started to feel something.

Time flew. The mid-term test had long been done, both passing with flying colours. It was mid-February now, the weather cold and windy and raining most of the time. Still, they would walk the streets, passing over the Mathematical Bridge, visiting King's Chapel, the church of St. Catherine's College, the Church of Our Lady and the English Martyrs; they did it all.

On the evening of the 2nd of March, they went for their last dinner, made love afterwards, and went to their respective beds early. Tomorrow was the day, the final exam. Paul worked his way through it without being too nervous. He thought it went well; Ingrid had the same impression. In the afternoon of the 3rd, students were officially dismissed, results to be released on the 5th at 10 a.m., respective diplomas handed out to the successful. Ingrid had her flight booked for the morning of the 4th, not having found a flight back to Bergen for the 5th, so they said goodbye, swearing to write and call, stay in touch, maybe even visit each other.

Paul checked into a hotel nearby. He would stay until the 5th, taking his diploma, and head straight back to Zürich. Ingrid's would be posted to her.

The auditorium was packed. Names were announced class by class and diplomas handed out. When Paul's name came up, he almost ran to the stage, took it, shook hands with the headmaster, and bolted off to take a cab to the hotel. He grabbed his bag, the taxi waiting, and off he went, straight to the main bus station. He made it to Heathrow on time, caught the flight, and was back by 9 p.m. Opening the door to his flat, he sat down, had a beer, and smiled to himself. "Well done." Tomorrow he'd start looking for that new job.

CHAPTER 9

However, the first thing he did the next morning was phone Director Brunner's secretary to arrange for a brief meeting. He wanted to show him his proficiency certificate personally. She called back, confirming tomorrow at 8:30 sharp, and don't be late. "She couldn't help herself, stuck-up bitch."

When he started to work, noticing that nothing had changed during his absence, he examined the LCs Mueller had already dumped on his desk with the usual sarcastic smile. "Idiot," Paul thought, but he knew this situation, with any luck, would not continue for very long. He started to examine the LC documents, big bundles of sheets held together by a rubber band. He made comments and approved or denied as appropriate.

At noon he went to lunch in the internal canteen, and after that for a brief walk. He sat down on a bench and began reading to-day's papers, which he had bought earlier. Not much in them, but Paul was not interested in local affairs and gossip; he went straight to the job section, making sure none of his colleagues were nearby watching him. A few Swiss banks had openings and offerings, a Jewish bank was looking for a teller, an Arab bank needed a bilingual secretary, etc. Nothing that caught his eye. Paul realised he needed to be patient. This could take weeks, if not months. He had to bear with Mueller and smile at Brunner. That was OK for the time being.

Walking back to the office, he sat down at his desk and called Tin. He had not seen him for almost five months. Tin answered on the second ring, pleased to hear Paul's voice. They agreed to meet at Jack's Bar at 6 p.m. Jack's was located near the Bellevue Square, at the very beginning of the Niederdorf, the lively bar and restaurant quarter. At 5:30 p.m. Paul called it a day, handed the files, now completed, back to Mueller, put on his suit jacket and raincoat, and left the building.

It was cold, but not raining or snowing. He did not take the tram, instead deciding to walk. Shortly after six, he arrived at Jack's to find Tin already sitting at the bar, a large beer in front of him. "Hi old sport," Paul greeted his friend, shaking his hand and giving him a hug.

"Hi, Mr. Winter," Tin answered, and they both sat down again, drinking their beers and chatting away.

Tin said he was very happy with his new job, no problems so far, sticking to the rules after the lesson he had learned from the disaster of his previous job. It was OK. He had swapped his car for a newer Toyota model, to which Paul responded that on Friday night he would get the rest of his cut, a neat 50,000 plus. Tin was pleased. They continued to talk, exchanging ideas, and agreed that they would travel to Frankfurt by car in July, just for a change of scenery and to have some fun. After this was agreed, they paid the bill and said goodbye, Tin walking back to his car and Paul taking the tram home.

He needed to get out of his current job. He also needed a new apartment, the old one beginning to annoy him. He realised he could afford it now, one of those upper class flats overlooking the lake, in a posh neighbourhood. He had to move up in life; it was about time.

There were many things to resolve in the next weeks and months. Sitting on his couch watching the news, he suddenly felt an urge to call Ingrid in Bergen. He had not checked the time difference, but luckily she was available. She answered on the fifth ring, pleased to hear from him. She confirmed receipt of her English diploma, very happy about it, and said she missed Paul and their time together in Cambridge. Paul said he missed her too, and they vaguely agreed to meet in summer, probably July. Paul promised to stay in touch and hung up.

The next few weeks dragged on, but Paul had managed to rent a top notch apartment in Seefeld with a large terrace overlooking the lake, within walking distance of the centre and financial district; but it came with no garage, the only drawback. He paid a hefty security deposit of SFr. 8,000 to seal the deal. He was happy and content with his new address, but still no new job. He and Tin went to Frankfurt for their dirty weekend, had more than enough fun, and one day after they returned, he saw it: one of the biggest Canadian industrial companies had recently opened a banking subsidiary in Zürich, and were looking for a qualified loan officer to work in their international loan department. Competitive salary package, sporadic travel required, and long term career prospects, in a quickly expanding environment. That was it. He must get it, depending on the terms, of course. He phoned the head-hunter right away and set up a first meeting for the day after tomorrow, at 9 a.m. That gave Paul two days to prepare himself, putting together his application and reference file. He also worked on his application dossier, bought a new dark grey suit, a new pair of black leather shoes at Bally's, had his hair cut, and asked Brunner for an interim reference letter, which was promptly provided. With that, he was ready.

At 8:45, he sat in the reception area of the head-hunter's office. At 9:02, the secretary asked him politely to come through to see the Managing Director, one Mr. Keller, who greeted him warmly. Paul politely and cautiously answered all of Keller's questions and handed over his file, which Keller studied with interest. He said he would talk to the Director of the HR department and call him within a week. When Paul heard the salary range, he almost fell off his chair. It amounted to at least double the salary he got now, slaving for Mueller and Brunner. They shook hands, and he left the building.

Taking a tram back to his office, when he arrived it was already 11:15. Mueller asked where the hell he had been.

"Dentist appointment," Paul responded.

"Next time, you advise me beforehand!" Mueller shouted.

"Asshole," Paul thought, "with a little bit of luck, I'll be giving you the boot very soon now."

The next few days dragged on endlessly, but then, after exactly seven days, Keller called to inform Paul that the bank wanted to meet him. He should report tomorrow at 8:30 a.m. and ask for Mr. Armstrong, the head of HR – if that was at all possible at such short notice. Paul said it was, said goodbye and hung up.

He then stood up from his desk and went straight to the gents, smoking a cigarette. He was nervous, but at the same time very excited; this was his chance, the job was his, must be his.

Next morning, shaven and shining in his new suit and shoes, he arrived at the bank at 8:10 and was asked to sit down and wait for Mr. Armstrong.

"It won't be a minute," the very cute assistant informed him. When Armstrong called him into his large office, Paul shook his hand and sat down. Armstrong fired away in Canadian English, testing Paul's capacity to communicate, and it seemed the two men hit it off immediately. Armstrong asked a lot of questions, why and how and what could he contribute to the bank's goal; Paul answered it all in a cool, professional tone of voice.

Armstrong said, "Very well, give me 15 minutes please," and left the office, undoubtedly to talk to his colleagues and superiors about Paul's case and file.

After a nerve-racking 20 minutes, Armstrong re-entered his office, sat down, and asked, "Do you want the job?"

Paul said, "Very much so."

"You've got it, congrats," said Armstrong, standing up and shaking Paul's hand. "Documents will be sent to you within two days for your signature and return. You will start two months from now, on the 1st of June, respecting the demission period at your present employer. My secretary will be in touch. All the best, and bye for now."

With that, Paul left the man's office, said goodbye to the assistant, and went straight to Bierhalle Wolf, at the other end of the Niederdorf. He ordered a large Hürlimann beer with a sausage and sat down, savouring his triumph. After a while he went home, writing his resignation letter ready to hand it to Brunner once he had signed his new contract. He had no time to waste now. He then phoned Tin, breaking the news.

"You lucky bastard, you!" was all Tin said.

A few days later, he handed his resignation letter personally to Brunner, who could not conceal his disappointment and rage. "And l sent you to Cambridge, you lousy ungrateful son of a bitch. l should have listened to Mueller when he warned me about you. Get out of my office and don't ever call again."

Paul still had to complete the remaining weeks of the contract, but this did not bother him. He fulfilled his duties professionally until the very last day and said goodbye to his colleagues. The next day he would start his new job. They all could go to hell, especially Mueller. Less so Brunner, who had sent him to Cambridge, something he would remember for a long time to come. He also had made quite a few good friends during his stay, and not least had learned a lot in the letter of credit department, knowledge that would come handy now in his new and, he knew, very demanding job. They would not pay double for him to sit on his arse, watching paint dry.

Next morning, at 8 a.m., Paul arrived at his new employer and was welcomed by Armstrong, with a smile on his face. "I will introduce you to the CEO, Urs Tobler."

With that said, they went up to the top floor, walked through the reception area, passing a very attractive brunette secretary, and entered Tobler's office, decorated with thick, dark blue carpets, a dark wooden bookshelf and a large desk, behind which sat the big boss, talking on the phone. He waved to Armstrong and Paul and gestured for them to sit down in the two visitors' chairs.

Having finished his call, he extended his hand to Paul. "Welcome on board. Armstrong told good things about you. Do your job well, and we will look after you." With that, he said goodbye, and the two men left the office.

Armstrong then took Paul down to the second floor, where the HR department was located. "Lilly here will show you around, anything you need or want to ask, give me a buzz," he said, and left Paul in Lilly's care. Lilly, a dark-haired, plump girl in her late thirties, showed him around the bank; the facilities, all the departments, lots of new faces, the whole tour was exciting. Finally, she opened the door to the loan department, situated on the ground floor. She introduced Paul to the department head, Vice President Fritz Elmer, a man in his early forties, a bit heavy set, with greasy hair, oily skin, and fat lips, wearing gold-rimmed spectacles.

"Welcome Paul, let me introduce you to your colleagues." With that, Lilly left, and Fritz introduced him to: Greta Bieler, a skinny mid-forties looking woman; Sven Selman, early thirties, a sporty looking, rather short guy; Frank Oehler, a tall, bearded, black-haired man, again in his mid-thirties; and Bill Doller, a short, rather fat man wearing thick glasses and a reddish beard. "That's the crew. Greta here will show you the ropes, but you ask me anything you want. This is your desk. Welcome."

It was a nice desk, in the far end of the large room, facing fat Doller's back. Greta, for the next few hours, showed him the files, the computer system, the secretary pool in the adjoining room, and explained some of the syndicated loan cases and put him to work. Over the next few days Paul spent his time asking questions, lots of questions, which Greta, a capable, well-instructed professional, answered easily, without ever getting tired or bored. Elmer was a procuration holder, along with Bieler and Selman. Doller was mandatory, the lowest signature power of them, and Paul, for the time being, could not sign to bind the Bank at all yet. The next few months passed by in a flash, with Paul putting all his efforts, strength, and knowledge into the job, working long and hard hours. All these efforts were recognised, and by the end of that first year, the bank promoted him to mandatory status. He could now co-sign documents binding the bank legally. Along with the promotion came a raise in salary.

To celebrate, Paul had arranged with Tin to meet up tonight to hit the streets and bars, and hopefully something else. But by 4 p.m., Tin called to say that he could not make it. Tonight was the annual meeting and dinner of the Association of Private Guards and Security Companies, Zürich chapter. His boss' wife had fallen ill, and the boss asked Tin to come along, replacing the wife. Tin had agreed, free booze, good food, and lots of ladies. Paul said he understood and asked him to give him a call tomorrow. Then he phoned Sophie, a very good-looking blonde 18-year-old girl he had befriended over the last few months. He took her out to Jacky's Stapferstube, a fancy restaurant specialising in steaks, a real treat. They arrived in his new dark grey Alfa Romeo GTV 2000. He loved that car; it was a real eye catcher, and fast as hell. During the excellent dinner, consisting of two superb 400g veal steaks, two bottles of Chateauneuf du Pape, and a few brandies, Paul told Sophie about his promotion.

She was delighted, kissed him fully on the lips, and said, "Take me out of here. I want to show you something."

They left Jacky's and walked to the car, parked in a small, dimly lit alley nearby. Entering the car, Sophie lifted her blouse, showing Paul her big, round breasts, nipples already stiff and erect. She took out Paul's cock without saying a word and started sucking it immediately.

"This is only a teaser," she said, his hard cock in her mouth. "Don't come yet. I want to fuck your brains out."

It took Paul a great deal of effort and concentration not to come, but he managed, kissed her, and off they went, roaring down the road in his shiny new toy. The rest of the night was promising; knowing Sophie, she would live up to her promises.

Next morning, around 9:30, Tin called. "We need to talk urgently. I met a very interesting guy named Anton Novak last night. Head of security at Cartier, Bahnhofstrasse."

Hearing that information, Paul almost dropped his phone. "Meet me tonight at that bar behind the public Hallenbad. Six o'clock sharp."

Paul had arrived almost half an hour early, keen to hear Tin's story. Shortly after six, Tin entered, looking a bit roughed up.

"Long night," he said and ordered a pint. Paul had chosen a quiet table at the far end of the bar room. They said "Prost!" and then Tin started his story. "This fellow Novak sat next to me, drank a lot, and started to talk a lot, too. He is in his early thirties, kind of tall, rather skinny, with long blond hair that he wears in a ponytail. He tells me he is chief security officer at Cartier, has worked there for over a year. He has a big nose, and we hit it off, laughing a lot. We exchanged numbers and agreed to meet soon for drinks. What do you say to that?"

"Interesting," Paul said, "set up a meeting in two days' time, say you will bring a friend. Let's see what this Novak guy is willing to tell us. We will have to probe hard."

Having said that, they continued talking for a while, and then said goodbye. After two days Tin called, having set up the meet at the Savoy at Paradeplatz, at seven o'clock that night.

"I'll be there, and Tin, wear a suit. We have to impress the man."

Shortly after seven, Paul entered the Savoy Bar and Grill, an elegant venue facing the Paradeplatz. The bar was beginning to fill up, the pianist playing soft tunes on the shiny black instrument. Lots of suits and girls in expensive dresses, candles on the black marble bar, waiters in white aprons, and waitresses dressed in equally white outfits. Absolutely the right surroundings to chat up Anton Novak, head of security at Cartier. Paul spotted Tin, who sat at the bar. He ordered a gin and tonic, and they both waited. A few minutes later, Novak entered the bar. Paul spotted him immediately, the long blond hair and the big nose.

He walked towards Tin, they shook hands, and Tin introduced Paul as his long-time friend and drinking buddy. The Nose ordered a double Jameson Irish Whiskey on the rocks, and they saluted. Paul then started to talk, wearing his social, friendly, buddy-like hat, trying to read the Nose, getting information. Novak said he was of Czech origin, his parents having emigrated to Switzerland in the early sixties, fleeing from the upcoming communist coup and the power struggles that had already emerged. He was not married, believe it or not; he still lived with his parents in a northern suburb, to save money, as he said, and had been working at Cartier for over two years now. He said he liked to go out, having a good time, meeting with girls, drinking and having fun.

What he did not reveal was that he was a degenerate gambler, mostly poker and blackjack, owing over Fr. 20,000 to the local German gambling hall owner, just over in Schaffhausen. The German was leaning on him to get his money back. The Nose also did not reveal that he was a cocaine addict, snorting away some 10 grams a week. But for the time being, this intel did not matter. Paul and Tin worked the Nose, trying to gain his confidence, making him laugh, having a good time and relaxing. They hit it off, and after some three hours of steady drinking, agreed to meet again next Saturday for a night out. The Nose also told them he played tennis at the WTC (Wollishofen Tennis Club), when asked what kind of sports he did. Paul knew the club very well, having played there a few times himself. Paul suggested a match in the next few days, and the Nose agreed, but first was Saturday's meet, taking it step by step.

They said goodnight, and Paul and Tin walked to Paul's car. "Check his address, see where he lives. He mentioned Schwamendingen; I'll check out Cartier and his routine, etc. Drive to Solingen in Germany, try to find the gambling club, see whether you can get some more info on the Nose, but be discreet. Let's have lunch before we meet the Nose on Saturday. See what we know by then."

With that, Paul drove off, and Tin walked to his car, parked not far away. Next Friday Tin and Paul met for lunch and exchanged the info they'd got so far on the Nose, with Tin confirming that he owed money in the gambling club over the border. They then went on to prepare for Saturday night. They needed him to talk, especially about the details of his job at Cartier, and gain his confidence. It would take time, but Paul was confident he would get the info he needed to do one more job, a robbery and heist, and also to deal with the Nose, the stakes being much higher now – equal to the reward he was expecting. Cartier was the leading French jeweller. He had no idea how much they had in their safe yet, but judging from their window display, it must be well over a million Francs on any given day. A vague scheme began to form in Paul's head. This time it would involve getting rid of the Nose, no other way; he had to work Tin on that one, and work him good.

On Saturday night, right on 8 p.m., Paul and Tin sat at a table in the Mascott Restaurant and Bar overlooking Bellevue, where they could make out the lake in the near distance. Paul was wearing a sports coat, casual blue silk shirt, and dark grey trousers, no tie. Tin was dressed up equally sportily in a grey flannel trouser, red and green shirt, and a blue sports coat, no tie either. They had ordered two Hürlimann beers, waiting for Anton Novak, the Nose. Paul told Tin they needed to make a point to mention to him that they both were in dire straits, financially, and desperately needed some cash. A brave lie; they both were extremely well off after the Migros job, but they had to make the Nose think that they needed cash as desperately as he did.

Tin spotted the Nose entering the restaurant. Long blond hair loose this time, no ponytail. He was smartly dressed in a black sports suit and light blue shirt. Tin waved to him, and the Nose sat down.

"How are you, Tony?" Paul asked.

Tin just asked, "Want a beer?"

"Yes." Then they started talking about sports, cars, girls, and finally their jobs.

Tin informed the Nose that his job paid too little, and he was behind on the instalments on his car loan. He needed to help his sick mother with increasingly expensive medical bills the social security benefit would not pay; he was also buying all her food and clothing, etc. Paul told him that he had just rented a flat he could ill afford, bought a car on finance and had to pay in hefty monthly instalments. Summarising, the two were in desperate need of cash. Over dinner, the Nose began to reveal that he himself was in deep shit, liking cocaine and the women too much, but worse, had a run up a debt gambling that he did not know how to pay.

Paul asked, "How much?"

"22,000 Francs," the Nose responded, being honest there.

"That's a lot of money. I'm afraid if you don't come up with it, they will lean on your family, your mother," Paul said, putting fear into the Nose's heart.

"I know, I need to pay by the end of the month," the Nose responded, almost in tears and visibly shaken and afraid, "which means three and a half weeks from now."

"I might have an idea to sort you and us out for good," Paul remarked. The Nose looked at him with his big blue eyes full of hope and curiosity. "Me and Tin here, we have a plan, but first let's finish our dinner, and then go upstairs to the club, dance, relax, enjoy. I even brought a line or two of blow, if you are interested," Paul went on, making his eyes shine and raising his curiosity even more. "The plan I'm working on will be ready in a few days. I'll tell you about it when we meet next week at the tennis club. Play a match and then get to business. How does that sound?"

"I can't wait to hear it!"

Tin smiled, Paul raised his mug of beer, and the three saluted. The Nose was smiling like a child under the Christmas tree. Little did he know that he would never see another Christmas tree.

After a great night at the nightclub, snorting away the coke, having a few more drinks, and dancing with some girls, having a ball, Paul said he had to leave, having an early meeting tomorrow. Tin also needed to go, mumbling something about his mother's health. The Nose stayed on as the two left.

Instead of going home, they walked to Paul's car at the public garage up the road, and drove to the Carlton Pub, a quiet, business-like venue that stayed open until 3 a.m. Sitting down at one of the small wooden tables, the pub almost empty, Tin asked, "What's the plan?"

"Well, as security chief, he must have the combination codes for the security door and the safe, since it's him, as he himself said, that shuts down the shop for the night and opens it in the morning," Paul started. "We do a robbery, the three of us, all with masks on and camouflage overalls. The cameras will register three men entering the safe room before we can destroy them, but that's exactly what I want. Police will look for three men, one of whom must have had the safety combinations since nothing was broken or damaged. They identify the guy with access to the codes, the Nose, but the Nose is nowhere to be found. He is gone, vanished from the earth. He will be the main suspect, and the scapegoat, the thief to be blamed and accused. Police will focus on finding him; the other two suspects were just unidentified bag carriers. I need to figure out how the Nose disappears. l am working on it. Need to do research on the place we'll go to after the heist. I already have something in mind. Meet me tonight at my place, say 9 p.m., l have an idea."

Tin was getting excited. "How much do you think we can score?"

"I figure the loot will be worth some 1.5 million, at 30 cents to the Franc. We will get a clean half a million, split equally into two. How does that sound? Worth taking the risk and doing him?"

Tin stared hard at Paul, taking his time. "Yes, let's do the job and the Nose. Never liked guys wearing gold bracelets, they all look like bloody fags. Besides, he is Czech, should've stayed where he belongs."

They shook hands and departed, each one walking to his car. The night was cold, but not rainy. Tomorrow, Paul would drive to Greifensee, the lake northeast of Zürich. He remembered swimming there as a child, many summers ago, with the old KIBAG cement factory right there at the shoreline. It had been decommissioned long ago for environmental issues; the perfect spot to do the Nose and get rid of him forever. As Paul remembered, the lake was some 80 metres deep there, KIBAG having dredged it for sand for decades.

The next morning, a grey, rainy day, he took his Alfa Romeo and headed north. Nobody would be at the lake in such foul weather. When he arrived there, he drove around in circles to find the service road leading to the cement factory. Eventually he found it: No Exit Road, the rusty sign read. He turned onto the gravel road, and after about 600 metres the cement factory came into sight. He parked the car way out of sight beneath some thick bushes and stepped out, umbrella in hand. The gate said "No Trespassing" and was overgrown with weed. The building was a greyish colour, all the windows broken and gone. The cement grinding tower still stood tall but was broken in parts. The ground was gravel, littered with glass, some tools, and machinery long broken and abandoned. The place was deserted. Paul stepped inside and looked around.

The air smelled damp and rusty. Assembly lines, broken metal carts of all shapes and sizes, the huge oven still visible, grinding machinery, and four cement blocks lying around scattered on the floor, each weighing some 25 kilos, Paul judged when he tried to lift one, which he barely managed. Each one of them had a metal loop big enough for a metal chain to fit through. All four together would make some 100 kilos of dead weight, enough to keep the Nose on the bottom of the lake forever.

Searching the shoreline in front of the factory, rain pouring down, soaking his clothes and making it hard to make anything out clearly, Paul thought he had spotted a small boat tucked away in the undergrowth, probably wrecked and long forgotten by some local fisherman. When he approached to take a closer look, the boat, being of aluminium hull, looked intact. The hull was bent and full of bulges and bumps, but still useable. Inside, it was full of water, though, with the oars missing. He needed Tin to clean it up, get two new oars, lanterns, a heavy, five-metre-long metal chain, a good lock, and a large knife. He entered the car, soaked through, put on the heater and drove straight back to his flat. He needed a hot bath, and then a few hours of quiet, hard thinking, putting some details to paper. He was excited and, at the same time, thoughtful, worried and remorseful; he held nothing against the Nose, it was just business. He didn't even know the man, he was just a tool – a tool that would have to disappear forever, otherwise he and Tin would disappear for a very long time behind prison bars. Although Switzerland had no death penalty, murder in the first degree for greed and low motives would sentence them to life in prison, that is, 30 years.

With these thoughts, he phoned Sophie to see whether she could cheer him up. However, it was to no avail. Paul watched the news and went to bed early. Tomorrow he'd meet with Tin, explain the risky plan, go into more detail, make the list. He slept badly that night, waking up all the time, seeing the Nose's long blond hair gently sweeping back and forth at the bottom of the lake.

The next evening Tin arrived at Paul's flat, punctually. "Great place you got here, old man," Tin said, "and look at that view! Must be costing you a fortune, place like this."

"It's not cheap, but worth every penny. Girls love it." With that, the two men sat down at Paul's dining table. No beers tonight. "Here's the deal. We do the job on Friday night, i.e. early Saturday morning, like 3 a.m. That gives us a head start of two days before they find out on Monday morning. Tomorrow I'll talk to the Nose, you come along. There must be at least two steel doors before we get into the security vault with the safe. The Nose must have all the combinations, otherwise the whole plan falls apart; a no-go. You organise a dummy gun, the ones that look real on camera. This is extremely important. The security cameras must show, at least before we knock them out, that the nose was held at gunpoint, being forced. Police will concentrate on Anton Novak, the fall guy, the victim, but they won't find him. They'll also look for two bag carriers, but they'll only know we're tall –no identification possible if we're wearing gloves, ski goggles, and ski masks. They'll only identify Novak, because he's got the combinations and he works there, and also because a strand of blond hair is poking out from under his mask. This is important, remember it when we all get dressed up for the heist." Paul went on to tell Tin about his plans for the Nose at the old cement factory.` I ve got the place where we do him, a deserted KIBAG factory, at Greifensee. Checked it out, it s perfect. I ll show you next week .There is an old boat, and 4 cement blocks. We ll tie him with a chain, to the cement blocks, and throw him into the lake, together with the blocks, dragging him down. Gone. Nobody will ever find him, lake is very deep there. Then,

"We'll drive to Milan and unload the loot there. I'll talk to my army pal, Moretti, this week. He's got relatives down there, if I remember correctly. I hope he can give me a lead. According to my calculation, we'll get some 30 cents to the Franc, half a million plus, clean. I want you to get a metal chain, some 4 meters long, a knive ,at least 30cm , a gas lantern, the ones being used for camping ,and a scale. That s all.

"I want you to pay cash for the stuff we need, and buy item by item in different stores. I'll get the overalls, gloves, goggles, and heavy boots, the stuff I can buy in any retail store. I will also get the oars. Once we empty the safe and the shelves in the strong room, you will drive with the Nose to the safe house, I take the loot and drive in my car to the meeting point where we are supposed to split, and then it's each man on his own. We tell him we'll drive him wherever he wants to go, probably a railway station or something, him being careless. That's more or less it. What do you say?"

"I say it just might work. I want to see the KIBAG site though, check it out to see whether I like it; apart from that, OK." Tin was not going to ask who would kill the Nose; it was clear from Paul's outline that this part would fall into his lap. It did not matter too much to him. They were in this together, whatever might come. Besides, it was Paul's plan; he wasn't going to argue.

"Tomorrow at 4:30 p.m. I will play tennis with the Nose at the Wollishofen Tennis Courts. Be there by six, we'll talk to him after the match, see how he takes it. After that, next week, I will drive you to Greifensee, show you the place. Clean the boat, get rid of the water inside, make it seaworthy, and test it. See you tomorrow."

"See you." With that Tin left, and Paul laid down on the sofa, staring at the ceiling, going through everything in slow motion to make sure he hadn't forgotten anything.

Paul arrived at the WTC at 4 p.m. The club was squeezed between the railway tracks on the one side and the Seestrasse on the other, giving way to the lawns of Mythenquai and the lake. The club consisted of five tennis courts, one after the other in a row, court number 1 being the centre court, with green banks for the spectators to watch from; the other courts had none. There were showers, dressing rooms, and a cafeteria. Paul had already changed into his pants and white Lacoste shirt, plus Adidas shoes. He was sitting at one of the tables, waiting for

Anton Novak. He spotted him immediately when he entered the room; long blond hair tied in a ponytail, Lacoste shirt, blue pants, and Puma shoes. The Czechs were known for being good tennis players, and he looked the part.

They shook hands and went straight to court number 5, the last one. There was nobody there to watch their game. They warmed up for several minutes, then got down to business. Anton was a strong player, fast, with good legs and a strong forehand, and Paul had to play his best tennis to keep up with the Czech. After five sets, Anton had the break, and made the point. He won. Great match. Paul was satisfied. He wanted him at ease, relaxed and proud at having beaten Paul. They were also getting to know each other better, starting to trust and rely on each other.

After the match, the two men drank some water and then went to shower and change. After a while, they walked out of the changing room together, dressed now in suits, but no ties. Instead of the cafeteria, Paul suggested sitting down on one of the banks, far away from anybody else. It was 6:15 by then, the club almost empty. It would close in about two hours, time enough. They both sat down.

Tin entered the club and joined them. "Who won?"

"He did, the lucky bastard," Paul answered, going on to say he enjoyed the match very much, complimenting Novak on his formidable forehand and speed. Novak started to smile, liking what he heard.

Paul then looked the Nose straight in the eyes, with Tin very close by, all three of them leaning in. Paul then outlined the job, the plan, the timetable, the getaway car; the clothes they would wear, the gun, the cameras, the bags. From time to time, Novak would ask a question, making a suggestion, but agreeing in general to Paul's plan. He asked where the safe house was.

"It's a short drive north," Paul said, revealing no more, and then asked, "You've got the keys and the security combinations, right?"

"Yes, I have the locks and keys, all the combinations, and the timing device."

"Do they change over the weekend?"

"No," the Nose replied, "they stay the same. I'm the only one that's got them, plus, the regional manager is based in Geneva. No problem there."

"How much is kept there, in the store?" Paul asked.

The Nose said, "Depending on the day's sales, at least SFr. 1.7 million worth of gold watches and jewellery. There're also small bags of loose cut diamonds, used for replacements, and some gold bars. All in all over 1.7 on any given day."

"Good. With that we can all sort out our problems for good."

To that, Novak only said, "Amen."

They then talked some more about the details, the security doors and locks, the cameras, the safe and so on, the plan now falling into place. At last, Paul informed him that he was arranging for an Italian buyer to unload the product, and Novak was free to join in, or take his cut and do whatever he thought best. Novak replied that he would take his cut and disappear.

"OK, sure," Paul said, "your choice." With that out of the way, they agreed not to meet for the time being, with the date set for Saturday the 27th, giving them a good three weeks; not long enough for Novak to get cold feet, and not too close for them to organise the preparations. "Tin will contact you. Stay low, work your routine, don't go gambling, and don't get sick."

With that, they left, Novak to the bus station close by, and Paul and Tin to their cars. Earlier they had agreed to meet at the Old Fashion Bar near Bahnhofstrasse for a quiet beer. Both of them arrived at almost the same time, and sat down at the far end table, ordering two large ones.

"Do you think he'll do it?" Tin asked.

"Oh, he'll do it. He has no choice. He's in way too much trouble with the gambling hall owner. You can't walk away from a debt of SFr. 22,000. They will start hurting him and his family, and he knows that. He will do it, 100%."

They drank their beers, going through all the details, once again making sure they had not forgotten anything, checking the buy lists and so on. Paul then said, "We will go to Greifensee early Saturday morning, clean the boat, dry it, carry the cement blocks into the boat, leave the oars in place, camouflaged in the undergrowth, and do a general inspection and search of the place."

With that said, they both departed, heavy thoughts on their minds. It could just work, but Novak was the weak link; without him there was no heist, and to worsen it, he now knew of the plan. That was the risk they had to take, though, for him to get on board. This was one variable Paul could not control – he had to rely on the Nose being convinced that the desperate situation he found himself in left him no choice. Concerning Tin, he had no worries. He was in a 100%.

On Saturday morning, at 3:30 a.m., they drove out to the lake, this time in Tin's car. It was dark and windy, the cold air getting to their bones. They emptied the boat and put the oars and cement blocks in it. The cement blocks were heavy, and it took them a while to carry all four of them over. After that, they camouflaged the boat, throwing dead wood and leaves and mud over it. One could not make it out any more, at least not from a distance of a good ten metres. It was now very well hidden.

Satisfied, they started to check the factory floor, and found two metals crates and a rusty fridge. They put the old fridge on its side, serving as a table, with the two crates opposite each other as chairs. It was there where they would show the product to the Nose, distracting him with it, while Tin fetched something – but the sequence of this would come later. There'd be time enough to sort out the details of this nasty part of the whole story. Satisfied with their inspection of the factory, they left the ghostly place and drove back, each one left to his own thoughts, not saying a word.

On Thursday evening they met for the last time. It was 7:25 p.m. Paul had chosen Joe's bar, the big, loud place where their meeting would go unnoticed.

The two were sitting at their table, unable to speak, checking their watches every other minute, when the Nose entered the bar. "What a relief," Paul thought. Novak sat down.

"Everything OK? You're good?"

"Yes, I'm OK, let's do this, can't wait any longer, I've got the shits, I'm so nervous."

"Relax, everything is under control so far. Have a sip, smoke a cig. Everything OK at the shop? Nothing out of the usual?"

Novak started to cool down. "No, everything's cool, smooth. Tomorrow I'll put the goods in the safe, as I do every day. It will be full.

"Good. Tomorrow night, at 2 a.m., Tin will pick you up at the Schwamendingen Tram station number 9. Be punctual. You will then drive with Tin to the parking space under the bridge at Enge quarter. There we will change clothes, boots, etc. I've got all the stuff in my car. You may want to bring a sports bag along, to carry your cut."

The Nose said, "OK," visibly delighted with the thought of packing his share. "I'll be there on time."

Paul asked where he would go after they split the loot, to which the Nose responded, "Drop me at the Main Railway station. I have made travel arrangements."

"OK, no problem," Paul answered.

Anton Novak, chief security officer at Cartier, began to smile and drink his beer in hasty gulps. His face was sweaty, with a two-day beard showing, deep lines around his eyes, and bags underneath. He looked like he'd had no sleep for at least three days. His hands were shaking slightly when he gripped his beer glass; his big nose was reddish and swollen.

"Get some rest, tomorrow is the day. It will work out just fine. Just don't raise any suspicions until then and be punctual."

"OK, OK, I understand," he said, "goodbye," and left the bar.

"Hope he won't crack before tomorrow. He looks like shit."

"No, he'll be there. He'll make it," Tin responded. "Needs the money more than anybody else, poor bastard."

Paul then informed Tin about his meeting with Moretti some days ago. "He got me the telephone number and address of a certain Dr Guido Alberti of Milan. We will drive straight down to Milan in the Alfa, with the product in a false bottom of a suitcase." He had arranged for the case to be full of clothes and travelling items. Everything going to plan, they could leave the cement factory at around 4 a.m., hit the motorway, drive south through the Gotthard Tunnel, have a coffee in Bellinzona, and cross the border at around 8 a.m. in Chiasso.

At that time, the border crossing would be full of early commuters; the police would not have enough time or interest to check every car. Anyway, even if they did, all they would find was a suitcase and two guys in a shiny new Alfa Romeo heading south, minding their business, or so Paul hoped. He had crossed at Chiasso many times before, and not once got stopped. He further informed Tin that he had spoken to Dr Alberti already, who confirmed that if the product was as he expected, he would pay 30, no problem, he himself being an official appraiser for the big insurance companies in Italy and Germany. He also said he would bring along one of his fellow appraiser colleagues, just one, nobody else. No weapons, no guns, a quiet appraisal in his office in downtown Milan, handing over the cash, and that was that. Still, it was risky, but Alberti had sounded cool and business-like on the phone, only interested in making a very nice profit out of the transaction. Besides ,they had no choice ,Alberti was vital. Moretti, his Army pal, did not know about Alberti; all he had given was the telephone number of his distant cousin, who lived in Verona. This cousin had made the connection, no loose ends there. To Dr Alberti, Paul had introduced himself as Werner Teichmann, a German businessman out of Munich.

Tin said, "What about the Zürich plates on your car?"

"What about them? I will tell Alberti it's a rental, doubt he will even notice, too keen on seeing the product and getting the deal done."

"OK."

But then Paul said, "wait a minute, too big a risk to take, when one can avoid it. You've got a point. We will park the Alfa somewhere near the Railway Station, take the case, and hire a cab, getting off a block before Alberti's. Deal done, we take a cab back. Good point there, Tin."

With that, they finished their beers and went off into the night.

Saturday, 1:40 a.m. Tin sat at the tram station waiting for the Nose, his car parked a few blocks away. There was no one at the station, with only one last tram scheduled to pass through. Bitterly cold and windy, a fine drizzle was starting to fall. Finally, he saw the Nose walking across from the corner, just barely visible in the mist and drizzle. When the Nose got to the station, Tin stood up, said hello, and they walked to the car. Looking out the corner of his eye, he saw the Nose's face all red and swollen. The bastard looked miserable.

"Hurry up, l got some hot coffee in the car."

With that, they drove off to Enge. When they arrived, it was already 2 a.m. Paul was there waiting, and he handed out the overalls, boots, masks, and goggles. They all put the overalls and boots on, with the masks and goggles left in the car, ready, together with the tools and the fake pistol.

"I'll drive first, you follow." Paul got into his car, with Tin and the Nose entering in the second car, not a living soul around. It took them only eight minutes to arrive at the back street near Bahnhofstrasse and the jewellery shop. Pitch dark, nobody in sight. They parked the cars and put on each other's masks, with Paul making sure that a nice strand of blond hair was sticking out under the Nose's mask, visible at his neck.

Putting on the goggles, they marched quickly to the steel back door, the Nose opening it with his special key. Closing the door, they now approached the second heavy steel door, this one giving way to the storeroom, with the first camera there.

Paul made sure that the gun was visible, pointing at the Nose's back as they entered the door. Then, after some five seconds, as if the Nose remembered something, he slowly turned and smashed the camera with a wrench he had brought along. OK, camera gone; they now walked to the third door, the Nose opening it without a problem. Finally, they got to the strong-room, with the shelves full of the less-valuable items, and the safe standing there in the corner, facing the far right wall. Cameras smashed again, the Nose kneeled down in front of the safe, concentrating hard. He worked the dial, visibly under strain; he could not miss the combination, otherwise the safe would shut down on the third attempt. After about two long, nerve-wracking minutes, the Nose stepped back and slowly opened the heavy safe door.

It was full of shiny gold jewellery; diamonds in all shapes and colours; gold bars; and all kinds of watches, bracelets, earrings, and other valuable items; it was a sight for sore eyes. They had never seen such a vast amount of wealth in one place.

"Quick now, step aside. Tin, give me a hand, hold the bag open – you, Anton, you empty the shelves."

The bag was full in under three minutes. Paul zipped it, turned off the lights, and left the safe door open. The Nose closed the first door, then the second, and finally they stepped out into the night, the Nose carefully closing the last door. Taking off the masks and glasses, they walked quickly to the car, Paul throwing the bag into the Alfa's boot while Tin and Nose entered the other car, all of them already having taken off the overalls, now wearing their normal clothes that were hidden underneath.

"Meet you at the safe house," Paul shouted, and drove off. A few seconds later, Tin sped off as well, keeping a safe distance between him and Paul's car, dimly visible in the rainy, foggy night.

At the roundabout and entrance to Greifensee, he lost sight of the Alfa, the Nose getting worried. "Relax, we just arrived," said Tin, entering the gravel road. All of a sudden the factory came into sight, the Alfa sitting in front. "You see, all cool. Let's have a look. Check what we've got."

Entering the plant's large main floor, they saw Paul sitting on one of the crates, having lit the gas lamp already, opening the bag, and emptying all the Cartier goods on the fridge/table. "Have a seat Anton, look at that, and Tin bring me the scale please, it's in my car."

The Nose stared at the diamonds, his eyes shining, an almost shocked expression on his face. "We made it," Anton said, still staring at the gold, while Tin silently approached from behind. Instead of the scale, he held a large fish knife in his right hand.

Paul gripped both of the Nose's wrists hard and held them down while Tin slit his throat from ear to ear in one strong, vicious movement. Blood gushing, eyes bulging, his body trembled hard for a few seconds and then went very still, Paul still holding his wrists.

Tin put a large plastic bag over the Nose's head and tied it with a rubber band, while Paul put all the treasures back into the bag, ran to the car, and threw the bag into it. They lifted the body and carried it to the boat, dumping it in there. Tin fetched the oars, while Paul fit the chain through the loops of the cement blocks, and then around Anton's body about three times. He then tightened the chain as hard as he could and locked the loose end with the heavy lock. They heaved the boat into the lake's grey water, a few tiny waves rocking it gently. Tin rowed about 90 metres out onto the lake. Not a sound, not a light, total darkness and stillness. They slipped the body over the side of the boat and then lifted the four cement blocks over the side as well. With all the weights together, the body sank immediately with a gushing sound, dragging the nose down 80 metres to the bottom. The whole operation had taken no more than 12 minutes. They sat still for a few seconds, listening to nothing, and then made it back to the shoreline, leaving the boat where Paul had first found it. The rain would fill it up quickly, cleaning all possible traces of their actions. Then they threw some dead woods and branches over it, and the oars they threw into the undergrowth. They walked back to the factory, moved the crates in opposite directions, and put the fridge back where they had first found it. Then, for good measure, Paul swept the floor with a broom, leaving no traces. They had washed their hands and faces in the lake's water, and now put on fresh, smart suits and social shoes. The overalls, masks, boots, and glasses they would get rid of later in a dump at a rest parking area on the motorway. The knife had already gone to the bottom of the lake, along with the gas lamp. Paul checked the area one last time, all OK.

They looked at each other, not saying a word. Paul headed out first, with Tin following in his car. At 3:55 Tin parked his car in the public parking space near Enge, entered the Alfa, and they sped off to Motorway A1, southbound. Two hours later, they were in the 17 km long Gotthard Tunnel, heading towards Tessin and Italy.

When they exited the Tunnel, the sun came out on the south side of the Alps. They took this as a good sign. Forty minutes later they stopped in Bellinzona, eating a big breakfast, with lots of coffee to go with.

An hour later, they had crossed the border at Chiasso without being stopped. They then drove down to Lecco, and on to Como, heading for Milan.

Entering Milan, Paul headed towards the main station. He remembered it well. He parked the car, took out the suitcase, a blue Samsonite, and hailed a cab.

When he gave Alberti's address, the cab driver nodded and smiled. "A goode neyburhud," he mumbled as they drove off.

After a ten-minute ride, they arrived at the address, Via da Roma number 351, an elegant office building with an imposing entrance of steel and glass.

"Drive on a bit to the corner there," Paul told the cabbie, "behind it, out of sight of the building." He paid the cab, took the case, and they walked quickly back to the address given.

Entering the hall, they crossed the marble floor to a black reception desk with a pretty brunette receptionist. They asked for Dr Alberti.

"Whom can I announce, please?" she asked in a low, polite voice,

"Herr Teichmann, and associate." Paul responded calmly.

The girl spoke into the intercom, nodded, and hung up, looking at Paul and saying, "ninth floor, office 921, the Doctor is expecting you." With that she showed them to the lifts.

They rode up to the ninth floor and, stepping out of the lift, found Dr Alberti's office immediately, ringing the bell. The door opened, and there stood Dr Alberti, a short, heavyset man in his early sixties, very well dressed in a light blue silk suit with matching tie and shirt. Even his fine Italian leather shoes were of almost the same colour, a light blue. He was wearing glasses and a very thin, black moustache, looking smart and professional.

"My dear Teichmann, please come in, and that must be...?" he asked, looking at Tin.

"My associate Herr Nebel," Paul introduced him.

"Please have a seat," said Dr Alberti, gesturing to a large black leather sofa with a gold-plated coffee table in front of it. "How was your trip?" he asked, not expecting an answer. Alberti, at this point did not know about the heist at Cartier Zürich, but undoubtedly had made up his mind that the product he was about to see, was of unknown, if not illegal, provenance. "What can I offer you? Whiskey, brandy, wine?"

"Just coffee please, and still water."

"Of course." He summoned his appraiser colleague to fetch the drinks.

When the coffee arrived, black, sweet and very strong, Alberti chatted away about the weather, the high taxes in Italy, rising inflation and the socialist government, which did nothing but interfere and cause trouble for his modest business.

"Now then, let me check what you've brought," he said, but before he handed over the bag, Paul pointed out that his other colleague waited in the car on the street below, in front of the building, in an "unfortunately, no parking space area." Hearing that, Alberti frowned, took the bag, put the contents on the large desk, turning on a strong headlamp and magnifying glass, and said, "This won't take a minute, don't worry."

His colleague sat down on the opposite side of the desk, starting to examine the goods. There was an electric calculator and a precision scale. Slowly, item by item, the two men appraised the jewellery, weighing each piece, noting down the results on a sheet of paper, examining them carefully with the magnifying glass while the calculator was doing its work. Paul and Tin, standing close by, watched the men work.

After 15 minutes, Alberti stopped, looking at his associate, and said, "Che cosa buona." He checked the calculator again and again, showing it to the other man, him nodding and saying something into his ear.

He checked again, and then said, "My dear Teichmann, I don't know where you got all this from and I don't want to know, but you have got a fine load here. My colleague and I appraise that," he held his breath, looking around, for maximum effect, "this fine merchandise is worth US$1.72 million. At 30%, you get US$516,000. Would that be agreeable?"

Paul had to control himself hard not to show any excitement. "That would be about right, Dr Alberti." Tin said nothing, just looked at the goods and the two men.

"Well then, since I was expecting more or less this amount after our telephone conversation, the money is almost all ready. Just a minute, please." With that, he turned and left the room, closing the door – no doubt entering his other office, where he held the cash – and left the three men alone. A long silence ensued, the men ignoring each other, but watching every move.

Six minutes later, Alberti re-entered the room holding a black sports bag, which he put in front of his desk. He then opened a drawer, Tin watching nervously, and took out an electronic cash counting machine. He connected it to the outlet, asked Paul to step over, please, and started feeding bundles of 10,000 dollars each into the machine, the machine doing its work. It took a while.

When it was all counted, with Paul observing closely, he put all the notes back into the bag, handing it over to Paul. "Un secondo, Dottore," Paul would go, and felt his way into the base of the bag, taking out bundles of $100 bills from deep inside. He took the notes to the window and examined them. From his days back at Kreditanstalt, he knew a true note from a fake one. Having finished his exam, he put the notes back into the bag. "Perfect, Dr Alberti, delighted to do business with you."

They shook hands, and he and Tin left the office. They got to the lift as quickly as possible, rode down to the ground floor, waved goodbye to the pretty receptionist and exited the building, not quite running, but almost. When Paul looked back over his shoulder, he thought he caught a glimpse of Alberti standing at his window, staring down at them, or maybe it was just his imagination... The bag was heavy, but soon, just around the corner, they spotted a cab, the driver smoking a cigarette and reading the sports papers. Paul gave the street name near the station, and they drove off. A few minutes later, having paid the cab, he opened the boot of his car, then the doors, and they drove off.

The two men started laughing, almost crying, out of satisfaction and excitement. "Well done. What a day."

As much as he appreciated Italian cuisine, and both of them were hungry, he could not risk having lunch and leaving the car unwatched with over half a million dollars cash in it in front of a restaurant, somewhere in Italy. They first had to cross the border, and then, back in Switzerland, grab a bite to eat, car in sight. But before that, he had to find a quiet spot to unload the cash and put it into the false bottom of the suitcase. Outside Milan, hitting Como already, they found an abandoned truck stop. Paul turned the car so that the boot was out of sight of passing cars and unpacked the cash. Alberti's sports bag was thrown into a trash bin nearby.

They then headed immediately to the Chiasso border, passing through customs without a hitch. The police officer waved them through, both of them sweating profoundly. Paul sighed in relief, while Tin lit a cigarette. Shortly after customs, they found a restaurant with a car park in the front. Paul parked the Alfa where he could see it and then entered the restaurant. It was just about 2 p.m., the kitchen almost closing. When Paul said to the waiter, they were both very hungry, and also wanted to drink wine, the waiter shouted something to the kitchen at the back and took their order. First, two large beers, then another two, while ordering their lunch. Penne al arrabiata, pork steaks with fries and vegetables, two side salads, a bottle of Rosso de Montepulciano, then another one, and finally two double espressos with grappas to go with. After the meal, they sat for a while, smoking their cigarettes, looking at each other and just smiling; both of them aware that they were now considerably richer than a few hours ago, and a whole new world would open with all its temptations and dangers.

To be exact, they were each US$258,000 richer, with the cash sitting there in the car. Paul paid the bill and left a generous tip. He then drove the Alfa to the next gas station and filled her up. No more stops until Zürich; he would drive as fast as he could, and traffic conditions permitting and everything going OK, they would arrive by nightfall. Paul had advised Sophie beforehand of his arrival – he was in desperate need of a good fuck or two, or three. Tin said he had made arrangements with one of the whores he saw regularly, and they agreed on meeting next week, around Thursday, to split the cash. Tin was OK with that; he was still flush with the result of the Urdorf heist last year.

CHAPTER 10

Paul entered his brand new flat, stashing the suitcase in his wardrobe under a pile of towels and bed clothing. He then undressed and ran a hot bath. He was exhausted. The last 48 hours had been hell, and were taking their toll. He opened a can of beer and got into the hot water. He took a sip and almost immediately fell asleep. He was still sleeping in the water when the doorbell rang. Stepping out of the tub, his skin hot and red, he grabbed a towel, put it around his waist, and went to the door. "This must be Sophie." He checked the kitchen clock, almost 8:30 p.m. Opening the door, there she stood in all her beauty: 1.7 metres tall, good hips and arse, large round breasts, curly natural blonde hair falling to her shoulders; a good face, with full lips, big blue eyes, and a nose a touch too big.

"Hello stranger, let me help you with that towel," she said, stepping inside and closer, taking off the towel and feeling his cock and balls. They kissed, Paul barely managing to close the door then, still kissing, stumbled to his bedroom, falling onto the large king size bed. Sophie took her clothes off immediately, showing Paul her naked beauty, fondling her big tits and caressing his cock. She then took him into her mouth, sucking it like no tomorrow, licking his balls and his arsehole. She got him so horny, he almost came in her mouth, but then slowly took her head and began kissing her again. "What a girl," he thought. She then lay flat on her back, opening her blonde-curl-covered, wet, pink pussy, and pressed his cock inside her. He hammered away, staring at his cock going in and out. When Soph came, with a long deep sigh, she took Paul's cock out of her pussy and made him come in her mouth. It always ended like that, he had to come in her mouth. She loved that, and would swallow all of his cum, showing him her empty mouth and clean tongue afterwards. She loved the taste of cum; for her, it was like eating her favourite dish. Both were very satisfied for the time being and happy to be together again. Adoring each other's company, and having lots of ground to cover, they kissed long and hard and held each other tight for a while, neither saying a word.

He had met Sophie a couple of weeks ago in the Silver Ball, a nightclub in Glattbrugg near the airport. She was there with her brother Tom, a nice skinny fellow, blond hair too, good looking. Soph, at the time, was just 17, and when they set eyes on each other, it was love at first sight. Having met her on a Saturday night, three days later, on Tuesday night, they had fucked for the first time. She lost her virginity, or so she said, loving it and insisting on it. Her initiative made Paul wonder how many cocks she had sucked already, being such a seasoned expert in the matter. After a few meetings, Paul found out that she also loved it up her arse. Paul was definitely a sucker for that. She was technically a virgin when he met her, but was definitely no stranger to sex. Even so, she insisted Paul was her first.

This went on for a few weeks, at which point she announced she wanted Paul to meet her family. Paul was happy and agreed; he had started to have strong feelings for Soph. One night they drove to Wallisellen, a small town just outside Zürich, 30 minutes' drive from the city centre.

Soph's family had a nice, big house: swimming pool; double garage; four bedrooms on the ground floor, as well as a kitchen and living room, plus the master bedroom on the first floor; and immaculate little gardens in front and back, which her mother, Anna, kept in perfect shape. The father, Hans, a short man with little hair, welcomed him. He smiled a lot, making him feel comfortable and welcome. Originally from Basel, he had a small shop in a side street behind Paradeplatz. He sold mostly electronic devices; radios, tape recorders, and so on, as well as TV s. He catered to tourist from all over the world, who did not mind paying his steep prices, the location being his strongest point, and by looking at his big house, Paul gathered he did well.

So, the first family meeting went nicely, and Hans, being a liberal man, from that point on allowed his daughter to sleep at Paul's on the weekends, and sometimes Paul would sleep over at their house in Soph's tiny bed.

"I am thirsty," Soph said. "Do you want something?"

"A beer."

Soph stood up, took a quick shower, and handed him a can, opening her own one. They drank their beers still in bed, kissing from time to time, whispering nonsense in each other's ears, Paul nearly falling asleep again.

"Let's go out, grab a pizza at Antonio's."

"Great idea. I'm starving," Soph answered. They dressed, left the flat, and walked to Antonio's arm in arm; two lovebirds, having eyes only for each other. They ate their dinner, chatting away, making plans for the future; a trip to Spain in the summer, a weekend in Italy. Paul liked the idea; Soph, full of energy, loved it.

When they walked back to the flat, it was way after midnight. Paul said he liked her, liked her company and everything else. In response, Soph kissed him, saying, "Me too, and a lot more." They fell into bed now, both of them very tired but happy, way too exhausted for any action, falling asleep immediately. When Paul woke up the next morning, he realised his cock was in Soph's mouth again. What an awakening. They fucked like animals, this time in her arse, but again, she did not let him come in her arsehole, instead sucking him off, swallowing every drop.

"Nice," she said, "let's have a real breakfast now," and stood up, showing her beautiful round arse. Sunday went by, more or less in the same rhythm, and by nightfall he drove her home, satisfied and tired, worn out and sore.

"Call you tomorrow!"

"Great, love!" she said, stepping out of the car and opening the gate to her house.

Monday morning, he showered, put on a good suit, fresh clean shirt and tie, black leather shoes, combed his hair and closed the door behind him. He would take the tram, too much driving lately. Arriving at Limmatquai station, a stone's throw away from his workplace, he sat down in his favourite cafe, ordered a double expresso, a water and a croissant, and started to read the papers. There was no mention of the heist. They must have found out just about three hours ago when the jewellery shop opened with no Novak, but instead an empty safe and shelves. Far away, Paul heard the screaming of police sirens, but could not connect that to the case. He paid for his coffee and went to work; the evening papers would surely be full of it. When he stepped into the bank's reception hall, the doorman greeted him.

"Good morning, Mr. Winter. Have you heard the latest? A massive robbery at Cartier was just reported on the radio."

Paul said no and took the lift to the first floor, entered the loan department's large room, and sat down at his desk.

"They cleaned Cartier out," Tobler shouted, "close to two million was stolen, police are sealing off the shop, going about their investigation, saying it is one of the biggest heists in the last ten years, it's all over the radio."

With that, Tobler sat down, and so did the others. Paul allowed himself the slightest smile and put his mind to work. He still had lots to learn, showing performance and interest, putting in long hours, arriving almost first, and leaving last. He liked his job so far; it was interesting, demanding new work. His colleagues in the department were CK, especially the lady who explained lots of the work and requirement and procedures, and still did.

The men were OK, apart from Doller, who regarded Paul as a threat. Never mind, hopefully, by the end of the year or, at latest, the following, Paul would be promoted again; this time to holder of procuration, passing Dobler's rank and getting equal with the others in the department.

He liked the job, but had already set his eyes on the Marketing department on the same floor. Being separated only by the joint secretaries' pool, it was there where the real action took place. It was there where the big money was made, by far the most profitable department of the bank, and, most importantly, it was very profitable indeed for the members of that department. Rumour had it that the Directors there made close to Fr. 10,000 each, every time they structured a new syndicated loan deal, in addition to their salary. It was there where the real money was made, but Paul realised, that for his ambition to one day come true, with him being transferred, he first had to befriend all of the directors and secondly have a degree in Economics. Without that degree, no way, but studying economics at the University of Zurich meant hard work and a long four years of dedication; plus the fees had to be paid by the bank, he hoped, with the economics degree being a very expensive course. Well, these were plans for the future, but Paul, being both ambitious and ruthless to the bone, had always been a man with a plan. Why not this time? Nothing seemed impossible for a 24-year-old motherfucker with close to SFr. 350,000 to his name.

Having worked hard the whole day, going out just for a quick sandwich at his lunch break, Paul was eager to call it a day. He left the office shortly after six and went straight to the newspaper stand just across from the office. The headline of the night edition screamed: MASSIVE AUDACIOUS HEIST AT CARTIER

Paul took the paper and sat down at one of the tables inside Odeons Bar and Restaurant, ordered a glass of Pinot Grigio and started to read while smoking one of his Marlboros. The newspaper informed that when staff arrived early this morning; they found the place upside down, shelves in the strong room empty, and the safe open. They searched for Anton Novak, Chief Security Officer, but could not find him. They called the regional Manager, who flew in from Geneva, arriving shortly after 9:30. All attempts to locate Novak were to no avail so far. Estimate of the robbery, over 2 Million Swiss Francs. The CCTV recording system was intact, but all the cameras had been smashed. Police were going through the recordings. The report then went on to say that efforts were continuing to be made to locate Novak.

Chief Inspector Keller, at the press conference at midday, informed furthermore that Cantonal Police and the special branch of the Criminal l Police had joined in, and a special task force had been set up to help solve the robbery. They were searching for Anton Novak, a 32-year-old Czech born resident of Zurich, and two unidentified males of tall build, probably in their mid to late twenties.

An Interpol search warrant went out on Novak. Police felt confident they could bring him in within the next few days. A local search for the two unidentified other men continues with no trace yet. Police are interrogating the staff, and are confident they will solve this heist. Joint efforts are under way, no cost to be spared to bring the criminals to justice. With that, he folded the paper and put it on the table, sipping his wine and smoking. His thoughts wandered. Confident my arse, they have shit.

Nothing to go on. With that, he stood up, walking down the small staircase that led to the gents, with a telephone booth in front of the doors. He called Tin; it was 7:30 p.m.

On the third ring Tin answered... "Have you heard? It's all over the news."

"Yes, I did. What do you make of it?"

"They have shit. Their efforts are concentrated on locating Novak. Good luck. This Keller guy and his team, they got nothing. Shit is what they got."

"Yeah, I agree. Give it a few weeks and the whole thing will die away."

"OK, good."

"Don't worry. Meet me Thursday night at my place to split the loot. And bring a bag. You will need one."

With that he hung up and went back to his table, ordered another glass of wine and a salmon carpaccio to go with it, ate his dinner in silence, enjoying the moment and watching the patrons at the bar, mostly male, with a few females thrown in for good measure; nothing, or nobody that caught his eye. He settled the bill and left the Odeon. It was a cold, but rainless night. He put on his overcoat and decided he would walk home, enjoying the fresh night air, getting his thoughts sorted. They got nothing he assured himself repeatedly, his thoughts drifting away to Alberti of Milan. By now the crook must have heard about the heist, and would already have come to the conclusion, obviously, but he had no real names, no telephone number, no addresses and so on. It was also not in his interest to reveal what he thought he knew. No, Alberti would keep his mouth shut, wait a few months and then start to unload the product, making his cut; being professional about it. But still, it was a loose end, and he never trusted anybody, let alone Alberti.

Thursday night, at 8 p.m., the doorbell rang. This must be Tin. Speaking into the intercom, he said, "Yes?"

"It's me, you silly bugger, open the god damned door, it's freezing cold out here."

Paul let Tin in, and there was his pal, sweatshirt, old Jeans and a dark green sports bag under his arm. "You came prepared, good." He hugged him. "I got US$ 258,000 waiting for you, but before that let's have a beer."

Opening two large cans of Hürlimann Lager, putting some nuts, sticks, and crackers on the table, they made a toast, both smiling and shouting obscenities at the cops. After a while they got tired of that, and Paul took the blue Samsonite suitcase out of the wardrobe, putting it on the table, his cut he had already stashed away, leaving only Tin's cut in the case. "Let's count it again." With that, he put the stacks of Notes next to Tin on the table.

"This will take a while, take your time." Sitting down now, sipping his beer, smoking a cigarette and watching Tin counting his cut. Smiling but concentrated, at ease and visibly happy, Tin took his time, Paul observed. Not so much because he didn't trust Paul, but because he savoured the moment, or so Paul thought. A good 25 minutes later, having counted it twice, Tin announced, "258k, to the cent. You are a genius. Marvellous, great, what a success, we pulled it off alright." Not mentioning the nose, lying in his wet grave at the bottom of the lake. Taking Paul's hand, he shook it wildly.

"If you say so," Paul said in mock modesty, "but without you, I could never have pulled it off. You were as much, if not more important than me. We did this together."

Hearing all this, and visibly pleased and emotional, Tin said, "You're right, we did it together. Anything else coming up? I am your man."

Paul opened two more cans, and they sat in silence, sipping and smoking. "Tin. You know, we have to give it some time, let the investigation go away, cool things down, remember that the police are looking for Novak, yes, in the first place, but also for us. I want you to lie low. No splashing of cash, just the normal routine. If you want, we can go to Frankfurt next month for a dirty weekend. If you can find the time, we could drive into Poland, Gdansk and Stettin. I heard the girls are just crazy up there. What do you say?"

"Sounds just what the doctor ordered," Tin replied. "I am game. Let me know when you want to go. Before that we can still hit the High Life Night club again, get wasted, say. Yes, let's do that." He then turned on the TV, but the local news had already finished. They watched some sports shows and at around 10 p.m., Tin said he had to go, long day tomorrow.

"Sure, take care now, and don't forget your bag."

Tin was already at the door, bag under his arm, holding it tight. "Talk to you soon. See you." And with that, he was gone.

Paul watched TV a little longer, but then turned off the set and went to bed, being tired and worn out, but happy.

CHAPTER 11

Paul went to work next morning, and the days and weeks went by. He concentrated hard on his job, putting in long hours, paying attention to every word his boss, Tobler and his colleagues threw at him. It was precise, methodical work with lots of reading and calculations; sometimes the loan agreement documents would run over 120 pages, with all the terms and conditions, eventualities, penalties, instalments, interest rate fees, adjustments and corrections, fines, and so on. This was fed into the bank's computer system and calculated to create a new file. It was work that required all his attention; no fiddling about, but also extremely interesting and very lucrative to the bank.

Sometimes, Schultz, the German, would step into the loan department to bring a new deal, a new loan, to Tobler, explaining the outline and conditions. Tobler would give the new transaction to one of the loan officers and often a new deal would land on Paul's desk. Sometimes Paul would go to the marketing department, mostly talking to Schultz about a new transaction, asking questions. He got along well with Schultz and the other Directors, they even invited him to come along with Imbach and Schultz for a beer one night. Paul enjoyed the company of these two senior Directors and learning from them. But on these nights out beer drinking, it was mostly chatting away, jokes and laughter, having a good time and chilling out after a long day's work, commenting on the looks and bodily attributes of a new secretary, or clerk or whatever pair of tits that ventured into the bank as a new employee.

Rumour had it that Schultz had screwed them all, and all, in this case, meant some 20 plus women, with him being married, but that seemed to bother nobody, least of all him. Schultz was definitely the woman eater of the bank, tall, good looking, 36 years old with already white, full hair, and dressed impeccably, the man must have over 15 suits, wearing a different one every day. He also had a pot belly, no doubt because of the litres of beer he consumed every day together with his best pal, Imbach. Schultz would say to Paul that his belly had cost him a lot of money, and in his opinion a man without a belly was a cripple. The Jovial German there, but underneath all that friendly smile and loose talk was a very capable, ambitious executive, that would step over dead bodies if it brought him a new deal, or better still, a promotion. Schultz definitely liked women, money, food and beer.

Imbach, on the other hand, a giant friendly bear of a man, was tied down with his girlfriend, and had no time or interest in other women. He had, however, time to structure the most incredible new loan deals in the whole of the country and he was extremely well respected in financial circles and the banking industry. Nobody would mess with Imbach; not even the CEO, or the owners of the Bank. Imbach made them all so much money that he became untouchable. He owned a house near Baden, and rumour had it that more than once a month he would miss getting off the train at his station, being asleep and drunk, and ride down to the end of the line to Basel. At Basel, the attendant would wake him up. He would then check into one of the hotels nearby to sleep it off and next morning, punctual as always, with a new shirt on, he always kept one in his drawer, he would command a new day of deal making as if nothing had happened. The only thing that gave him away, as Schultz confided to Paul, was Sepp wearing the same tie as the day before. Schultz would secretly call this the Basel tie.

On one of their beer nights out, Schultz asked Paul how he liked his job, and bank work in general; and what kind of plans he had for his career. Paul answered, having waited for this moment for months, that he was in his first semester of studying Economics at Kaderschule, Zurich at the University, and hoped to be able to show his certificate in two and a half years' time, at which time he hoped for an opening in the Marketing department. Schultz saw Paul's potential and ambition, and already envisaged an eager Paul helping and furthering his own career.

"Paul, old sport, nine months before the end of your course, I will have a talk with Tobler and the head of marketing, Meier, get them to agree and transfer you to work under me at the German Central Desk, and of late, ever more important Eastern European desk. Leave it with me. You bring me the Economist title, I will get you the job."

Having heard these words, Paul almost fell off his chair, but managed not to. He had a large gulp of his beer and replied, "Thank you for that, Helmut; that would be just great."

Imbach, who had overheard the conversation only said, "You are the new man, don't worry, if Schultz can't pull this one off, I will. And forget about the other two in the department, Rosen and Karen, they will come along. Tobler will require special convincing, but he too will come round, so don't worry. Have another beer and relax."

From that moment on, Paul had become almost a member of the team. Imbach Letting him in on many of his new syndicated loan deals, bringing handsome profits to anyone in the department and the bank. He also taught him the wonders of dealing in American T Bills and T Bonds, who were negotiated down to 1/16 of their price in Dollars, but when one made an average of 6/16 to 7/16 on a minimum $100,000 contract, these were nice profits, and they rolled in almost overnight, within 24 to 48 hours upon completion of the transaction. Everything went well. Paul studied and worked hard and things with Soph were going just great, and the occasional hang outs with Tin continued. Paul studied the newspapers every day, but slowly, slowly, no news came out any more and the Cartier assault had died away.

Until one day, Keller, the head of the task force, informed in a news conference that they had managed to locate Anton Novak. When he read that, he immediately threw up into the trash bin next to the bench he sat on, trembling and sweating, hardly being able to catch his breath again. When he did, he continued to read and started to cry... out of relief. Keller informed they had located Novak in Thailand, and the Thai police had him flown over to Zurich where he was expected to land next morning and be interrogated by Keller and his team. Whoever this Novak fellow was, poor bugger, it was not the one Paul and Tin had dumped into the lake, long gone eaten by the fish. There goes the promising career of Inspector Keller, who would probably end up writing parking tickets in some godforsaken long forgotten town, if not worse. Paul called Tin and gave him the news. They agreed that the case of Keller called for a heavy night out celebrating, indeed.

Two nights later, on a Friday night, Paul and Tin met. This time, they had chosen the Kreis 4 Bar again, a loud and lively hang out at Longstreet, in the rough District 4. Paul arrived at 7 p.m. and waved to the bouncer who was at the door smoking. The bouncer waved back and let him in at once. Paul had seen him before but forgotten his name. The place was already packed. Happy hour, two drinks for one. He spotted a small table at the far end of the room and sat down, ordering a pint of Hürlimann Lager to kick it off. Tin had not arrived yet. Paul checked his Breitling, 7:12 p.m., and then observed the room and the drinkers. There was the usual local crowd, boys having a night out, smoking and telling jokes, laughing loud. Regular office girls, two or three together, doing the same. Tin probably had problems finding a parking space, Paul thought, sipping on his beer while smoking another cigarette. Three men entered the bar, leading them was a short, strongly-built guy with very dark eyes and long black hair, the two others, following him, both of smaller build, but the same looking; probably Bulgarians Paul figured. Minutes later, Tin entered the bar, smartly dressed in a dark grey suit, creme coloured shirt, no tie. He spotted Paul and walked over.

"Hi old man, everything cool?"

"Good to see you. Yes, great, have a beer."

With that, Paul waved the waiter over and ordered a large one for Tin.

"A toast to Keller. Poor bastard, won't hear from him any more. Prost."

They both took a large gulp. They then talked shop, work, planning their trip to Frankfurt, and possibly further north. This went on for a while, the bar being packed now, loud music playing, when two girls entered the place. They were good looking too, reasonably dressed, one brunette with a great figure, tall, in her mid-twenties, the other slightly shorter, good looking too, dark hair bound in a pony tail, both wearing rather short skirts, blouses and high heels. They were looking for a place to sit down, but there wasn't anywhere. Paul went over, introduced himself and offered for them to sit down with him at the table and they gladly accepted. One called herself Natascha and the other one, the one with the pony tail, was Svetlana. He introduced them to Tin, who stood up and shook hands with them both.

Introductions done, Paul asked what they wanted to drink, and they settled for Vodka on the rocks with a slice of lemon; Tin having the same. Paul ordered a gin and tonic. The girls explained that they were both Russians, being there for the summer, studying German at a local school, which Paul believed he knew. It could just be true, or not. Who cared? The four of them were in for a great night, not too many questions asked. The two Russian girls were steady drinkers, holding their liquor and starting to laugh a lot; and getting closer to the two men. They were getting into the mood, their hands touching, Paul had settled for Natascha, the taller one, while Tin was busy with the Pony tail, they started kissing, not too wild, just feeling the ground.

It was, by now, 11:30 p.m. and things began to heat up between them, when all of a sudden a ball of paper was thrown at them, landing in Svetlana's drink. Paul caught the movement out of the corner of his eye. It was the short, heavy Bulgarian who had thrown it. Paul just looked at Tin without saying a word. Tin stood up and slowly walked over to the table of the Bulgarians. With his 1.82m height, dark complexion, large shoulders and strong arms, a no-nonsense face, staring at the three men, no smile and well dressed, he drew attention. Wearing gold-rimmed spectacles, sporting a dark black moustache with its ends pointing slightly down, men had respect for him, and the women, some women, liked his pimpish, bandit look. He slowly approached the table with the three men staring at him, the two sidekicks taking a step back, but the leader holding his ground.

He then asked, "Is there a problem you Bulgarian cunt?" While putting his cigarillo out in the guy's beer mug. With a swift move, he grabbed the man's long hair and smashed his head violently on the edge of the table, breaking the front teeth, blood spilling out of his mouth and nose. He then turned his face towards him, but holding a distance, not to soil his suit, and said, "The ladies feel disturbed, and my friend and me are pissed. It's time for you to get lost."

With that, he grabbed the man's head even harder, made him cry and whimper, not being able to say a word, and dragged him to the exit door. At the door, he loosened his grip and kicked him hard in the stomach; the guy falling down the entrance stairs into the street, lying there crying and bleeding while his two companions had watched the whole scene from a few metres away.

"If I see you again, you better run." With that he straightened his jacket, waved an OK to the bouncer, and re-entered the bar, going straight to the gents to wash his bloody hands before returning to their table and sipping his vodka as if nothing had happened. The whole bar had watched the scene with full attention, and total silence, and now that it was over concentrated again on their drinks and the music started playing. The two girls looked at him in awe while Paul smiled slightly, proposing a toast.

The night ended in a nearby hotel. Next morning, they all exchanged telephone numbers, hugged and promised to stay in touch. Paul was not sure whether Tin had given his correct number, but his was definitely a fake, leaving it as it was. Maybe they saw them again, maybe not.

For the next few months Paul worked even harder in the loan department, being given ever more complex loan transactions to analyse and work the documentation. Sometimes he had to refer to the internal law department, with a question or a particularly difficult clause. His studies at the university went well, and he passed the mid-term exams with an average of 4.8 out of six. He had also made two new friends on the course, Franz Rischer, Head of IT at a bank, and Beat Zimmer, an accountant at Price Waterhouse. Sometimes, after their class ended, they went to a Vietnamese eatery near Enge Station that stayed open late, for a bite and a chat. Rischer was a good ten years older than Paul and was married with a one year old baby son; while Zimmer was Paul's age, single and determined to stay that way. The three went along well, having lots of common ground and topics, discussing some of the course content, and problem exchanging ideas; and answering each other's questions, they had become close and good friends, even made plans to make a prep week before the exam. It was by now early December and the final exams were set for mid-February.

In one of their after-hour sessions, they decided that they needed extra preparation time and would therefore draw a 12-day leave from work; but where to go? A secluded place with no interference. Paul suggested a remote hotel in the Graubünden Alps, but Zimmer came up with an even better idea. A far away relative, an uncle of his mother's brother, owned a cabin in the Appenzell mountains, Ebenalp, a far away place. He had been there once or twice as a boy in summer, and remembered it as very remote and secluded with no human civilization around for at least seven kilometres. Paul said perfect; Zimmer said he'd make enquiries with his uncle, but it should be available in winter; there was no need for it to be used.

If it was OK and available, he would let them know the next week. They settled for the last ten days in January, the final exam being scheduled for the 7th and 8th of February. Rischer offered his car, a Mercedes sedan, with a large boot, good winter tires and chains, as transport. Agreed, and thank you.

A week later, Zimmer informed them the cabin was available for the requested period. The price agreed was. SFr. 100 for the ten days and keys would be under the mat at the entrance door. A very precarious energy connection and supply was available, other than that, wood for heat and cooking, and a lavatory hut outside the cabin, hidden in the woods. They were also required to bring their own sleeping bags, since temperature at this time of winter would easily drop to minus 12 degrees, along with all the maintenance and supplies, books and charts, and food for the ten days. No stores available anywhere around.

It was a grey and bitterly cold winter morning when the three men set off. Everyone had brought along what he thought he needed. The Merc was packed to the roof, as they drove off in an easterly direction, heading towards Winterthur, then on to Wil, Herisau and further on in the directions of the Säntis mountains. At first the roads were OK, the highways being kept clean of snow and ice, but the further east they got, the more snow there was, which led to slower driving. The secondary roads were now covered with a good 15 cm of snow and increasing. The heavy Merc swayed on the road, fishtailing. It had taken them more than three hours to get near to Ebenalp with snow falling ever harder; the wipers had trouble keeping the windshield clean. It was very cold and very dark, difficult to see or make out anything outside.

Paul and Zimmer consulted the map. The road led to a small intersection where they had to turn left, steeper up into the hills towards Ebenalp and Schwende. When they reached the intersection, barely visible in front of them, Paul suggested stopping the car, pull over at the small space at the right side of the road. The car came to a slithering halt with the direction signs all snowed over and unreadable; but Zimmer said this was the turn, he was sure about it; remembering it from a long time ago. They had to drive up left, up that tiny road leading to Schwende and even further on to the cabin they would hopefully find in the heavy snowfall; in complete darkness, and with no natural light. The heavy clouds had blocked any of it and visibility was down to about six metres. Paul said they had to put the chains on the tyres or there was no way to get up there without them.

The army drill max time for two chains on the two rear tires was set at eight minutes for a staff of four. Let's see how the three of them were managing here. Rischer took the chains out of the boot together with the jack and a torch light. The three put on their gloves and went to work. It was hard work but, according to Paul's Breitling, they managed to finish the job in 11 minutes. Not bad considering the difficult conditions and being short one pair of hands. Rischer now put everything back into the boot and started the engine. Paul and Beat sat in the backseat to give extra weight on the rear wheels.

With full headlight on, Franz turned the car left and slowly began to drive up that narrow, winding snowed-in steep mountain road. It was a dangerous, laborious task, with the car swaying heavily from the left to right, but the chains gave the extra grip, and slowly, slowly they kept going up the mountain road; just managing. Another small intersection came up, no signs, nothing more than two tracks in the snow, and Zimmer said to turn left, and go straight for another five kilometres, when hopefully the cabin would come into sight. Five kilometres up and no cabin. Rischer stopped the car but left the motor running. Zimmer stepped out with the torchlight on and set off up and out into the snow. After ten seconds, they could not see him any more. He had vanished into the grey and white surroundings. They looked at each other, tension rising, tired and worried.

"I got it. Found it. Just over there behind that group of big, tall trees," Beat said. "Franz, turn the car round, facing down."

He managed to turn the Mercedes with some difficulty, and then the three set out to inspect the cabin.

There she was, a low lying, small construction of wood and concrete not more than a hut, but looking inviting and cozy. Beat had found the key and opened the door. There was a small room with a big wooden table and four chairs, one small window, and two doors, one led to the kitchen and dark grey metal stove (with a front opening to put in the wood), a sink and a window, the other door led to a bedroom with a bathroom with a sink, holding four single, army style metal beds. The light came from a bulb in the kitchen, a lamp over the wooden table, with no light in the other room. It was perfect. Earlier on, the three had agreed on the role of each one: Rischer was the cook, Zimmer was cleaning, and Paul was the wood man.

They set out to take their belongings from the car. It was a lot but everything was necessary and served a vital purpose, this was wilderness, as remote as it gets, just what they needed to prepare undisturbed for their exam. Once their belongings were safe in the house, Paul set out to inspect the wood supply. It had to last for at least ten days; there was a stash of already chopped wood that would suffice for tonight. Tomorrow he would start chopping to keep the stove and heating going. The wood was not that dry, but he managed to keep a fire going that would not go out until they left the cabin, hopefully fully prepared by then for their final exams. Rischer was already busy preparing a soup served with bread, while Zimmer was cleaning and sweeping the floor.

Paul had set out into the open to inspect the lavatory, which consisted of a wooden bench with a hole carved out in the middle, old style. OK, but no toilet paper; but he had brought along a supply – good thinking. It was bitterly cold outside, and pitch dark at 4 p.m. He hurried back into the cabin and sat down. Zimmer had already organised and separated the academic material and books each one of them had brought along. He had put them into three neat piles on the wooden side table. Good man, organised, well done. They sat down to eat their soup; Rischer had opened a bottle of Veltliner, a local wine he had brought along, and they made a toast. After eating and then reading for half an hour, they all went to bed, happy and very tired.

Next morning, they rose at 6:30 a.m. Rischer got busy making coffee and breakfast. Paul set out to clean the pathway to the toilet shack, and to the small road; it was all snowed in again, and to clean it might take him a while. After breakfast, they started with their routine, established earlier for the days to come: 7 a.m. – breakfast; 8 to 11:30 a.m. – studies; then lunch break until 1 p.m.; afterwards studies until 4 p.m. with dinner set for 6 p.m. The days passed quickly, and they made the best of it. Rischer had even invented some sort of quiz, consisting of seven questions thrown at each other – the winner would get a sip of his special reserve Kirsch.

On fine nights, they put on their heavy coats, boots, gloves and hats, and ventured out into the moonlit wilderness in the total pitch dark; the surrounding mountains barely visible on the horizon, lying there majestically. Beat pointed out tracks in the snow; rabbits and foxes, different types of birds, deer (small and big), wild boars. It was magic, the stillness total, only broken now and then by the typical, repeating sound of the owls communicating with each other, warning of the three intruders. Sometimes they could spot the mountain eagles flying high above their heads, or a pair of crows crying out loud. Paul felt at ease, very peaceful, content and happy. He knew this preparation marathon would yield the result he needed. He did not know what the others felt, only guessing here. Zimmer was focused and concentrated. Paul was sure he would make it, with Rischer he had second thoughts, not knowing exactly why, something, sometimes was off with him, spending long intervals and hours in the kitchen, staring out of the window without moving his head. Just a hunch, Paul thought; hopefully he was wrong and all of them would pass with flying colours in their final exam, now only days away. It was to be a game changer for all of them.

His thoughts wandered back to the mid-term exam, and the loss of a good 40% of students who did not pass. Anyway, he brushed his thoughts away and asked Zimmer about a track he found and could not identify. They marched on for another 40 minutes, enjoying the pure cold air, and then went back downhill in the direction of the hut, a good 60 minutes still to go.

When they arrived back, they sat down at the table; it was their second to last night. Paul opened a bottle of red Chianti he had brought along, and they made a toast. Tomorrow, was question-and-answer day the whole session, and afterwards, weather permitting, Paul suggested facing the one hour plus march down to Schwende to see whether they could find a restaurant and have their last dinner there; a suggestion wildly approved by all of them. So the next, and last, day brought the hours long question-and-answer session, all three doing reasonably well.

At 3:30 p.m. they called it quits and started packing, ready for leaving early the next morning.

After an hour of packing, they put on their outdoor clothes and started out at 5 p.m.; it was pitch black already. They marched down the road towards the tiny village, six kilometres down in the valley; all three of them smoking – Paul his Marlboros, Zimmer his cigarillos, with Rischer having lit a pipe; the sweet aroma lingering in the pure air. The small pathway was snow-covered and icy, and was tricky to walk at times, leading downhill for a good hour, they reached the village, "altitude 1710 metres", a sign at the outskirts read. The first tavern was closed, they passed by the small cemetery with its stone crosses, and the small church, turned left after the butcher shop, that was long closed, passed the bakery, also closed, and finally got to the Goldenes Kalb, the local eatery; it was open, its lights shining out invitingly from the small windows in the front.

They entered gratefully and stepped into the only room, wood panelled, dark from years of smoke, where four people sat around a large table, drinking beer and eating some sort of cold cuts. The three sat down at one of the two remaining tables and started immediately looking at the menu, desperately hungry as they were. It consisted of two options for dinner: Rösti mit Bratwurst (i.e., mashed potatoes with pork sausage), or macaroni with local cheese and bacon. All three went for the sausage with potatoes, keeping it simple, three large pints of local Appenzeller beer to start with as the first dish, the cheese platter with bread, arrived; brought to the table by Anni, the owner's daughter. They dug in immediately, the cold air and march having made them starving and thirsty. Paul asked Anni whether there was a telephone. She answered yes, down the hall and to the right. He took a piss and then dialled Soph's number, it had been a while since they had spoken and he was in need of hearing her voice, telling her about his stay and preparations at the secluded hut in the wilderness, arranging the time and place they'd meet tomorrow. After having spoken to her, he returned to the table happily, a smile on his face.

"All going to plan, and with a bit of luck, I think I am getting laid tomorrow," Paul informed them with a grin on his face.

"You lucky bastard, not that you deserve it," Zimmer said.

They then had another round of beers followed by a bottle of Merlot, and then another one, enjoying the meal and each other's company. After a round of coffee and Schnapps, and having split and paid the bill, they stepped out into the cold again. An uphill march of a good one and a half hours before them. They set out, rarely speaking. It was much too cold for that; each of them lost in his thoughts. Finally, tired and exhausted, they reached the cabin. All of them went immediately to bed. Tomorrow was departing day, a long journey, starting with cleaning the hut, packing the car, and then hopefully managing the snow-covered icy road downhill, a not less dangerous task than when they drove up 11 days ago.

Next morning, Rischer turned the car key and the engine caught first time; not surprising since he had had the motor running every day for a good five minutes to prevent the battery from running out of juice. Everybody and all the luggage safely in the car, key left in the same place they found it, they started their journey downhill. It went surprisingly well. When they reached the same intersection, hitting the larger, cleaner, cantonal road, they took the chains off the tires – piece of cake – and drove west, towards the cities and population.

They reached Zurich three hours later, all safe and sound, finally entering the large car park and stepping out of the Merc, Paul and Zimmer headed for their own cars. There was no snow in Zurich, the air smelling foul and damp, the roads and streets being a dirty brownish colour. Having grabbed their stuff, they all said goodbye, remembering that if any question came up, they should all call each other immediately with the final exam being only three days away.

With this agreed, they all left. Paul drove home as fast as he could. He entered his flat, unpacked, took a long hot bath, then prepared himself a gin and tonic, watched the 8 o'clock news, and started to relax and feel good, waiting for Soph to arrive; eager now to embrace and kiss her and all the rest that would most probably come to their minds.

He was keen to catch up with her and tell her all about his stay. The prep. studies, his two friends, the cabin and the wilderness. The beauty of nature, untouched and pristine like the first snowfall in November, the animals they discovered, and he learned to identify, thanks to his pal Zimmer, who was a real nature enthusiast and knew everything about it; having spent many summers at his uncle's hut up there, when he was a small, and then not so small boy, being taught many things about the mountains, the seasons, and all the wildlife that lived there, and the mushrooms and other food they would harvest.

Tuesday morning, Paul walked up the stairs leading to the entrance of the university. Exam day, going from 8 a.m. until 1:30 p.m. He walked through the foyer and headed right to the cafeteria, bought an espresso and a water. Searching for a free table, he saw Prof. Meier and two of his assistants. Paul greeted them. They would take the oral exams. While sipping his coffee and smoking, looking out for Rischer and Zimmer, both nowhere in sight. A few minutes later, he spotted Zimmer.

"How are you? Everything cool?" Zimmer asked.

"Fine, but still no sign of Rischer. Have you seen him?"

"No," Beat replied.

It was now 7:50 a.m. He finished the coffee and took hold of the water bottle. Standing up now from the table, wearing a dark blue pair of Levis, sneakers, a grey cashmere sweater and a black Parka jacket, he said, "I am going to the gents, take a leak, check whether I can see Franz. See you in the exam room."

While he headed for the WC, he looked around; Franz was nowhere in sight. He did what he had to do, washed his hands, combed his hair, and went straight up to the first floor. Entering the exam room and sitting down at one of the small desks, he took out paper and pen and gave Zimmer a questioning look. Zimmer returned his glance the same way, no Rischer in sight.

At 8 a.m. sharp, the doors closed, Mueller welcomed them all, wished them good luck, and had the exam papers handed out by one of his assistants. Paul stared at the door.; still no Rischer. There must be something wrong. This could not be true, not after all they went through together, he thought; but still no Rischer. That only left three explanations:

1. His car broke down and he was late. Unlikely, him being so fond of the Mercedes, and keeping it in good shape at all times.

2. Rischer had decided not to take the final exam, for one reason or another. Again, this made no sense. Why would he do something like that?

3. Rischer had never passed the mid exams, but opted to finish the course and hang on, without ever being able to take the final test and obtain the certificate; without telling his friends for reasons only known to himself.

"What the hell," Paul thought, and concentrated on the exam.

The first day of exams went reasonably well. He asked Zimmer how he had fared and he replied, "Fairly well, I think." They did not mention Rischer. It was too embarrassing. The second day of exams went OK too, the same perception, more or less. Paul felt he had done great on Math and his dissertation on the 19th century industrial revolution. The verbal exam on Stochastic, applied statistics, and its interpretations, he was afraid did not go well. He had screwed up this one, giving halfway answers or none at all, but still, with strong results on the other subjects, these might just compensate for that very weak one, and allow passing the exam, still reasonably well overall.

At the end of the second day, Mueller informed them the results would be announced in three weeks' time; Friday the 28th at 6:30 p.m. They all would meet in the audience room number 3, and this would be followed by a cocktail reception in the Foyer. Candidates who had passed would receive their diplomas that evening from the Minister of Education of the Canton of Zurich, Mr. Escher, personally, Mueller proudly announced.

Paul and Beat headed for the door and out of the university, which had been their place of dedication and hard work for the past four years; four long years. They were both relieved and happy that it was finally over. They headed straight to the Vietnamese eatery nearby and ordered two large ones, followed by the same, and again the same; chilling out and beginning to relax.

Paul said he had to go, having promised Soph to take her out for dinner. "See you on the 28th," he said.

With that, he stood up, shook hands with Zimmer, and headed for his Alfa parked nearby. He roared away, happy and relaxed that this ordeal was finally over. He was thinking about Soph and their night out together, but also remembering Rischer. He would call him next week, invite him for a drink, and try to find out what the hell was going on with his friend, who had been helpful and vital in the cabin a few days ago; helping to make this all happen and yet, obviously, having no part in it at all, and never being able to get his diploma.

Weeks later, Paul walked into the audience room number 3 wearing a dark navy blue, double-breasted suit ,white shirt, black leather shoes, and a blue and white striped tie. He spotted Zimmer and sat down next to him. As in Cambridge, which seemed a lifetime ago, Mueller read out the names of the successful students, and asked them one by one to step forward.

Mueller handed out the envelopes containing the final results, while

Escher, a tall, slim, elegant man in his late sixties, handed out the diplomas; shaking the hands of each of them and congratulating them. Paul had to wait a long time until his name was called, the calls being made in alphabetical order. But finally, yes, Paul's name was called, and he approached the front desk, almost crying with relief and very proud. Zimmer had to wait even longer, but finally his name was called out, too. When the two sat down again, they opened their envelopes: Paul had scored 4.7, while Zimmer had bettered that with his 4.9; these were very good results indeed for both of them. From the initial 71 students, only 28 names had come up tonight, a rather small proportion had made it.

They went to the cocktail reception and had their drinks, canapes of smoked salmon, and a variety of cold meats and cheese that were offered. They both dug in. After Paul's third G&T he called it quits. He had to have a clear head, showing his certified economist diploma to Schultz and Imbach, and everybody else who was interested in seeing it. If Schultz was true to his word, Paul's days in the loan department were numbered, and a whole new ball game was hopefully to start very soon, with all its pains and glories yet unknown to Paul Winter. Next day, early, he sat down with Schultz and Imbach in one of the bank's conference rooms, proudly showing them the results and diploma.

They both said, "Well done."

"Well done indeed," said Schultz. "I will inform Tobler, your boss at loans, and we will also talk to Meier and the other two in our department. Tobler might take a bit of convincing, but don't worry, it will work out just fine. You are mine now," Schultz went on with a large grin on his face. What this exactly meant was yet unclear to Paul, but he was soon to find out. The day passed without any further developments, until sharply, at 6 p.m., with all his colleagues at loans long gone, Tobler approached his desk, briefcase and raincoat in hand, ready to leave for the day.

"I have reluctantly agreed to let you leave my department and start working at marketing in one month's time. During that period, you will train a new colleague, who will hopefully start working here in the next few days. I will give you your interim qualification document in a few days, and I thank you for your collaboration and excellent work you have shown here in the loan department."

With that said, he shook Paul's hand and left the room. It was clear to him that Tobler did not want him to leave his department, and it must have taken a great deal of persuasion from higher up to let him go. But still, now he was out, and soon, and that was all that counted for him just now. In one month's time he would sit behind Schultz, and in front of Meier, in the most exciting and lucrative department of the whole bank.

CHAPTER 12

It was Thursday morning, early March, when Paul finally sat down at his new desk behind Schultz, excited and eager to learn all there was to learn. His relationship with Soph continued well, the investigation of the Cartier heist had died away for good, so he hoped, and he and Tin had met a few times in the last weeks, and agreed to take the car in the second week of April to hit Frankfurt, drive up further north, to Hamburg, then take a swing to the east and head for Stettin, and maybe Gdansk, two cities in Poland. When he had told Soph about his forthcoming trip, she was not very understanding, saying it was a waste of time and what on earth would they do there in the first place. Still he said he was going, and that was that.

Sitting at his desk, he studied the files Schultz had given him. He had spoken earlier to Rosen, who normally spent most of his time in London, drumming up business there, and Karen whose task was to solve all problems, of any kind, being the angel of the department, and also in charge of booking all trips, hotels, rentals, Visas, and anything else that came up, which Paul was soon to find out. She was liaison with the other departments, bilingual, English and French, with a few German swear words thrown in. She was a tough cookie, and Paul took a liking to her immediately.

Schultz took him to a luncheon meeting with the subsidiary of a Japanese bank. This pattern would follow during the next week. Lots of meetings, mostly in Zurich, and sometimes Geneva. Imbach also took him out to business meetings, showing him the ropes and introducing him to a lot of people and his connections, that were many. He seemed to know everybody that counted. These were powerful meetings at guild houses, where new transactions were signed and celebrated. Only the very best of food and drinks were served at these venues and meetings.

He then started to travel with Schultz, mostly to Germany, to visit local and regional banks, starting out with Munich, Baden-Württemberg, Hessen, Frankfurt, Bonn, Köln, Bremen, Hamburg, and on it went.

Schultz would only stay in 5-star hotels, each having his suite, very elegant, with the finest food for breakfast, lunch and dinner. They travelled outside the big cities too, visiting small banks, regional head offices and their affiliates. Paul paid very close attention to all the details and what Schultz had to say in these many meetings. He learned a lot, right on the spot. It was very valuable training indeed; he needed that if he was to travel on his own in the future – something he was most keen on doing. Paul also made notes, wrote down everything he thought was vital. Learned the craft of deal-making, convincing, exaggerating, putting everything in the best possible light, sometimes omitting some facts, or numbers that were not too favourable to the bank. Schultz was the master of deal-making. With his elegant, imposing stature, cultivated manners, and perfect speech, he was very convincing. He could sell a car to a blind man, no problem there.

Paul had found his master and showed respect. He was very glad that Schultz took him along and seemed to trust him sometimes over a quiet beer, confiding that he foresaw a good career for Paul, and would help him to achieve it.

These regional banks all had an excellent credit standing but were unable to tap the interbank market; that was where Schultz came in, arranging for bridging loans that the banks on their own could not manage due to lack of expertise and connections. These loans varied from short to medium and even long-term transactions, always with almost no risk to Schultz and the bank back in Zurich, and very profitable indeed.

Paul learned a lot, with Schultz doing most of the talking in the meetings, Paul making a comment here and there, providing some numbers, interest rates, etc. Schultz was a master in representing his bank and a top-notch negotiator; mostly in Germany, his home turf.

He was king, having a strong physical presence, with his impeccably tailored suits. When he entered any room, everybody immediately looked up and paid attention. And he soon dominated the conversation. He was also quick with a joke, was witty and charming, competent, and utterly competitive.

Rarely did he have to call his boss, Meier, about anything. He disposed of large discretionary limits, he could negotiate on his own.

Besides the banks, sometimes they would visit medium to large German companies. There too, Schultz was able to conclude business and bring home new deals; but less so. Paul took all this in. He was proud of being in Schultz's company, and very determined to learn as much as he could, and as quickly as possible. And never let his boss down. He realised the potential and possibilities all of this presented to him, so he would make the best and most out of it. Schultz appeared to be pleased with Paul, slapping his shoulder or making an approving comment.

Back in Zurich, Paul processed the negotiated new deals, put them in a formal form, sometimes even went over to the loan department and outlined the new deal to his former boss, Tobler. This gave him immense pleasure.

All the travelling was always done together with Schultz, never alone, yet. When Schultz took his holiday break, Paul was bunkered down at his desk in Zurich. But he did, though, take that trip to Frankfurt and Poland, together with Tin. They set off on a Thursday morning in mid-April and drove straight up to Frankfurt in Tin's Corolla.

Up north, the Autobahn had no speed limit, and they took everything out of the Corolla's motor. There was no heavy traffic, and they arrived at midday in Frankfurt and had lunch. After that, they checked into a small hotel, breakfast included, just opposite the main railway station, with a garage to park the car. They took a one hour nap and then headed for the big Frankfurt entertainment area, with its hundreds of bars, restaurants and big blocks full of pussy.

They ventured into the buildings, block after block, up the stairs, down the stairs, and along long halls, with dozens of doors open, bright lights shining out; the women presenting themselves in a variety of outfits, mostly wearing almost nothing, or being completely naked, bar a pair of fishnet stockings.

It was fun to drink lots of German beer, do people watching, in this case whore watching, sometimes stopping at one of them, chatting them up talking nonsense and bullshit, and hear their sales pitch. After a few hours of this very entertaining nonsense, they became hungry and headed for a Greek restaurant nearby that Paul vaguely remembered from an earlier trip to Frankfurt.

They sat down, smoking and drinking, studying the menu, which was brought by a fat Greek lady with a moustache. Paul ordered Mezes, a variety of small plates filled with all kinds of delicious starters consisting of cold and hot meat, olives, cheese, roasted lamb and chicken, grilled vegetables, Tzatziki, a Greek spicy sauce, roasted bread, small Greek sausages... it went on forever and ever. The Greeks surely liked to eat; it was a feast that went on and on.

After the beers, they had a bottle of red chilled Greek wine, a bit too sweet, but OK. They then ordered grilled lamb chops with rice and a mixed salad. Good food, great company, the two enjoying each other, drinking, eating and laughing their socks off.

After the third bottle of that red wine, Paul ordered Greek coffees, together with two large shots of Metaxa the Greek brandy; delicious. Being too full of all this food and wine, tired and a little bit tipsy, too weary to climb the god damned stairs again to see the offers, they stumbled back to their small hotel, falling straight into bed and sleeping it off.

Next morning, around 9 a.m., they had their breakfast, settled the bill, and drove off towards Hamburg, further north. The plan was to have lunch thereabouts, without actually getting into the city, and turn east towards Stettin. Having had lunch, they re-fuelled the car and set off again. It took them another three hours until they were finally approaching the Polish border; it was 7 p.m. and dark already. Tin was still driving. Paul had offered to take the wheel, but he refused, saying he was OK. The custom building came into sight, brightly lit on both sides of the border. They got closer with almost no cars or trucks in sight. The German side waved them through, having looked at the car's registration plates.

They approached the Polish side and Tin was driving a bit too fast for Paul's liking, and then it all happened very quickly. Tin, in his wisdom, had taken the truck and lorry lane leading into Poland. He entered the wrong lane and was already past the guard's booth when sirens began screaming, and two Lada Police cars sped off chasing after them.

"Stop the bloody car, immediately, now!" Paul shouted. But the Polish Police had already blocked their car, bringing it to a screaming halt.

The two Police officers stepped out of their car, machine guns pointed at them, and shouting, "Freeze, hands in the air, no move." Approaching now, frisking the two of them, demanding to see passports, car documents, driving licence, all produced immediately.

Paul was shaking with rage and fear while Tin had put on his "excuse me Sir", smile. The Officers examined passports and documents carefully. They then noticed the red colour, with the white cross, saying Switzerland. They started laughing, relaxing, dropping their weapons.

"What on earth is happening with you guys? Had one too much, or need glasses?" They handed back the passports and documents.

"Now get out of here fast before Colonel Andrezey arrives." They urged them back into the car. Laughing nonstop, loudly. "Try to read the signs next time." They slapped on the Carolla's roof, sending them off. Tin accelerated and sped off as fast as the Corolla would go.

When they hit the main road, they looked at each other, starting to laugh. "Of all the people on earth, only you are capable of pulling that one off," said Paul, giving him a push and slap on his shoulder. "Now let's get the hell out of here before the Poles change their minds." Off they went down the road and into the night, towards Stettin.

Hitting Stettin shortly after 9 p.m., they drove into its centre, searching for a hotel with parking facilities; they found one near a Tram station. Stepping out of the car, still shaken after the border incident, Paul asked Tin to wait in the car. He entered the swinging doors of the establishment and asked for a room, two beds, one night.

"We have one, yes, daily rate is US$15."

On hearing this rate, Paul said, "OK, we will take it."

He had changed DM 300 into dollars while still in Frankfurt, and was expecting something like $60, but hell, $15 sounded great. He paid in advance, filled in a form, signing with Smith, and they walked back to the car. Tin was smoking one of his cigarillos to calm down.

"Park the car over there, right by that tree," Paul said.

That done, they took out their overnight bags and entered the hotel. The clerk handing out the key now. "Second floor, last door to the left. I am afraid the lift is broken."

They walked up the stairs, it was not exactly the Waldorf Astoria, old carpets with holes in them, greasy windows, wooden doors that looked like they would fall apart any minute; but so what! For 15 bucks, it could have been worse. Inspecting the room more closely now, two small single beds, one small side table with a lamp on top, with broken glass, two chairs and one wardrobe, with part of its two doors hanging awkwardly off the hinges. Throwing his bag on the bed, Paul inspected the bathroom, consisting of a lavatory with no lid, a sink, brown with a large fissure, and a bathtub of a greyish brown colour, cracked. Well a shower would have to do. No way he would lay down in that bath. Getting his toilet bag out of the bag, he used his own soap and showered, brushed his teeth, and laid down on the creaky bed, smoking a cigarette.

His thoughts wandered back to the incident at the border, them narrowly having escaped being shot. There was no point in giving more shit to Tin about it. He got the message; he had been sloppy, careless, and negligent, not paying attention to where he was driving. But it had passed now. Tin was a good chap, the best, so he would not say any more about it. When they both had dressed, they went down to the reception, asking the night guy for recommendations for restaurants within walking distance. They had done enough driving for one day.

"There is the Stettin Keller just around the corner, and down 300 metres."

"Thank you. We will give it a try."

They hung on to the key, not trusting this reception guy. After walking for about seven minutes, they found the place straight away. It was packed and smoky, loud as hell. They sat down at a vacant table.

A fat waiter with a beard came up to them. "What can I get you?" he asked in Polish.

Neither of them could speak Polish, so Paul said, "English, please, OK? Two large beers and the menu."

On hearing that, the waiter turned and walked away. Paul looked around the noisy large room, packed with all sorts of people, couples, workers, office clerks, suits, overalls, clean and dirty too, some women, mostly fat, nothing attractive. When the beers arrived, they both took a large gulp, almost emptying the mugs in one go. "Another two, please," Paul shouted to the waiter, who nodded.

Beers arriving, they studied the menu, which, thank god, had a Polish and a German section. When the waiter came back to the table to take their orders, they both went for pork cutlets with potatoes and beans, nothing fancy. When the meals arrived, they both dug in. It was good food, in very generous portions. After two more rounds of beer, they agreed to call it a day, wanting to leave Stettin first thing in the morning and head straight to Gdansk, situated on the Baltic Sea; a much larger, and hopefully more lively town than Stettin. Bill arriving, the amount was the equivalent of West DM 18, very cheap indeed, they both agreed. They then stepped into the cool nights air ,smoking ,and walking around for about 30 minutes. The town was already very quiet, nothing going on; no action. Arriving at the hotel, they greeted the night watch, who, to their surprise, was still hanging at the reception. They went upstairs and straight to bed, still chatting for a little bit, about Frankfurt and the great time they had there.

Paul consulted the map, showing it to Tin. By his estimate, it would take them about three hours to drive to Gdansk; piece of cake. Next morning, they had their Polish breakfast, a big affair again, took the car, and drove north. The Motorway was in reasonably good shape, no problem there. They stopped at a gas station, filling the Corolla up; which was slightly more expensive than back home, and continued.

The landscape was mostly agricultural, with large fields, trees, now and then a small town, some industry, not much of it, basically all agriculture. Entering Gdansk shortly after midday, they drove to the railway station to ask for directions and get a map or something. This was a much bigger town now, large roads, traffic intense, trains and trams, and in the distance, the sea. Paul spoke to a woman who ran a newspaper stand, asking about hotels and directions. She indicated a few, with Paul marking them on a map. He showed it to Tin, and they agreed to settle for a slightly better place this time, not so much in the city centre, but located more towards the sea. They chose the Anker Hotel and Restaurant and headed for it.

After another 25-minute drive, searching around, they finally found it. It looked good, big and stylish from the outside. Parking the car in front of it, trees lining the sides, they stepped out, collected their bags, and entered the hotel. They saw a large reception area, leather chairs to the left, with a bar to the right, and the reception desk. Stepping up to the desk, behind which was a tall man in his sixties.

"Can I help you?" he asked.

"Yes, please. We would like to have a double room for two nights."

"Let me check, please. Yes, there is one available on the third floor. The daily rate is $45. Would that be alright?"

"Perfect, we will take it."

After filling in the form and handing over an American Express credit card, they were given the key. "Breakfast is from 7 to 10 a.m. in the dining room, next to the lobby. Anything else, don't hesitate to ask."

"Thank you," they said and, taking the bags, they went up to the third floor. Opening their door, they stepped in. This time was much better, two good beds with clean sheets, functional furniture, and a good-sized bathroom; OK. They unpacked, both taking a shower, and went straight out, exploring the city. Walking up to the seashore, some 200 metres away, they saw a promenade and walked towards it. There was a splendid view of the sea and surf with a fresh wind blowing, seagulls flying and screaming above their heads, and ships passing by slowly.

Now and then, there were resting tables and benches, where people sat talking or having a snack. They walked another 20 minutes along the promenade when they spotted two girls who must have been in their mid-20s, sitting on one of the benches, both smoking, and both blonde, well dressed, and chatting away. Paul and Tin approached slowly. Getting closer now, they realised that both girls were rather tall, with full, curvy bodies. Paul smiled, and one of the girls smiled back. When they got to them, they all shook hands, Paul making the introductions. The two girls replied in English and gave their names as Lena and Zofia, both medical students on leave for the next two weeks.

They all sat down again, Paul and Lena on one side of the table, Tin and Zofia on the other side. Paul offered more cigarettes and explained that they were from Zurich, passing through, staying two nights. Lena said she had been to Switzerland once, visiting the capital, Bern, and passing through Zurich too. She said she found it beautiful, very clean and tidy, the mountains and all, wanting to visit the country again. Paul now started to look more closely at them. They were both dressed the same, pleated blue skirts ending above the knees, white blouses, blue socks and black shoes with medium height heels. They looked very cute; the dresses appeared to be some kind of a uniform or dress code. They chatted away happily, mostly about studies, university, work, family and so on and so forth. It all went very well indeed between the four of them, and Paul felt attracted to Lena, wanting to get closer to her. But it was too soon, not the right time yet. Instead, he suggested lunch, and were they any hungry? Did they have any suggestions for a lunch venue? Zofia suggested the Lighthouse, one kilometre down the walkway, right alongside the sea with a veranda overlooking it.

"Sounds great. Let's go. I am starving," said Paul.

With that, the four started walking in pairs, Paul and Lena taking the lead, with Zofia and Tin following right behind. After a short walk down the shoreline they reached the Lighthouse, entered and chose a table outside, close to the wall separating the outside section from the internal dining room. It was spectacular surroundings, sea and ships, the wind mildly blowing, and the sun shining. There were a few people scattered at the other tables, minding their own business, and not paying much attention to the group of four. Then the waitress, a brunette in her forties, white apron and black skirt, come to their table, greeting them warmly. They ordered four large beers and started to check the menu, which was in Polish and, thank god, German. No problem here. The restaurant specialised in fish and seafood; all four said they liked seafood a lot. When the first round of beers arrived, Paul ordered the seafood platter as a first course. It consisted of pieces of fish, shrimps, squid, mussels and other types of shellfish. When it arrived in a big bowl, they all dug in. It was delicious.

After the third round of beers, they were ready for the main course, all ordering the daily special; sole with potatoes and green salad. They stuck to beer for the time being, the girls keeping up with the guys, Paul observed.

When the two girls went to the ladies to freshen up, Paul said, "I am hot on that Lena girl. She's a stunner. Did you see her arse? Perfect."

"I don't need to see no Lena arse," Tin replied. "I've got the hots for Zofia."

When the two came back to the table, Paul had ordered four vodkas on ice with lemon. Again, the two kept up with the men, liking it and laughing. After the third round, Paul asked for the bill; it was by now, 4:30 p.m. After settling the bill, he suggested a walk on the seashore to freshen up. They walked along the walkway, now already hand in hand, for a good 20 minutes, when they spotted a table and bench a little bit further up, under a tree and overlooking the scenery.

They walked to it and sat down, this time all on the same side of the table. Paul started to kiss Lena. It was a passionate kiss, full of lust and drunkenness. Lena slid her hand down to his cock, starting to squeeze it. When Paul's hand went down Lena's back to caress her arse, he noticed that she wasn't wearing a slip. He stroked her arse, still kissing her, and then started to caress her arsehole. She started to moan, not objecting. Encouraged, Paul put his middle finger into her hole. She continued to moan, now even harder, taking out his cock and stroking it hard under the table. They both were completely unaware of the other couple beside them, but these two did more or less the same.

Then Paul could not take it any more. He was about to shoot off his jism right there. No way. He slowly took his tongue out of Lena's mouth, closed his zipper, stood up, and stepped back from the bench, trying to cool down. He was two steps behind Lena, with her right in front of him, overlooking the scenery, and all of a sudden Lena slowly raised her skirt, bending over slightly and opening her cheeks with both hands, showing him her arsehole, knowing that he was staring at her back. Paul had to control the impulse of putting his hard cock right into her hole and sodomising her on the spot. Breathing heavily, he turned his face around and tried to concentrate on something else. Managing more or less, and halfway composed again, he sat down and looked into Lena's eyes. She looked back at him with a challenging look, kissed him fully on his mouth, and said, "Let's get up and walk. I am thirsty. There is a kiosk down the road selling beer. It was very clear to him how this afternoon and night would end; clear to all four of them.

When they reached the small stand, they sat down at one of the two tables and had their beers; after that they went back to the hotel. Paul fetched the key and they entered the room. He fucked her from behind, hard, immediately, and screaming loud. Paul stared at Lena's gaping arsehole and they fucked again, and he came right there, while Lena moaned loudly and came too; again he stared at her round arse. After maybe half an hour of lying still in each other's arms, they went to take a shower together, cleaning themselves, kissing from time to time, less urgent now, just kind and tender, like old long-time lovers.

Stepping back into the room again, they observed the other two with Zofia's arse hanging half out of the bed while Tin lay on his back, snoring loudly. Lena walked towards Zofia and shook her gently.

"Go take a shower, you love bird, clean yourself up. We've got to go."

Hearing that, Zofia, half asleep still, managed to stand up and stumble awkwardly to the bathroom, her pussy oozing whitish liquid running down on one of her thighs. Later, Paul walked the two girls down to the lobby and asked the receptionist to please call a Taxi. They all sat down in the lobby chairs, too tired and drunk to stand, and waited, not saying too much either. Paul handed a $20 note to Lena, asking whether she felt this would take care of the taxi. She said yes, perfect. Paul knew that if he had tried to give her more money, something extra maybe, she would feel offended. They then kissed goodbye and agreed to meet again the next day, at the hotel at 10 a.m. Paul was keen to get to know Gdansk, and Lena agreed to act as their guide. He kissed her lightly on her cheek, and off they went, walking towards the taxi that had just arrived. Paul smiled and waved at them as they departed.

What a day. He had heard that Polish girls were wild and beautiful, but not that much. He turned and waited for the lift to arrive, tired, happy and very keen and eager to see the two lovely wild girls again tomorrow. Entering the room, he collapsed on the bed and fell asleep immediately.

Next morning, showered and shaved, the two men walked into the dining hall to have breakfast. Paul was wearing a dark blue navy blazer, Levis, a white and green striped sports shirt, with black leather moccasin slippers, looking sharp and ready to engage the world again. Tin was dressed sharply too, wearing a light brown sports jacket with grey flannels and a white shirt to go with it.

When they entered the breakfast room, two elderly ladies, past their prime, smiled and greeted them. Paul smiled back politely, being in a good, light mood. They sat down and had their breakfast, with juice and coffee, lots of it. They talked about the previous day and what a great day it had been, both keen to spend an equal one today. Having finished, they slowly went over to the lobby and sat down in the chairs, smoking, trying to read the papers, which were all in Polish, waiting for their companions to arrive. The weather was similar to the previous day, a mild sun and a steady breeze blowing from the sea. It was by now 10:10 p.m., and no Lena and Zofia in sight, only older couples and single men. Paul did not think that the two were a no show.

He asked Tin what he thought. "They will come. Relax, probably wasting too much time doing their make up."

A few minutes later, a Taxi drove up. Paul went out to see whether it was them and, if so, settling the fare. It was them alright, smiling and waving, stepping out of the cab. Lena kissed him on the lips, a nice scent engulfing him, and memories of last night came back. He paid the cab driver, and the three entered the hotel lobby to greet Tin. Kisses done, Paul suggested a walk, keen to visit the harbour, the old part of town and the Polish National Museum. Lena suggested the harbour first, then the museum and finally the old town. That agreed they set out. Today the two were dressed in red skirts with pale blue shirts and black shoes, no high heels; fit for walking. Lena had brought a map and an umbrella, just in case, while Zofia had brought the weather. It was a nice stroll, chatting away, all in good spirits, happy and cheerful, not a worry on their minds; and all curious how this second, and last, day would progress.

They reached the harbour and walked up to the ticket counter. Paul bought tickets for the harbour discovery tour on a vintage wooden bark with bar service; the ticket lady informed them drinks were not included. Before they stepped on board, Lena asked the deck hand to take a picture of them, with the vessel as background. That done, they settled on a bench outside on the forward stern, enjoying the scenery, the wind blowing in their faces, and the smell of salt, diesel, and high hopes in the air.

The harbour at this time of day was busy with barges transporting wheat, medium-sized tankers, general transport vessels, some sails, pleasure boats, and ferries. As they sailed out further to the right side of the harbour, the captain pointed out three frigates and a destroyer anchored and docked in front of a grey navy compound.

Taking all this in, sitting in their chairs, sipping beer, they talked about their private lives and duties. Lena explained she was in the seventh semester, five still to go to complete medical school. She was on an 80% scholarship for merit; without the scholarship, she could never complete her studies, the parents being in no position to support her and come forward with that kind of money. Her father was a steel worker with another 20 years to go, her mother tended the household. She had a younger sister, Paula, aged 19, and an older brother, Janick, serving in the army. She said she loved studying medicine, and intended to become a general surgeon one day. Paul, in turn, talked about his degree in economics, just having finished a few months ago, his career in general terms, and the probability of travel, which he loved, making deals and money. Lena listened with attention to all this information, apparently interested in what he had to say. Then their boat, after the more than three hours tour, finally docked at the jetty. They walked to a nearby cafe and had a quick lunch. Time was short.

Having finished their lunch, Lena pointed out the directions to the national Museum. They could either take a 30-minute walk or go by bus. They all opted to walk, enjoying the mild sun and clean air. When they reached the museum, an impressive 18th century building, Paul paid the modest entrance fee, and they all set out to discover. There was one entire floor dedicated to WW2, when Gdansk was called Danzig, under German occupation. The Poles then found themselves between a rock and a hard place, hating the Germans, but hating the Russians even more. They managed and put up fierce resistance, but were overrun and beaten by the Germans, who ruled them mercilessly.

After defeat, they managed to build and organise the Polish foreign army in the UK. Whole regiments fought alongside the British against the Germans in Europe. Most notably though, were the Polish fighter pilots, being organised in squadrons, along with the Canadians and British, who fought together from their airbases in the south of England. They fought fearlessly and very bravely. As Churchill had put it, "Never in the history of mankind, have so many owed so much to so few." All this was taken in and had an impressive impact on the four. They discussed and commented on it while the girls gave stories they had heard from their parents and grandparents, Zofia commenting that her family had lost their grandparents, and all male relatives during the war.

They then strolled on, discovering the Polish history in general, until its present day, culminating in the Pope being a Pole and the recent solidarity movement, led by Lech Walesa, whom Zofia said her father knew personally. After hours of history, they'd had enough, and sat down in a nearby cafe, in the shadow of old oak trees, drinking beer, along with shots of ice-cold vodka.

After this mostly serious and sombre experience in the Museum, they were keen to strike a lighter note. Paul telling the story of their border crossing a few days earlier, being almost shot. They all laughed at Tin's expense, who blushed, saying that he could not read Polish traffic signs. Now they all laughed even more and left it at that. The sun now was almost setting, so they headed for the old part of town, Lena leading the way, with both the girls commenting now and then on some building, bridge or landmark. It was pleasant to walk the mediaeval cobble-stoned narrow streets of Gdansk, with its many shops, cafes, hotels, governmental buildings, bridges, small parks, banks and commerce in general. It was by now dark and noticeably colder.

It had been a long day, and they were all tired, a little bit cold and hungry. Lena asked what they wanted to have for dinner. Paul suggested meat, they all agreed, and Zofia this time pointed out a Restaurant she knew well, just around the corner, and 400 metres down the road. Paul spotted an empty table, and they all sat down. When the waitress, a heavy-set woman in her early sixties, brought the menus, she suggested the day's special, a goulash served with potatoes and vegetables.

Paul said, "Thank you. Bring four beers please, and the wine list."

When the beers arrived, he said they had all agreed on goulash, and ordered a bottle of Châteauneuf du Pape to go with it. They then talked about their impressions of today's excursion, Lena from time to time squeezing Pauls hand and thighs, also kissing him lightly on the cheeks to warm up. After the delicious dinner and three bottles of wine, they rose and stepped out of the fine restaurant. It was 11 p.m. by now, and Lena, tireless as she was, suggested a night cap in a nearby bar and club. The place was packed and noisy, but they managed to squeeze in at the far end of the bar. After two drinks, they started to dance, some disco music pumping away. The DJ then decided to slow things down a bit, giving the love birds a chance, and put on Je t'aime moi non plus, the iconic song bringing them into the right mood, with Paul's hand stroking Lena's arse while she squeezed his dick, kissing away.

After two hours of this warming up, they all decided it was time to go. Leaving the club and walking down the now deserted streets, they found a cab, and Paul gave the hotel name and address, arriving there in under 20 minutes. He got the key from the same night receptionist, who was smiling when he saw them and the girls. Paul was actually thinking of asking for a second room, to have more space and privacy with Lena, but discarded it; the hotel must be fully booked, and he had no time to discuss prices and fill in another form, handing out credit cards. So the four took the lift and entered the one room; Lena and Zofia went to the bathroom to freshen up, while Paul dimmed the lights, opened the mini bar and took out four mini bottles of vodka.

They made a toast to friendship and love, and promised to meet again someday, some place; but in the meantime, they all had more urgent tasks in mind. Paul saw Zofia bending over, sucking Tin's cock, while at the same time, he was stroking her pussy with one hand. After having kissed Lena, Paul whispered in her ear that he had to piss.

"Let's go to the bathroom. You can piss in my mouth. I love it," was all she replied.

Hearing that, Paul almost dragged Lena to the bathroom, both taking off their clothes and Paul, standing over Lena, who had knelt down on the floor, slowly started pissing into her mouth, she swallowed it all, from time to time sucking on his cock.

When he was done, she stood up, bent over the bathtub, and offered her back, showing her wet pussy and arsehole. He put his cock into her cunt and fucked her hard, moaning and breathing heavily, while she uttered words in Polish he could not understand. It did not matter. Then she came with a loud sigh and Paul was about to do the same, but just before he came, she took his cock out and put it in her mouth

"Tonight I want to taste and eat it. Cum into my mouth, you filthy dog."

Hearing that, he shot his load into her mouth almost immediately. She swallowed it all, satisfied, showing her clean tongue and empty mouth as proof. They held each other for a while, then took a shower together, dried themselves, and, when they heard a knock on the bathroom door, it was Tin holding Zofia, wanting to take a shower.

"Go ahead, Tin. It's all yours."

Closing the bathroom door, they laid down on the small bed, embraced, whispering words and holding each other tight, kissing from time to time. There was no more vodka, so they settled for

Whiskey instead, drinking it in small sips, enjoying the moment and quiet after climax. And what a climax it had been. After a while of embraced happiness, the others walked back into the room. Paul offered whiskey, which they accepted, then Tin and Zofia laid down on their bed. They talked for a while, and then all of them fell silent.

The beds were too small to hold them, let alone have a night's sleep. So, after maybe an hour, it was 3 a.m. by now, all of them dressed, took the lift, and sat down in the empty lobby while Paul asked reception to call a Taxi.

They exchanged telephone numbers and promised to call and keep in touch, and meet again, maybe in Poland or Germany, or even in Switzerland in a few months' time. It was clear, at least to Paul, that this, unfortunately, was unlikely to happen. When the Taxi arrived, he gave money to the driver, and they all embraced. It was sad and satisfying at the same time. Paul thought he had seen a tear in Lena's blue eyes. They waved goodbye as the taxi took a bend and disappeared into the night. The two men did not say a word and went up to their roam and fell into bed. A long drive back home awaited them tomorrow.

CHAPTER 13

By eight o'clock they were in the car after having had a big breakfast and settled the bill. Paul was driving. No bullshit on the border this time. They passed through customs at Stettin and this time it went smoothly, no problem The Polish officer was not interested in looking at them or their papers. Back in Germany, Paul drove straight to the outskirts of Hamburg and there took the Autobahn. Heading south, traffic light, they made good progress, stopping once to fill the Corolla and have a coffee. By 2 p.m. they hit Frankfurt, passed it by and, at the next gas station, had a light lunch, then drove further south. Tin, in the best circumstances, was not a great speaker, normally saying about five words in a whole day. This time, though, he was more talkative.

"I think I'll call Zofia in a few weeks' time, see what she is up to. I like the girl, what a no-nonsense broad, going all the way nonstop, just the way I love it."

"I know," Paul replied. "Lena's a very hot number too, and good looking, pretty, witty, with a good sense of humour. It was great, to say the least," Paul went on. "Yes, maybe we will and can arrange to meet them in Germany somewhere, sometime. Zurich is out of the question. Soph is too jealous, and I don't want to have any more problems with her. She is already pissed about me travelling so much now on business, and my travelling on business will only increase. I like, maybe love her, and want to keep her happy and on my side."

Tin said, "Yes, you're right. Keep her afloat. She's a hot piece of arse."

Anybody else making this kind of remark about his girlfriend, Paul would have hit the guy immediately, but with Tin it was different, he had the freedom and space to get away with such a remark. The two had known each other far too long, and had gone through some pretty hairy stuff, so it was just OK. Paul even managed a smile.

Tin then went on to ask whether there was any action in sight other than girlie stuff; to which Paul said, "No, not for the time being. If anything comes up in the future, you will be the man."

Hearing this, Tin smiled and said he was ready for anything Paul would suggest, Anything.

After another two hours' drive, they crossed the Swiss customs at Basel. Traffic was heavy now, evening rush hour. Here again they were not stopped at the border, and Paul drove straight to Zurich. Just outside the city, they filled the Corolla one more time. It was 9 p.m. by the time they stopped in front of Paul's flat; he stepped out of the car and collected his bag. He was tired and worn out, sore on many parts of his body, in desperate need of a shower and a quiet evening. Looking at Tin, he knew he felt the same. They hugged and said goodnight, not without making a dirty Joke about Polish female attributes, but in a funny, light way.

"I'll call you," Paul shouted as Tin sped off. He went up to the third floor, opened the door, dropped the bag in the hallway and entered the bathroom, taking a good hot shower, washing the filth away from the hours of driving. He then opened the double glassed windowand the door to his veranda. He grabbed a beer and sat down in one of the blue and white covered summer chairs, and enjoyed the view. It was dark, but relatively mild, overlooking the lake; he saw some pleasure boats still cruising out there on the water, their red and green position lights still visible. He would call Soph in a minute, promising to take her out next day, meanwhile preparing himself mentally for tomorrow's work day, looming just around the corner. His thoughts wandered back to Gdansk and to Lena. What a great time they had, with Tin on his side, enjoying every moment. But tomorrow was reality, remembering Schultz saying that, if approved, he would have some news for him by Tuesday. Paul wondered what that could imply but could not yet figure it out. With that, he finished the beer, called Soph and went to bed to sleep off all his sins; or so he hoped.

Next morning, at 8 o'clock sharp, he sat down at his desk to read the papers. First the local *Neue Zürcher Zeitung*, and then the *Financial Times* and *The Wall Street Journal*. Half an hour later, Schultz walked into the office immaculately dressed in a black double-breasted suit, looking sharp. Imbach had arrived earlier and greeted Paul already.

"Good morning, Paul. Good trip? Take a break and let's go to the conference room. Sepp, come along If you could. I have news for you that can't wait a second."

With that the three went upstairs to one of the minor conference rooms. Having sat down, the secretary brought them coffee, and then Schultz got started.

"The board of Directors have agreed, last Friday, to allocate a country, or better, regional limit of US$300 million for the east bloc countries, namely Romania, Bulgaria, Czechoslovakia, Hungary and East Germany. They have accepted my recommendation, with the support of Imbach here to be fair, to go out and get these loan transactions done. It is our intention to syndicate some of the volume out, and Imbach assured everybody that there was great interest from many local and international banks, to participate in these transactions." For extra dramatic effect, Schultz stood up and walked to the window, looking out like a captain might look out to the sea from his bridge. "Initially, it is up to you, young Paul, to visit these countries, starting with the lesser acceptable risks such as Romania and Bulgaria, but still, within the limit agreed by the board. Hence, the first trip will be to Romania. We are already working on a shortlist of banks and companies to visit there. It goes without saying, all of them are 100% state-owned. Plan is to get you started at the end of the month. Karen will coordinate the itinerary and visa requirements. Let's get this thing going right away. I am very excited for you Paul, this is your chance to make it all happen, under my supervision of course."

It was immediately clear to Paul that Schultz would not enter this boat until it was proven that it could float. He also did not want to travel to Romania and the likes, extremely poor and under-structured countries, without the amenities Schultz was accustomed to. If it went wrong, the blame would be on him; if it went right, it would be Schultz's merit. But still, it was a huge chance, travelling alone, negotiating on his own, and bringing back the deals he was supposed to bring.

"I am delighted for the trust put into myself and thank you sincerely. I will give my best to make this a success," Paul said.

"Good man, that's the spirit," Schultz replied. With that, he rose again and walked out of the room, leaving Sepp and Paul alone.

"This is your chance, Paul. Make it happen. I will instruct and explain to you which banks and companies we are most interested in, these being also the ones I will be able to sell and load off to my friendly bank friends. You've still got two weeks till the end of the month, time enough to get acquainted and familiar with this, no doubt, pretty rough terrain."

With that, he too left the room, leaving Paul sitting alone at the table, absorbed in deep thought. He was excited, but at the same time aware of the risks and dangers this venture was about to engulf him in. But he would give it his best. After all, he had been in much worse situations and come out clean. He spent the next two weeks studying the countries he was about to visit; economics, political structure, country risks, ratings, balance sheets, if available, and so on.

When his three-day itinerary was completed, Karen asked for his passport to get the visa. He handed it to her, and after a few days, Karen handed it back with a one month visa for Romania, stamped by the Foreign Ministry of the country. Little did he know then what this all meant and included.

By now it was the end of May, a Tuesday, shortly after midday when Paul called a cab. It arrived a few minutes later, and Paul stepped in. He was wearing a new dark grey suit, white shirt with a blue tie, and dark black leather shoes from Church, London. He had a light beige raincoat with him and a rather large brief-case, no suitcase. The brown briefcase consisted of two parts that were held together with an on and off mechanism on the back. The upper half held his working tools: instruction papers; itin-erary; a Hewlett-Packard pocket calculator; agenda; pens; a map and information; and material, charts, and data on Romania's struggling economy. The lower half contained his personal be-longings: socks; underwear; clean shirts; two ties; toilet bag; and keys (held together by a key ring that had a golden horse-shoe attached to it, for extra luck - a gift from Soph for his 27th birthday earlier this year).

When he arrived at the embarking section at Kloten Airport to the north of Zurich, he paid the cab, kept the receipt, and went straight to Terminal 2, and the Swissair desk. A sizeable queue had already formed in the economy section, but he was booked in business class, with very few people queueing.

"Ticket and passport, Sir," the brunette attendant addressed Paul. Checking his documents, she asked, "No luggage to check in?"

Paul said, "No, no luggage. Just the briefcase."

She looked at him suspiciously, a man in his mid-twenties with no luggage, flying unaccompanied to Bucharest! But after a short while clicking away on her computer, she handed back his passport, gave him his boarding ticket, and told him the departure gate and boarding time. "Have a pleasant flight, Sir."

Paul found the gate and checked his watch. Half an hour to go, so he went to a coffee stall, ordering an espresso. He sat down on one of the small tables, observing the coming and going of people, hearing the announcements on the airports communication system, sipping his coffee, anxious to get to Bucharest and have his first meetings. He was keen to make it all happen.

Sitting now in his comfortable black leather chair, with nobody by his side and a nice stewardess in her late twenties walking by from time to time, smiling; the plane took off. After a good four-hour flight, they landed in Bucharest. Despite it being the month of May and springtime, a slight rain was falling, and the temperature was noticeably cooler by about ten degrees. Paul went through immigration, a rather lengthy procedure, but finally made it and stepped out of the airport building; a construction of the early sixties that would make any decent architect cry out in despair.

Waiting for a taxi; finally, it was his turn. A greenish Lada stopped in front of him. Paul opened the back door and climbed in. The car was damp and filthy; the seats stained and dirty; it smelled of cigarettes, booze, and vomit. He gave the hotel address, a supposedly 5-star hotel in the centre of the city. The driver nodded, saying something Paul could not understand, and drove off.

After a half hour drive, they arrived at the Grand Hotel Bucharest. Karen had given him some Lev Romano, the local currency, which was worth next to nothing. The driver refused the Levs, demanding dollars instead. So much for the trust they had in their own currency, but Paul, not having any other option, handed the driver dollars and entered the lobby of the hotel; a grand affair indeed, must be dating back to the twenties or thirties. After checking in, no problem there, he asked what time dinner was served and went up to his room; a rather large one, with a desk, bathroom and a double bed. The walls were painted in green and yellow, with orange curtains, a nightmare for any interior designer. To compensate, the bathroom was large, with a large bathtub and a double sink. Paul took a shower, feeling that he needed one.

The drive from the airport had shown nothing but endless rows of apartment blocks, all soviet built, all equal and exactly the same four storey grey buildings, few trees lining the streets, almost no green open space areas, all dull and functional. Having taken all this in, he had no desire to go out at all. Instead, he poured himself a whiskey from the minibar and turned on the small TV set. It was in colour alright, but only local stations talking in Romanian, no other language; a waste of time. He turned the TV off and instead, concentrated on the *Financial Times* he had brought with him from the airplane and started reading. But he could not concentrate, his mind wandering, so he put on his suit, left the room, and went downstairs, heading straight to the bar. He sat down on one of the bar stools, ordered a Gin and Tonic, and started observing the crowd.

It was, by now, 8 p.m., but despite the hour, few people sat at the bar or in the chairs around small tables. The patrons were mostly men sitting alone, or in groups of two, talking. There were two women, wearing sixties-style dresses, tight, with the skirts too short, smoking; no doubt local hookers waiting for their prey. Paul was not interested in them, not his style, not the right time, and not in the mood. He scanned the room lobby and bar again, this time more closely. His eyes fell on a man in his early forties, strong built, moustache and an ill-fitting suit. He wasn't sure, but he thought he had seen the man before, somewhere at the airport. With that, he signed the tab to his room and went to the dining hall. Stating his room number, he was led to a table at the far end, next to the large windows. He sat down, ordered another gin and tonic, and started reading the menu, which had a section written in English. When the waiter brought his drink, he said he needed a few more minutes and started to observe the other diners.

Again, it was not packed, with a good half of the tables empty, and again the diners were mostly men in their forties to sixties. Paul smoked a cigarette, and when the waiter came back to his table, ordered a soup for starters, and the beef wellington as main course, together with a bottle of Beaujolais. He was not very hungry. After coffee, he signed the bill to his room and walked through the lobby in the direction of the lifts. He spotted the same man, still sitting in the same chair, reading the local papers this time. Immediately, Paul rode up to level 5, opened the door and tried to call Soph, but either she was not at home or the connection did not go through. So he did some more reading, and after an hour went to bed.

At 7:30 the next morning, showered and shaved, he entered the breakfast room, had his breakfast, an unremarkable event, smoked a cigarette, and stood up. No newspaper had been delivered in the morning, so he went over to the reception desk, enquiring about an English language newspaper.

"I am afraid *The Wall Street Journal* will only be delivered at around noon, Sir," the chief receptionist said. He was a thin man with dark brown eyes and black hair.

"OK, I see," said Paul, "I will have to wait until noon then." With that, he grabbed his briefcase, consisting of only the upper part, put on his raincoat, and stepped out of the hotel. There were a few cabs waiting in front of the hotel and Paul approached the first one in the row and climbed in. When he showed the driver his itinerary with the first address to go to, the driver had already driven off without even looking at Paul's sheet. He seemed to know exactly where to go to. A shiver went down Paul's spine. How was this possible, or were the authorities aware of his every move? And if so, how had they managed that?

When they arrived after a 20-minute drive, he had already spotted the large building housing the Romanian Commercial Bank. He paid the cab, in dollars again, and walked into the reception area.

"My name is Winter. I am here to see Mr. Antonescu," he said.

"Have a seat, please. Mr. Antonescu will be with you in just a minute," said the greyish haired woman in a black dress, with golden spectacles.

Paul sat in one of the chairs, which had seen better days. After what seemed like an eternity, a young woman in her twenties approached him.

", Mr. Antonescu will see you now. Please follow me."

Paul stood up and followed the young lady into a labyrinth of endless halls. When she finally opened a door and stepped in, a rather fat man in a brown suit stood up from behind his desk.

"I am Mr. Antonescu. Welcome Mr. Winter." He stretched out his hand, which Paul shook. The man's hand felt sweaty and soft. "Let me introduce you to Mr. Boboc and Mr. Cercel, fellow directors of the bank." With this, Antonescu led Paul into an adjoining room, with a conference table and eight chairs around it.

Mr. Antonescu took the chair at the head of the table and asked all of them to sit down. A woman, who was not introduced, sat on a small chair at the far end of the room, undoubtedly to take notes. Antonescu then started his, no doubt, well-prepared speech about Romania's prosperity: its thriving economy, no unemployment rate to speak of, inflation well under control, exports increasing and stable currency. All this thanks to the efficient leadership of its economic Central Party and its Finance Minister. This rambling went on for a solid half an hour, with the little woman in the corner busy scribbling it all down. The two other men did not say a word, restricting themselves to nodding their heads from time to time, or writing down a figure or remark; they thought were worth noting down.

Paul listened carefully and intently to this nonsense, nodding here and there and smiling, knowing that Romania was on the brink of economic collapse – not divulging any useful information or data, trying to fool the outside world by presenting themselves much better than they were; supplying fake information and handing out manipulated data. As a matter of fact, their industrial machinery and technology was hopelessly outdated. They produced goods that no one wanted to buy, with the exception of their fellow eastern bloc countries, and perhaps Russia. But they all paid, if they paid, in their own weak currency, depressing the trade deficit even further. The Lev, Romania's currency, was worth next to nothing. Romania was hopelessly short of cash. What they needed was hard currency. But they would never admit that, not wanting to weaken their negotiating powers, if any.

When Antonescu had finished his endless rambling on the wonders of the Romanian economy, it was his turn. Paul stood up and addressed the audience, beginning with general information about his bank and principal shareholders. A powerful statement, and Paul was careful not to exaggerate, sticking to the facts, which spoke for themselves. When he turned his attention to outlining possible loan structures, terms, interest rates, additional costs and, most importantly, currencies. The three Romanians did not blink an eye, their faces devoid of any emotion or interest. They must have learned this type of behaviour in basic tutorial number 1, *"How to deal with western capitalists"*.

On the other hand, they were attentive, listening carefully and not once interrupting.

Paul, having finished, handed out an information sheet, which the three of them read carefully. Still they asked no questions, stood up, and thanked Paul for his time. On the way out, Paul mentioned to Antonescu that he would call him the next day, while still being in Bucharest, to see whether the directors were ready to sign a letter of intent and, if so, Paul would deliver it personally. Antonescu said he would be delighted to receive his call, by then having passed the terms to his board and them hopefully being ready for an answer.

They said goodbye, and that was the end of his first standalone meeting, in a very strange and unfamiliar set up. He said goodbye to the receptionist and exited the building to face another three meetings with other banks and Romania's largest finance company. He handled the three meetings bravely, with similar set ups and outcomes becoming familiar to him now.

Having finished the last one, he stepped into a cab, dying to get back to the hotel. He thought he caught a glimpse of the brown suit from the hotel lobby yesterday, sitting in a black Skoda three cars behind his taxi. Was he getting paranoid, or was it true? Was he being followed?

When he arrived, he could not see the black Skoda anywhere. Going straight up to his room, he took a shower, sat down in a chair, and went through his notes. He prepared and wrote his report on every meeting and every detail that had occurred while his memory was still fresh.

The next day went pretty much as the previous one had; four meetings, in total, mainly banks (an industrial bank, another commercial bank, and then the last and most important meeting with the Romanian Central Bank – the very bank that was supposed to guarantee the potential loan transactions.

This time, Paul found himself facing a committee of eight men, the usual stenotypist, and a ninth man, not looking like a banker, and who the Chairman was careful not to introduce. As always, he was first subjected to a this time even longer speech by the Chairman, about the wonders of the Romanian economy and its modern banking system. It took Paul quite some effort to remain interested and attentive. At the end of the speech this time, some of the other directors even applauded the Chairman. Paul was determined to make his mark, stood up, and gave his speech, which this time lasted double the usual time. It seemed one thing these eastern fellows had was time. No rush there.

When he had finished, the Chairman asked a few questions, first, about more detailed numbers of some of the general terms Paul had outlined. He was able to come up with accurate answers, but at one stage really had to search his memory to answer. Satisfied, the Chairman called the meeting to an end, and they all shook hands. An assistant appeared and let Paul out of the vast building.

On the cab ride back to the hotel, he had already started scribbling down notes on the last meeting. This last meeting was the key to doing business in this country. He could not afford to miss out a single small detail that had been mentioned in this last, most important meeting.

Entering his room, he went straight to the bathroom, took a hot shower, and sat down to finish his notes. It was already dark outside, and rain lashed at the windows. He went down to the bar, with the usual assortment of businessmen in their mid-thirties to sixties. Some Romanian ladies were thrown in for good measure.

He ordered a gin and tonic, smoked a cigarette, and let his thoughts wander free. When he had called Antonescu from the hotel earlier in the day, he had answered his call but informed him that the board had not yet reached a decision, that he had Paul's card and would call if a positive decision had been reached. Paul was realistic. He did not have too high hopes of this happening. It was their decision to accept the terms or not. He could yield a little here and there within his limited discretion, but the decision was theirs.

He ordered another drink and looked around. One particular woman in a yellow dress sitting two chairs down the bar, was looking at him and smiling invitingly. Paul smiled back, but made no move. Instead, he signed the bill to his room, left the bar, and went to the dining hall. Nothing fancy. No fancy business tonight. He was not in the mood and uneasy about the people in this country. The brown suit had changed into a grey one; Paul had spotted him earlier, sitting in the lobby. But he paid little attention to the man this time. Instead, he concentrated on his dinner, an ordinary affair. Tomorrow morning he would be on the 10 a.m. Swissair flight straight back to Zurich. That was all that mattered and counted at the moment. He was relieved and keen to get back to more friendly and familiar surroundings. It was only 11 p.m. when he called it a day, retreated to his room, and had a good, dreamless night's sleep; he felt that he had fulfilled his duty to his best knowledge and capability.

He arrived at Zurich Airport shortly after 2 p.m., went through customs, hailed a cab, and 40 minutes later was opening the door to his flat. What a relief. The weather being fine; he opened the door to the balcony and sat down sipping a cold beer he had fetched from the well-stocked fridge. He had called Soph earlier and invited her to go out and grab something to eat, and afterwards do what they both liked most, fucking each other's brains out, and anything else kinky that came to their minds.

Next morning, punctually at 8 o'clock, he sat down at his desk, again going through the notes and conclusions of each meeting. He then handed the notes to Lilly, the department's secretary, to be typed. Lilly had taken a shine to Paul, and when he said he needed the report in half an hour, she smiled at him and said, "Leave it with me, no problem my dear Paul."

Twenty-five minutes later, she put them on his desk, even before Schultz had arrived. He made himself a coffee from the machine, sipped water to go with it, and waited for his boss. He had already spoken to Imbach, giving a first rundown to which he only had commented, "It's rough terrain, nobody expects you to haul in a big million dollar deal on your first trip."

Schultz arrived 15 minutes later, shook his hand and asked how it went. He asked Paul to be in the conference room in half an hour to brief him. Paul was already seated in the conference room when the two men entered. He gave his speech, a good 20 minutes long, and he left no detail out, reporting everything to the two men. At the end, he gave his opinion on the potential. Helmut had most of the time nodded, while Sepp sat silent, and did not blink an eye.

Eventually, Helmut said, "Well done. I did not expect much from this round. It was warm up time. Keep the good work going, and by the way, your next mission is to Bulgaria in three weeks' time. Same time span, similar set up. Karen will start working on the itinerary in the next few days."

Having said that, he rose and left the room, dragging Imbach along with him. It was unclear to Paul whether Schultz had expected more out of this first trip; but if he had, he definitely had not shown it. So that was it, and now Bulgaria in only three weeks' time. What the hell! He had asked for being his own master, travelling on his own, proving himself; now he had got it. But Bulgaria, and so soon. Not much he could do about it. Think positive, embrace it, make the best out of it.

The next two weeks he studied Bulgaria's economic system, its banking system, political structure, and so on. It was much the same as Romania, only the language had changed, with Bulgarians writing in Cyrillic. The currency was much the same too.

He realised he would not understand a word of what they were saying, let alone read what was written, more complications here and there was no time for him to learn their language, nor had he any interest whatsoever in doing so. No, English and German would have to suffice.

So instead of getting into their strange language ,he concentrated on learning everything he could on the country ,and its financial system, if there was any. Their currency ,instead of Lev Romano, was called Lev Bulgaro, not much difference there and probably as worthless as in Romania.

After these two weeks of intense preparation, he was ready one more time. He had already handed his passport to Karen for her to arrange the necessary visa. His itinerary was ready. The duration of the trip was three days again no change. When he went to the internal cashier's desk to get some Bulgarian Lev, this time he took only the equivalent of Sfr. 100. He had a hunch that the Bulgarian Lev was not accepted there. They most probably did not trust their currency. Can't blame them, they want dollars.

On the eve of his flight, Swissair again non-stop – this time to Sofia – he gave Soph a treat, taking her out and promising that the next trip they would make together. She had mentioned that her father and mother, and two of her brothers, were set for Spain in mid-July and invited him to come along and join them a few days later, hoping very much he could make it, his commitments allowing. Her father, Hans, who had become rather fond of him, had reserved a room for them in the same hotel they were all staying. Paul promised Soph, over dinner, that yes he wanted to go spend the holiday with her and her family. He decided to take the car and drive down there to meet them all in Spain. Soph was delighted, and that night gave him the treat she thought he deserved.

Next morning, around 9 a.m., Paul was sitting in the seating area at gate number 35 at Kloten airport, waiting for embarkation to be announced and the plane's departure. A good five hours later, he found himself queueing for immigration and passport control at Sofia airport.

Riding in the cab to the Sofia Hotel Balkan in the city centre, he observed the landscape passing by. A few more trees lined the streets, a bit cleaner, but the same dull apartment blocks with no variety, endless rows, only broken by the intersections of the roads they passed. The car this time being a Russian model from the sixties, a brand name he could not pronounce. Anyway, they made it to the hotel and again Paul paid in dollars and walked the few steps up the stairway and into the lobby. It was very elegant, with chandeliers hanging high from the ceiling and had a large wooden reception desk.

He identified himself and was given a form to fill in. Having completed the check in and given his key, a man stepped up next to Paul. "Good afternoon. My name is Mr. Ivanov. I will be your official driver during your stay in Sofia. You most probably are unable to read the street signs written in our beautiful language, and the taxi drivers, in turn, are unable to read English. We don't want you to get lost."

Having said that, he informed Paul that he would be in the lobby tomorrow morning at 8 a.m., waiting for him. He shook his hand and walked out of the hotel, nodding to a man who sat in one of the chairs near the entrance.

Paul went up to his room on the sixth floor, number 614, deep in thought. What the hell was that all about? Official driver my arse. Ivanov had not said who he was, or for whom he worked, but undoubtedly he was with the Bulgarian police or, worse, state security. It was true that he could not understand or read any of their speech or writing, but had thought that the taxi drivers might help him out with that. As he saw it, the security police did not want to lose him, checking every step he made. He wondered whether Ivanov would join the meetings as well, but he was soon sure to find out. Creepy though, he did not like to be watched, had always loved his freedom and moving around unobserved.

He also had a thing about the police. Any police made him nervous, anxious and afraid. He did not like it at all. What could he do? Complain? But to whom? Complain to Schultz? No, he had to play this cool, just carry on putting up a brave face and not showing any concern.

The hotel room this time was bigger and much better decorated and furnished. It had a large wooden desk, two comfortable chairs, a large double bed, a small balcony opening to the Avenue, and a good-sized bath. He checked the mini bar, which was well stocked.

"OK, let's see how I can play this," he murmured to himself. After having showered, he sat down and read *The Wall Street Journal*, today's edition. OK, much better. Having finished with the paper, he felt like calling Soph, but restrained himself. He was pretty sure that all calls were being monitored and recorded. He did not want any link to him back to Switzerland. No, Soph would have to wait. He dressed, rode down in the lift, and sat down in the lobby for a while, watching the people coming and going while smoking a cigarette, and also observing the reception desk.

The man, Ivanov, who had greeted him earlier, was nowhere in sight, but that did not mean much. Undoubtedly, he had been replaced, but he could not make out anyone that looked like police; and even if he did, what could he do? Slap the man in the face, demanding identity? Ridiculous! No, he had to stay calm, playing along, but he really wished, for the first time, he was back in the security of his flat in Zurich. He stood up and went to the bar, ordering his usual G&T, smoking and observing his fellow bar dwellers, mostly men, but better dressed in well-cut suits, a few women, more discreet this time and much better dressed too, but undoubtedly here for the one and only purpose.

Having finished his second drink, Paul went to the dining hall; a large room, splendidly decorated with nice tables and chairs. The head waiter showed him to his table and passed over the menu, which had an English section,. Good He was hungry, so he ordered a mushroom soup, followed by a plate of smoked salmon with toast, and as main course, the roast beef with vegetables and rice. To go with it, and to wash it all down, he ordered a bottle of Brunello de Montalcino and still water. Enjoying his dinner, which was notably better that anything he'd had in Romania, he observed the other diners, groups of men, a few couples, no single ladies, a mixed well-dressed bunch of ordinary people, or so he hoped, his mind still on his so called "guide" for the next two days. He settled the bill, went up to his room straight away and into bed, sleeping almost immediately.

Having showered and shaved, early next morning, and even putting on a drop of Pino Silvestre, his preferred fragrance, he rode down to the breakfast room, carrying his briefcase, notes, itinerary, calculator, pen and everything else that would come in handy today. He even had a map with him, for good measure. Having finished his breakfast and smoked his first cigarette, he stood up and went to the lobby.

It was no surprise to him to find Ivanov already standing at the reception desk, dressed in a baggy black suit, raincoat hanging over his arm. Paul approached him, handed his key to the receptionist, and was greeted by Ivanov. "Lovely day today. My car is just parked outside. Shall we go?" He kept it light but scrutinised Paul's face and suit intensely.

"Good morning, and yes let's go," Paul answered. They walked out of the hotel and down the road some 50 metres, where the man opened the door for him.

Paul entered the car, a nondescript black sedan, while Ivanov sat at the wheel. Paul, just to test, gave the address and name of the bank of the first meeting, but his guide had already set off without even looking at it. They arrived at the Bulgarian Exim Bank 15 minutes later and pulled over. Paul thanked him and stepped out of the car, watching what Ivanov was doing.

Ivanov followed Paul a few steps back as he made his way to the reception desk. "My name is Paul Winter. I am here to see Mr. Grozdev."

"Yes, Sir. Mr. Grozdev will see you in a minute. Please have a seat."

With that, Paul sat down with Ivanov hanging around the reception desk. A few minutes later, a heavy-set man in a grey suit and white shirt stepped out of the lift, followed by a woman in her thirties, wearing a black suit and black shoes, carrying a folder under her arm.

"Mr. Winter. So nice to see you," he said as he shook his hand now with enthusiasm.

Paul followed Grozdev, leading the way, while Ivanov followed right behind them. "Let's see where this all leads to," Paul thought, when, after a quick walk, they reached a conference room with Grozdev's assistant opening the door. Paul stepped into the spacious room, followed by the bank executive and, believe it or not, Ivanov. "So that's how this will play out," Paul thought.

Ivanov was following Paul's every step, joining in commercial private meetings.

Four men, all in their forties, were waiting for them, with Grozdev making the introductions; then he started his propaganda speech. This very pattern repeated itself for the remainder of the day's meetings, and also over the next days; Ivanov not leaving Paul on his own for one single minute. The only place he had some privacy was his hotel room, but he made sure not to use the hotel's phone.

It was his last morning in Sofia, and he was glad it was all over, but he still had to make it to the airport. He settled the hotel bill, always looking over his shoulder to see whether his watchdog was around to drive him again. But, to his surprise, there was no Ivanov in sight. No doubt they had sent somebody else to see him off. Paul stepped out of the hotel and saw three taxis in front. He took the first one in the row, said, "Airport, quick," and they set off.

What a relief, but the real relaxation would only come with Paul sitting firmly in his business class seat aboard Swissair, heading home. 5 hours later, he landed at Zurich airport, and a good hour later was home, finally.

What a disturbing and unpleasant three days, and to make it worse, nothing to show for either. All his Bulgarian counterparts had seemed very interested, but none had signed any letter of intent or preliminary agreement. So not much to report to Schultz the next morning. But what could he do about it? He had given his best, but again, came back empty-handed.

Next morning's report and briefing went fairly well, Paul thought. Schultz did not criticise him, but did not slap him on his shoulder either, listening, and only saying good things take time. When Paul reported on his watchdog, neither of them spoke or

154

responded. Imbach only looked deeply into his eyes, then Schultz's eyes, and then back to Paul. Paul was not sure, and of course could never prove it, but he was under the impression that this piece of intelligence came as no surprise to them. Schultz called the meeting to an end, mentioning that the next trip would be to Czechoslovakia. He had not yet decided whether he himself would go, or Paul again. Anyway, he would let him know in the next few days.

Paul was not surprised to hear that Czechoslovakia was a much better developed country. Because of this fact, and much more favourable economics and politics, Schultz was considering taking the trip himself. There was nothing he could do. He had to wait; Helmut was the boss. After two weeks, however, Schultz announced that he could not make it, being too busy with important developments in Germany, and Paul would go again. Yes! The trip was scheduled for early autumn, a good two months away. That was very good news indeed, he could now make the trip to Spain with Soph and keep her happy, and gaining precious time before visiting his communist friends again. This time, he felt, he would bring the deal home; he had to.

During the next few weeks, he prepared himself for the next business trip, this time to the CSSR. He studied what could be studied and learned. There was much better data on the country's economy, exports to eastern bloc countries, but also to the West, a more modern society in general, and much better structured. But still a large trade deficit, weak currency, large unemployment, and a crumbling, outdated infrastructure. They were in need of cash, no doubt. He knew he could not come back empty-handed again; this time he had to bring home a deal, and by priority a large one that was on good terms for his bank.

He felt confident, for no obvious reason, but did not want to dwell on that point. CSSR had to wait a little while, he was in desperate need of a break, a summer holiday in sunny Spain with his lover by his side, and hopefully nothing to worry about for two weeks. He had the Alfa Romeo serviced, put four new tyres on, and gave it a general overhaul. He was looking forward to the drive; a good 1,400 kilometres of mostly highways, always heading south. Soph had already left three days before with her parents, flying to Barcelona, and then by coach to the Costa Brava. She had telephoned from the hotel, all glee and happy, saying that it was great. The hotel was just off the beach, beautifully located, the water warm and blue, with a good surf rolling in most of the time.

Their room was spacious, overlooking the sea, with a small balcony where they could sit and sip sangria, smoke cigarettes, and tell how much they loved each other. Yes, that sounded really very nice and inviting.

The day before, he had seen Tin for lunch at the Antinori, catching up with each other. Tin said he too was fine, no more walking astray to drink beer during working hours. He got along with his boss. Maybe there was even a raise at the end of the year. He was seeing Annie, a blonde whore he had met at the High Life night club.

Paul said yes, he did remember her. "Tall with big boobs and a horse's arse?"

"That's the one alright," Tin said, as they laughed this one off.

Paul then said he was steady with Soph, all things going smoothly in that department, thank you, and talked about his latest business trips; a dire affair, his watchdog Ivanov, to which Tin, in his wisdom, asked whether he saw any connection between the Bulgarian and Swiss authorities. Paul shrugged this one off, "no way," at which point Tin relaxed again, puffing on his cigarillo. Then Paul said good, yes, he would be in touch after Spain.

On the eve of his 16-hour drive, he packed his suitcase, keeping it light. The temperature in Spain was around 30°C. He packed a couple of short-sleeved shirts, Bermuda trunks, leather slippers, the dark blue navy blazer, a pair of chinos and one pair of Levis, Ray-Bans, Spanish Pesetas worth Fr. 2,000, toilet bag, and his jackknife. He closed his case and put it in the hallway next to the door. He then prepared a ham and cheese sandwich, grabbed a can, and sat down in one of the white and blue striped canvas summer chairs on his balcony overlooking the lake, shimmering blue and silver in the settling sun. It was full of boats with their red and white flags swaying proudly in the evening breeze. When all this became too cosy and sentimental, he went to the living room, slouched down on the black soft leather couch and watched the news. By 9:30 he was in bed, trying to get the strength for tomorrow's drive. He set the alarm at 3 a.m. and fell asleep, anxious and keen.

With the Alfa's 2-litre engine roaring down the motorway, he made the customs at Chiasso by 6:10 a.m., and continued south on the Italian highway in the direction of Genoa. Every other 50 kilometres or so he had to stop and pay the toll, a silly affair, slowing him down considerably. By noon he arrived at the outskirts of Genoa, where he filled the car and had a light lunch and two espressos; he also bought a large bottle of still water, the temperature getting hot, and even hotter inside the car. He listened to the local Italian radio stations, which, when the Italian presenter wasn't shouting, played mostly sentimental music; good for sleeping or crying, but not for driving. So, he put an AC/DC tape into the car's sound system, much better.

He then headed west, crossed the border into France near Monaco, no problem there, and continued west in the general direction of Marseille. He hit the city by nightfall, but kept driving on. The motorway was built above the coastline, and the sea shimmered darkly in the distance below. When a large petrol station with a rest sign came up, he filled the tank again, had his dinner, and sat down on one of the benches outside under the blue night sky in the rest area. Breathing in the warm night air, he smoked two cigarettes and walked around a bit, stretching his legs. He still felt fit and not too tired, ready to drive on. A few hours later he crossed into Spain, but this time the Spanish duty officer demanded to see his passport, driving licence and car registration documents. He ordered Paul to step out of the car and open the boot. Looking inside, searching for something, he saw only the blue Samsonite and nothing else; the boot was empty. He handed back the documents and waved him through.

Driving in a south westerly direction, he made Barcelona by 10 p.m., but drove on, finally reaching his destination, a small town at the Costa Brava. There was lots of action still, bars and restaurants full of late diners having a ball. He reached the Delmar Hotel and Resort in no time, parked the car in front, and took out the suitcase. The Alfa was sitting there, sleek and shimmering brightly beneath the powerful lamps of the car park. "What a beauty," he thought, looking at his car. He stepped into the lobby, still crowded, gave his name, and asked to ring Soph's room. The receptionist, a short man with a big dark moustache, gave him a spare key, 4th floor, number 427.

"Miss Soph is waiting for you, Sir," the receptionist said.

Running to the lift and taking the ride up to the 4th floor, when the door opened there she was in all her 20-year-old beauty, wearing a short, flowered dress, and slip ons. They embraced, fell on the bed, kissed and made love there and then. No time to waste. After this welcome, he took a shower, and they sat smoking on the balcony, holding hands.

Soph had ordered a bottle of local white wine, served chilled in a bucket full of ice, and then they toasted and drank, happy and full of energy, the way only very young lovers manage to do.

Next morning in the dining room, all six of them sat around a large table, having their breakfast, talking to each other non-stop. Her mother said that she loved the beach and sea, spending most of her time lying in the sun, showing a dark tan already; to which Hans, the head of the family, rebuked her, telling her not to spend so much time in the sun, her face was already full of wrinkles and spots, aggravated by the sunbathing. Age had not been kind to her, and she looked older than her 45 years, while Hans, with his intelligent small brown eyes, witty and always ready with a joke – sometimes on the dirty side – did not look his 55 something. He was short, but not fat – stocky maybe – and looked like a retired footballer or tennis player, which he claimed he was, but Paul had never seen him playing anything other than keep poor old Anna up and running. Her two brothers chatted away, the younger one taking the lead, a copy of his father, lively and outspoken, while the older one tended to be sullen, spoke little and kept mostly to himself, re-sembling his mother.

Hans and Paul now talked about cars and fishing, and Hans suggested a fishing trip in the next few days. Paul said, "Great, happy to join in, I like fishing." Soph said yes, she would join in, while Anna was not sure about it. Anyway, the hotel was great, the room very nice and spacious, their stay included breakfast and either lunch or dinner, all courtesy of Hans. They mostly had lunch on the hotel terrace overlooking the beach and sea. The hotel also offered a bar service at the beach, so for Soph and Paul, it was a seemingly endless supply of dry martinis, cuba libres and gin and tonics, while Hans would normally stick to beer and white wine, while Anna had water or nothing.

They swam in the sea every day, a couple of times, laid on the sand, or sat in the chairs sipping their drinks. They would go for long walks on the beach, Paul loving to walk and Soph joining in happily. After lunch, they always went up to their room for a little siesta, as Paul put it, but their siestas normally consisted of fucking and sucking, and afterwards, half an hour of dozing and a shower. It was the perfect "get-away-from-it-all holiday", and the two of them had a ball.

Paul saw Hans riding the lift up with Anna after lunch, giving the old girl a go, most probably. Old love never dies, or so it seemed. For dinner, he and Soph normally went out, sometimes, or mostly, they walked the streets on the sea shore, bristling with cafes and restaurants, open very late into the night. After dinner they usually went to their favourite bar, the Marlin, for a night cap. If they felt up to it, sometimes they went to a night club and disco, dancing the night away.

Paul had bought a map, he loved maps, and they would take the Alfa and drive up in the mountains, half an hour or so, to have dinner at a well-hidden Finca, or similar, away from the tourist crowd. He spoke no Spanish, and neither did Soph, but he made himself understood by using his passable Italian. The Spanish did not like that much, but what the hell, he was paying, and tipping generously, so the waiters mostly put a brave face on it and accepted Paul's Italian mumblings. Soph was a healthy girl, and a good eater and drinker, mostly keeping up with Paul.

Sometimes, when they arrived by car, in the half dark car park behind the small restaurant with no one else in sight, Soph would say, "Look over there, darling. See the silver owl on your left side." Then, with him looking out of the window, trying to see the bird, she would open his zipper with amazing speed and suck his cock, blowing him until he came. Afterwards, with her always swallowing the last drop, that was just the appetiser. "Sometimes I get tired of all these Tapas starters," she would say.

What could one say to a girl like that? Nothing, just treat her as the princess she was. These happy days continued and sometimes they were joined for dinner by Soph's parents, but rarely would they take the boys out with them. At the beginning of the second week, Paul suggested a trip up to Barcelona, visiting the big city. "A bit of culture," as he put it. What did they all think?

The boys said they had no interest in culture and preferred to stay at the hotel. Anna said, "Yes, a good idea. Let's break the routine for one day."

Hans said, "I will think about it. The four of us in your car?"

Half an hour later, all having finished their lunch, Hans came back from the gents and said that he had decided not to join them; preferring instead the comfort of the hotel. Anna tried to protest, but to no avail, it was a no go.

Soph said, "OK, then we will head to Barcelona tomorrow morning, early, and try to make it back the same day, or latest next."

At 7 a.m. the next morning, after having had a quick bite to eat, they drove off in a north easterly direction towards the big city. With both windows rolled down, listening to Led Zeppelin's Rock and Roll , they hit the city 90 minutes later. Paul searched for a public car park. Having found one, he paid the ticket and locked the car. They started walking, hand in hand, excited to be there, and exploring the city to see what it had to offer. They were keen and eager to discover as much as they could in less than 24 hours.

First, they went to the Spanish National Museum, interesting but too hot and sticky; and much too crowded. Forty minutes later they were out and sitting down in a nearby cafe, having coffee, sweet pastries, and water, lots of it. They then went on to the National Art gallery, a big, impressive building with Picassos and Dalis, and other famous Spanish painters on display. Wow, this was something Paul had intended to do for a long time, and now they were there it was very impressive and stunning.

When they got tired of all the paintings, they left and walked down to Barcelona's shoreline, full of people, restaurants, cafes, bars and the like. There were hordes of tourists too, lots of Japanese, following their guide who held up a stick with a round red sign on it, saying "Number 11". They observed all this from their vantage point at a table, digging into their Tapas and drinking a good bottle of Spanish Rioja wine. They then had their main course, grilled sea bass, with pepperoni and aubergine, and yellow saffron rice, another bottle of Rioja, with some salad on the side. Delicious lunch.

After the espressos and a brandy, Paul settled the bill, and they strolled on. Back to the inner city centre, and the Ramblas, full of people and traffic of all kinds; buses, cars, motorbikes, vans, bicycles – everybody seemed to be wired up and running from here to there and back. They took this in, sometimes stopping to take a photo of a particular subject that had caught their eye.

They then went on to the monumental Cathedral. The one that was not yet finished after all these years, with the cranes and scaffolding visible. The works had started a good one hundred years ago and there was no end in sight. Paul paid a small entrance fee, and they entered the cathedral, a mind-blowing construction, with the ceiling a good 80 metres above them. What a masterpiece of contemporary architecture. Soph was awed by the size, taking pictures non-stop, sometimes with Paul in it, but mostly not.

Gaudi was a genius, no doubt, with this masterpiece of human achievement and endeavour. Stepping out now, half dizzy with what they had just seen and experienced, Paul suggested sitting down for a moment, let it all sink in, trying to digest it and store it in their memories. They sat on a park bench, and for a good while remained silent, just looking around, letting it make an impression; something they would not forget.

"If only my mother could have seen this, she would have loved it. But anyway, I will show her the pictures and explain it all to her. Sometimes my father can be pretty selfish and dominant." having said that, Soph stood up and announced she was thirsty and in need of a drink, or two, preferably.

"Good idea. Let's go down the street here, see where it leads us to."

He took her hand and off they went, impressed and happy. It was by now 6 p.m., with a long walk back to the car park. He suggested not to drive back but rather stay the night, find a small pensión and head back tomorrow morning. Soph agreed. She wanted to hang on a little bit longer in that great city, exploring it more, tomorrow left time enough to lie at the beach again, at the Delmar Hotel.

They walked up and down the Ramblas in search of a hotel or pensión. It was not an easy task, there were few hotels to be found. Those they did find were fully booked with no vacancy. Paul weighed the options of heading back to the car and return today or keep on searching. They kept on searching and finally found one just off the corner in a small cobble-stoned side street; 200 metres off the Ramblas.

They entered the small hallway, which was dimly lit and smelled of not so fresh fish. An old woman, dressed in black, with spectacles and grey hair, was sitting behind the small desk, knitting. Paul went up and greeted her.

"One room for one night. Pay in cash now," he said in his improvised half Spanish, half Italian.

"50,000 pesetas, first floor, number 12, bathroom in the hall," she said, stretching out her old, tiny, wrinkled hand.

Paul paid, took the key and they went up the stairs searching for room number 12. It was small with one double bed, one creaky chair at the window, a wardrobe with one door missing, but apparently clean fresh sheets.

"That will have to do for one night," he announced, falling on the bed.

"I will go to the bathroom and freshen up," Soph responded, as she headed for the door.

When she came back some ten minutes later, Paul was already fast asleep, having taken off his shoes, socks, pants and shirt. She climbed into the bed beside him, careful not to wake him up, and minutes later fell asleep too.

Next morning, early, they stepped out of the smelly pensión, no breakfast to be had there, and strolled to the nearest cafe to get something to eat. Afterwards, they walked back to the car. Paul had to consult his map several times, but finally they managed. He showed his ticket, paid, and off they roared in a south westerly direction, towards the sea. Two hours later they reached the Delmar, parked the car, and entered the lobby, Soph getting their key. It was 11 a.m. by now, time to take a shower and meet the boys and parents for lunch on the hotel terrace.

Paul put his bathing trunks on, and a pair of white Bermudas, a flowery greenish summer shirt, together with his leather sandals and his black Ray-Bans. Soph was wearing her red bikini, with the tiny top, that showed her full breasts, a stunner, and when she came out of the water her nipples showed clearly.

Over the bikini, she slipped on one of her yellow and white summer dresses, ending way above her knees, straw hat on her head, and dark shades. She was a bombshell. Wherever she passed, men could not help but stare, with women looking on jealously. They embraced and kissed, rode down the lift to the first floor and the terrace, a very happy, healthy, good-looking young couple, having a ball and enjoying themselves to the max.

The boys were already seated at the table, fighting with each other, with Hans and Anna nowhere in sight. They sat down and Paul ordered two large beers for him and Soph. They chatted away until her parents arrived.

"Hello there you two love birdies. How was Barcelona? Worth the trip, all that mess and traffic?" Hans said as he sat down.

Soph did the reporting on their trip, excited and happy, full of drive and eager to not leave out the smallest of details. Anna listened attentively, nodding here and there, while Hans went to the buffet to fetch an appetiser.

When he came back to the table, he said, "Very interesting indeed, but let's concentrate on more urgent matters now. We have five more days until we fly back and our holiday ends. I have chartered a fishing boat for tomorrow; we'll depart at 6 a.m., at sunrise, and spend the day on the sea. Fishing tackle and bait is all provided. There will be the captain and one deck hand. Lunch on board, and the occasional swim in the high sea, captain permitting. How does that sound?"

Soph was excited and so were the boys, Anna less so. "That sounds just great, Dad. Let's see who catches the biggest Barracuda or Marlin. Winner can choose the venue for dinner. Agreed?"

"Deal done," Hans replied. "I look forward to being invited to El Farolito, my favourite restaurant. At your expense, of course."

They all laughed and dug into their lunch. After the meal, the parents went up for their daily siesta, or whatever. Paul and Soph went straight to the beach, spread their towels on the beach chairs, and ran into the water, enjoying the surf, the waves and the warm water of the sea.

After that, they went for a long walk along the shore, a good two hours. Returning, they both fell into their chairs, tired and relaxed. Paul ordered two dry martinis and a large bottle of still water. He suggested that tonight they go to a nearby pizzeria and return early to be fresh, rested and ready for their boat trip tomorrow.

Next day, after a cup of coffee and a light breakfast, they all rode in a cab to the town's small harbour. When they arrived at the Pier, with Hans leading the way, they walked down it in search of fishing vessel Esmeralda. Paul spotted it first, lying there in its blue and white painted beauty, a good ten metres long, and three metres wide.

Captain Jose greeted them warmly, and they all stepped on board. The deck hand, Martinez, waved a hand and stared at Soph's backside. Paul gave him a dirty look, and he went down to the engine room. They sailed off into the open sea; the sun having fully risen and beating down on them, shining her rays on the Esmeralda and the waves. Soph and Anna took out their cameras and started taking pictures, while Paul and Hans inspected the fishing gear, rods and baits; all in order. Two professional fishing chairs were fitted on the deck of the vessel, including the strapping belts to tie down whoever attempted to catch something. In front of the chair was the hole where the fishing rod was fixed to give it extra fixture. All perfect. After a good hour of sailing into the open sea, Jose stopped the engine and invited all of them to take a swim.

Everybody, including the boys, jumped into the water and swam around the vessel for maybe 15 minutes. What a delight, the sea being calm, small waves rolling inshore, seagulls screaming above their heads, and below them the deep blue darkness of the water. When they all climbed back on board, drying themselves, Paul noticed that Martinez had prepared the fishing rods and gear. He pointed to a freezer standing below the main window. Paul opened it and grabbed a beer for Soph, Hans and himself. Anna preferred a coke, so did the boys.

Each one of them took a rod, with Paul and Hans sitting in the two fishing chairs. They all threw their lines and the fun started. For a good half an hour nothing happened, so Jose fired the engine and sailed deeper into the sea, away from the coast, changing the boat's position. Anna struck lucky first, catching a red snapper, about 30 cm. Martinez took the fish off the hook and put it into the ice box. He then fixed Anna's fishing gear, putting fresh bait on the hook. The next one was Soph, who got another snapper, but this time a good 40 cm long; the men and boys had no luck so far, until Paul, a good hour later, felt a tickling on his rod, soft, but it was there. He reeled in to test the resistance, and there it was, pulling now strongly on his line.

Observing it all, Jose, the Captain, shouted, "Sit tight. Martinez, fasten his belt, and you, young man, keep on reeling in."

He heard all that, but it was easier said than done. Paul fought the Barracuda for a good 40 minutes, his hands and wrists in pain, but hanging on firmly. Finally, he brought the Barracuda alongside the vessel, and Martinez rammed a spike into it, hauling the fish on board. It was a big one alright, almost the length of Paul's height, and weighing a good 40 kilos, they all thought. The ice box was too small for it, so Martinez let the tale hang out. Paul fetched himself a beer, while Soph kissed him and looked deep into his eyes, proud and something else in her gaze.

It was now 1 p.m., and they all agreed to pause to have their lunch: bread, sardines, ham and cheese sandwiches, and afterwards, coffee. After lunch they continued fishing, with the exception of Anna and her older son, who got bored. They both preferred instead to lie on their towels, working on their tans. Paul sat firmly in his chair, and so did Hans, but no more luck. Jose had turned the boat and was heading back towards the harbour when Hans was almost pulled out of his chair; a big fish appeared to have taken his bait. Martinez ran to him and strapped him tight into his seat. Hans could not be helped; it was his task and efforts only to haul the big fish into the boat. He had to fight it, and that was exactly what he did. Paul observed him reeling hard and puffing and breathing heavily; struggling with a rather big one, apparently.

Jose cried out "Marlin" from his observation post high up on the bridge. It took Hans a good hour to reel the monster in. When he finally managed to get it close to the boat, Martinez then killed it with his spear, digging deep into the fish's belly. It took all three of them to haul it on board. By estimate the Marlin was two metres, and later measured by Martinez came out to be 1.94 metres, which made Hans the winner of the day.

Anna kissed him on his cheeks. "Congratulations."

Hans smiled and collapsed back into his seat. He was finished, exhausted, but a very happy man. Tonight's dinner would definitely not be on him. Paul shook his hand and congratulated him. They then had another two beers while the vessel made its steady way back to the small port. Getting off the boat now, the two men shook Jose's hand and told him that they were giving him the fish – the two had agreed on this earlier. They would give their catch to Jose rather than try to sell it to the local fish market. It was a token of appreciation for a wonderful fishing trip. Martinez got some cash from Hans and they all said goodbye. Paul hailed a cab and they rode back to the Delmar, tired but very happy indeed.

The last days of their holiday passed by quickly. They spent the remaining time keeping to their routine, beach, long walks, lunch, always together, and dinner sometimes. On the eve of the flight back, Hans invited all of them to the Cameron Restaurant and Grill, a popular spot for seafood. They had a feast, eating everything that could be eaten coming out of the sea, washed down with delicious local white wine. It was something to remember for a long time to come. Anna was busy taking pictures for her family album, she said. But as all good things have to come to an end, they left the restaurant and, instead of hailing a cab, they all walked back to the Delmar; the streets still busy and full of people having fun.

Arriving back at the hotel, they went right up to their rooms, but not before they all had hugged and said goodbye. The plane would leave at 9 a.m., no problem there, but Paul had said he planned to take the road together with Soph at around 6 a.m. With everything going to plan, they would be back home sometime after midnight.

The next morning, he took their bags to the car while Soph fetched some sandwiches from the breakfast room, together with two large bottles of water. They then handed back their key and said their goodbyes and promised to come back soon, while Hans would take care of the hotel bill. The day before, Paul had driven the Alfa to a nearby gas station to have the water and oil checked and calibrated the tires; he also filled her up.

Everything was in good order and they drove out of the car park, waved goodbye at the hotel and beach, with Paul taking the nearest entry to the motorway, now familiar with the directions he had taken two weeks earlier. They made it to the French border in good time, crossed without a problem or delay. They were in good spirits and so was the car, speeding down the highway, delivering its 160 horsepower in style. Paul loved the wooden steering wheel, the polished wooden dashboard, with its round silver and black instruments staring back at him. In Zurich, at his favourite Alfa garage, he had Sergio install a sport Abarth double exhaust pipe system, which gave the car a bit more horse-power and a low, sporty sound.

Near the border with Italy, he had filled her up, and they had a late lunch, stretching their legs afterwards, and smoking. Again, no problem crossing into Italy, with the border police having eyes only for the blonde Soph, and then for the car. Paul was ignored, and so were the documents in his hands. In Italy, they travelled strictly north, with traffic now heavier and queues at the toll gates. It was 11 p.m. when they crossed the border at Chiasso into Switzerland. Shortly after the crossing, still in Chiasso, Paul stopped, and they had a coffee and two Paninis at a bar he knew.

Refreshed and reinvigorated, they made their last leg of the journey and hit Zurich at 1:30 a.m. Paul parked in front of his flat, took out the bags, and they walked up to the first floor and entered the flat; with Soph staying over. Even before taking a shower, she called her mother and Anna picked up after three rings. There was an extension beside their bed. Everything was OK. Yes, they had arrived in good time, everybody was sound asleep. With that, she hung up, and they entered the bathroom together and showered. Then Paul had fixed them a drink, which they sipped in silence. Observing the lake in the distance, and the brightly lit small towns around it, Soph took Paul's hand and squeezed it tenderly.

"This was the best holiday I ever had, and I thank you for it." With that, she kissed him fully on his lips. "Come to bed you lazy dog. I've got a surprise for you."

Hearing this, Paul knew what was coming. He stood up, brushed his teeth and entered the bedroom, with Soph naked and spread out on the bed, her hand busy around her pussy, moaning. Paul kissed her and Soph guided him into her, eager and horny. She really was up for it, even after a good 17-hour drive. Paul realised there and then that he had fallen in love with her. This was a first timer for him, and he wondered where all this would lead to; but for now, he was just happy and eager to meet her expectations. Monday morning was hopefully still far away, but it would arrive, and with it the duty and obligation to make it happen in Czechoslovakia, bringing in that deal everybody at the bank was waiting for, especially Helmut. He felt happy and worried at the same time, and then fell asleep with the princess in his arms, hoping for the best, for them and also for him.

CHAPTER 14

Monday morning, sharp at eight, wearing a light grey summer suit, short sleeve white shirt, with a green and black tie, one of his favourites, Paul entered the Marketing department. Karen was there, greeting him with a big smile, and saying with her strong Canadian accent, "Morning Mr. Holiday maker. Time to work, don't you think?" and she gave him a big hug.

He shook hands with the boss of the department, Meier. No Imbach and Schultz in sight. He poured himself a coffee and sat down, starting with the *Neue Zürcher Zeitung*. After 20 minutes, he put the paper down and checked his inbox, statements, concluded transactions and balances. Overall, things were running smoothly. He had given Imbach a power of Attorney, together with a limit, so he could participate in the deals even in his absence; Imbach taking care of it. He then concentrated on the country limits and exposure data. The US$300 million limit was in place, of course; there for him to start using it.

He then walked over to Lilly in the typist pool and dictated a short internal memo. Imbach had arrived in the meantime and they shook hands. "Everything OK, Paul? Nice tan. Keeping the lady busy?"

Some 15 minutes later, Schultz arrived and greeted Paul. He asked how he was and announced a meeting in one hour's time in conference room number 3 on the second floor. Paul nodded. He knew exactly what this meant. He continued to study the statistics on CSSR, and any political and economic developments he should be aware of. He then checked his personal accounts status on his computer, all OK and satisfactory. He went to the toilet for a piss, washed his hands, combed his hair, and went up to the second floor, passing by another secretary pool, all smiling and waving cheerfully. He then sat in the conference room and waited. Shortly afterwards, Schultz arrived.

"Let me get straight to the point. I had a meeting with the Board of Directors last week, updated them, at their request, on our Eastern efforts, with unfortunately nothing yet to show for. The greedy bastards accepted my arguments, but hinted that the $300 million limit might be up for review in due course, due to binding lots of capital of the bank. They did not go as far as giving a deadline, yet, but clearly the threat was there."

Having said all this, he stood up and walked to the window, staring out as if he was searching for something; with the answer being somewhere out there. "You have three weeks to get ready for CSSR. Your trip is scheduled for the first week of August. Karen is busy with your itinerary, make good use of the remaining time, and bring me back a sack of new deals."

With that, he slapped Paul on his shoulder and left, looking back and said, "Make it happen, old sport, time is running out, for both of us."

Paul nodded and said he would give it his very best. With Schultz gone, Paul stayed on, trying to organise his thoughts. That was why Imbach had not joined the meeting this morning. There had been a clear threat. Either bring back the goods, or else take a long walk on a short pier. He was not a religious man, and praying was not his thing, but he appealed to higher powers, whatever they might be, to help him this time.

When he returned to the department, Schultz was gone and Imbach looked at him, thoughtfully. "Cheer up old Paulie. Join me at a lunch reception at the Guild House zur Waag, shaking hands with a gang of Japanese directors and managers who think they got the deal of the year. Poor bastards! Lots of food and drinks, short speech on my part, and hopefully an even shorter one from the Jap delegation, although I doubt it. Be ready in half an hour, and don't forget your business cards, lots of them. Them Japs love them."

Paul used the days before his CSSR business trip the best he could. He studied their economic data profoundly and in detail. He also delved into their political structure and organisation: leading figures, opposition, the whole apparatus. Although the Czechs were better off compared to Romania and Bulgaria, they were still a satellite state of the USSR, and firmly controlled by them. They had managed to export some of their goods, albeit on a small scale, to Western countries, earning some hard currency, but still their trade balance was utterly negative and their economic system needed hard currency rather desperately. That's where Paul would step in, or so he hoped. A week before his scheduled departure to Prague, he went to Brunos on Bahnhofstrasse, to buy a new dark blue pinstriped suit, together with two white, and two pale blue silk shirts, and ten pairs of black city socks. He also bought a new pair of black English leather shoes at Low's also on Bahnhofstrasse, together with a pair of dark brown leather mocassins. His raincoat was still new, and so was his leather briefcase. On the clothing part he was set, looking elegant and smart.

Karen had shown him the itinerary, a tight, fully packed schedule that this time also included some of the country's biggest manufacturing firms, but the focus was clearly on the four main Banks. He changed some Swiss Francs into Kroner at the Bank's internal till, together with some cash in dollars, the rest he would settle with his credit card. Two days before departure, he had lunch with Tin at Antinori, brought him up to date on his forthcoming trip, and also on Spain. Tin commented on his job, which was still going OK – "Thank god," Paul thought – and on his affair with the tall blonde, although, of late, the whole thing he thought they had, seemed to gradually fade away. They agreed to hit the Town when Paul returned, and then said goodbye.

His flight was booked for Monday, so on Saturday he took Soph out to the Lido at the lake; it was a sunny and warm summer's day. They swam in the clear water, climbed on to the float in the middle of the Lake, and lay on it, soaking up the warm sun. This was one of the places Paul liked most in summer, the Lake, the swimming and the people-watching. Getting tired of the water, they had their lunch at the Lido's restaurant – veal with fries and beers. Afterwards, they laid down on their towels, watching people and holding hands. Soph was looking stunning in her new yellow bikini, a rather tiny affair, which showed her generous curves only too well. In the past hour, the same two guys had circled their spot until Paul stood up and told them to fuck off. Then that was exactly what they did, poor sods.

"Look at some other birds. Mine is taken," he mumbled to himself when he laid down next to Soph again.

At around 5 p.m., sun still high up, they packed their bags and left the lido, strolling past Mythenquai at the border of the lake, heading towards Bellevue and the old town, where Paul intended to have dinner. He had left the car at his flat, preferring to walk instead. It was a lovely walk, the lake, blue and silver to their right, lots of folks doing just the same; some dog walkers, families with children, old folks walking on sticks, but still walking, lovers holding hands or sitting on one of the many park benches, running dogs barking, the seagulls crying, and the low, but distinct humming of the city in the distance.

After a good 40-minute walk, they entered the Niederdorf, Paul leading the way to the Restaurant zum Weissen Wind, which featured a lovely terrace overlooking the old city, and in the distance the lake. They found a table with a good view and ordered two large beers to kick it off, They then ordered the Tuna fish carpaccio, followed by a mixed salad and Eglifilet, with tartare sauce and spring potatoes. To wash it all down, white Swiss wine from the Valais, a perfect combination. Dinner was excellent and a success. They talked nonsense, two lovers enjoying each other's company. It was close to midnight when they left the venue and walked back home. Opening the sliding door to the balcony, they both sat down in the canvas chairs, enjoying the view and each other's company.

Tomorrow they would visit Soph's parents for lunch, and no doubt look at and admire the many photographs Anna had taken during their holiday in Spain. The next day it would be business again for Paul, and the high expectations weighed heavily on his shoulders and mind.

Monday morning, 7:45 a.m., queueing at the Swissair desk at Kloten Airport, Paul thought about the details of his itinerary, and how he would proceed. The board had given the OK to lower the management fee by an eighth of a per cent.

In a million-dollar loan structure, that would make a difference; anyway, it would give him a competitive edge and a strong negotiating position, which he intended to use fully and aggressively.

A good three hours later, Swissair flight number 3694 landed at Prague Airport, on time, as it usually did. He went through immigration, no hold up there, and walked out of the airport, heading to the taxi pool. After a few minutes' wait, he got into a relatively new white Skoda sedan, with clean seats and smelling of the green wonder tree that was hanging from the rearview mirror in front of the driver; a fat woman in her forties, talking nonstop. When Paul said, "No Czech, please. German or English," she switched to a hesitant German, informing that she had lived a few years in Switzerland with her parents, in the town of Winterthur, where her father worked at Sulzer as a machinist. Unfortunately, they had laid him off, and the family had to return to their homeland.

Paul gave the Hotel Pod Vezi as his destination, to which she nodded, shaking with her whole body, saying, "Very good place, elegant."

After that, the woman appeared to have run out of her German and they rode in silence. Paul enjoyed the ride. This was a much more modern, cleaner city, with trees and small parks, well-kept and organised, so it seemed. A big difference from Sofia or Bucharest. when they entered the historic part of town, getting closer to the hotel, Paul marvelled at the many old churches, and tidy, well-kept old houses. The whole city looked like it would have done in the 16th century, and he loved and admired it all. His first impression was extremely positive.

When the driver drove up to the main entrance of the elegant hotel, right in the city centre, and stopped, a man in a black suit with a black top hat opened Paul's door and welcomed him to the Pod Vezi. The cabbie gave him the fare price in Kroner and said she would take off 20% if he paid in dollars. Paul handed her the dollars and stepped into the lobby, followed by the top hat carrying his suitcase. There was no baggy suit hanging around the lobby this time, only a beautiful girl in her early thirties, with a name tag on her blue jacket saying "Dvorak, Receptionist". Paul introduced himself, looking straight into her light brown eyes.

"Of course, Mr. Winter. Welcome, we were expecting you. Please fill in this form and hand me your passport, won't take a second." Her English was good and fluent. "Here you go, Sir. Room number 509 on the fifth floor, a suite facing the bridge. I hope you will enjoy your stay. The dining room is to the left side, opening just now. Shall I make a reservation for lunch? You must be hungry, Sir." She smiled at him, waiting.

"That would be lovely. Yes, thank you," he responded, and walked to the lift.

The lift was wood panelled and lit by a small crystal chandelier, the top hat had followed him, opening the door to the suite, a spacious room opening to a balcony, giving a view to the Church ,the bridge and the stone cobbled streets below; and to the left the adjoining bedroom, large, with a good double bed and a black marble bathroom with golden taps and a silver mirror. Paul tipped the black hat generously in Kroner and received a warm smile in return .

He quickly unpacked his suitcase, checked the briefcase, and took the lift down and entered the spacious dining hall. He was led to his table by the head waiter, after having given his name. The waiter waved to one of his colleagues standing near the wall, who then immediately brought a flute of champagne to his table.

"Welcome, Sir, and here is the menu," he said.

Paul smoked a cigarette and sipped the very good champagne. First class impression of Prague so far, he hoped business would be as good too.

After lunch, he went up to his room, showered, and went through his itinerary. He had his first meeting at 3:30 p.m. at a leading industrial conglomerate. He hailed a cab shortly before 3 p.m., gave the address and off they rode, no suits, no bag carriers, and the driver did not know his destination beforehand. Paul relaxed and studied the city and landscape. After a good 20 minutes, they had reached the outskirts of town, and the green parks and trees gave way to grey office blocks and manufacturing sites, and some chimneys blasting their waste up into the air. At 3:29 p.m., the cab came to a halt in front of a large office building apparently built in the sixties, annexed to a plant that produced agricultural machinery.

He paid the driver in Kroner and stepped into the building. The lobby looked like the waiting room of a police station, with a large desk in the far corner against a wall, at which sat an elderly man in a grey, shabby uniform manning his post. When Paul introduced himself in English, the old fellow seemed not to understand a word. To help, he handed him his business card, said, "Svobotzka", pointing at his watch, showing the 3 o'clock finger. The old man seemed to understand him now and called someone on his black telephone. He nodded and hung up, gesturing to Paul to stand by. There were no chairs to sit on, so Paul kept standing near the desk, waiting. After a few minutes, a delegation of three men entered the lobby, led by a short, fat man, wearing a brown winter suit, despite the summer heat, and a greenish shirt.

"Svobotzka," he introduced himself, ignoring the other two men. Paul followed him into a large, shabby room, with a brown desk and four chairs around it. At least there were chairs, so Paul sat down. The meeting went fairly well, with Svobotzka giving an hour-long speech in English, or sort of, about his manufacturing plant, and the astonishing results it produced, year after year. This was a warm up. It probably would lead to nothing, but still he acted professionally, although a bit shorter on details and terms.

When it all ended, they exchanged business cards and promised to get in touch, see whether any points needed clarification, or further explanations. He gestured to the old receptionist clerk with his hands, imitating a steering wheel, saying "Taxi". The old man seemed to understand and made a call, gesturing for Paul to wait by the door, checking if anything with four wheels was appearing. Eventually a cab appeared, Paul gave the driver the name of the hotel and off they went. Shortly before arriving at the Pod Vezi, Paul spotted a park and told the driver to stop. He then paid and strode off into the park. The sun was still shining, so he took a walk, enjoying the scenery. After 20 minutes, he sat on a bench and smoked a cigarette, watching people and getting his thoughts organised. Tomorrow was the big day, meetings with three big important banks. This was his chance, and he intended to make the most of it, giving it his very best. He turned in early in order to get a good night's sleep, to be ready and sharp for the next day.

The Commercial Bank of Czechoslovakia was housed in an impressive, large 19th century building in the city centre, not far away from the hotel. When he stepped up to reception, he saw three attendants sitting behind it; two women and an efficient-looking man, no doubt the head of this little committee. Paul introduced himself, handing his business card to the man in charge.

"Of course, Mr. Winter. Good morning. Please have a seat. Mr. Novotny will be with you in a minute." This was all pronounced efficiently and businesslike. Paul sat down in one of the chairs and waited.

After four minutes, a tall, well-dressed man in his late forties appeared, introducing himself as Mr. Novotny, CEO of the bank, and shook Paul's hand. introductions done, he then led him into a large well-furbished room on the top floor, overlooking the square, which could be seen from large windows. He introduced Paul to his two colleagues and the secretary, who would take the notes of the meeting. Paul immediately realised that this was a professional outfit and acted accordingly. Novotny gave a short speech and then invited Paul to speak. After the usual pleasantries, Paul got down to business. He gave background information on his bank, the standing and financial power they had in Switzerland, Europe, and the US, their capacity for syndicated loan structures in all available hard currencies, terms and conditions, interest rates, spread costs, laws, timetable and availability.

Beforehand, he had studied the balance and profit-and-loss sheet of the commercial bank and was in a position to make them a substantial loan offer, right there in the first meeting. When he mentioned the nine-digit figure in US dollars, and stopping his speech for extra dramatic effect, everything went very silent. One could hear a needle drop to the floor; it was so quiet. After that strategic pause, Paul went on, giving additional details, and ended his speech by mentioning that funds were available immediately, but a decision had to be reached by close of business next day, when he was scheduled to leave Prague.

Undoubtedly, Paul's speech and its contents, including the offer, had made an impression on the directors, the very impression it was supposed to make. Novotny had a few questions, mostly technical, followed by questions from the CFO, mostly in a similar direction. Novotny thanked Paul for the excellent meeting, describing it as interesting and informative, and promised to present the proposal to his board immediately, and be back in touch by tomorrow. He asked Paul where he was staying, and with that they all stood up, shook hands, and the woman who had taken the notes opened the door and rode down with him to the entrance lobby.

"It was a pleasure meeting you, Mr. Winter; and we hope you enjoy the remainder of your stay in Prague."

Paul walked out of the bank's building, smoked a cigarette, and went around the block, just to calm down and relax. His heart was pumping, adrenalin was flowing, he thought he had given all he had in that meeting, and judged that in went very well, and the CEO and his colleagues were very interested indeed. Now came the long wait. Nothing he could do about it. No way to call Novotny, who had said that he would be in touch tomorrow.

Paul managed to calm down a bit, saw a cab, got in, and gave the address for his next meeting. After this one, there would be the last one and then his day was done. The last two meetings went well, but Paul's instinct told him that it was Novotny who would make his day, and very future.

Next morning, after an excellent breakfast, he sat down in the hotel lobby to read the *Financial Times*. He still had half an hour to kill before his next meeting, and then on to the last one, at the Agricultural bank. He had informed the front desk his plane was leaving in the late afternoon, so he would make a late check out. "No problem," they told him.

He smoked another cigarette and looked around, trying to control his anxiety. The next meeting had gone well, a routine he had gotten used to already. At 12:30 p.m., he sat down at the outside space of a small restaurant in the centre of the city and ordered his lunch, together with a bottle of still water. He then headed to his last meeting in Prague, and afterwards back to the hotel.

When he arrived, it was by now 4 p.m., and still no word from Novotny. After having checked the front desk for messages or calls, he rode up to his suite, and started packing, organising his briefcase and making further notes and annotations in his itinerary and reporting sheet. He then took a shower, put on his suit, sat down in a chair on the balcony and poured himself a double Glenfiddich, two cups of ice. He had to calm down, steady his nerves, catch the bloody plane; and still no word from Novotny. Having finished his drink, he called reception to please fetch his suitcase, and rode down in the lift and, reluctantly, handed back his key to the clerk at the desk and settled his bill.

It was now 5 p.m., three hours before his plane was due to leave. His suitcase had not been brought yet, so he sat down on one of the lobby chairs, smoking and looking around. The bellboy handed him his suitcase, and Paul stood up and walked towards the exit door. He was in the rotating door, the boy behind him carrying his case, when the receptionist came running after him. Already on the outside staircase, she caught up with him announcing he had a telephone call and stressing the word important. Paul ran back to the desk and was handed the telephone. It was Novotny alright.

"Mr. Winter, sorry to call you so late, but the board has only just now informed me that they have accepted your offer. You are kindly asked to come back to the bank this afternoon to sign the letter of intent and preliminary agreement of the terms."

Paul, having difficulty controlling his voice and excitement, said that he would be arriving within the next 40 minutes, and thanked Novotny for his call. He turned to the chief receptionist, telling him that something urgent had come up and he needed a room for another night; and could he please call Swissair and rearrange his 8 p.m. flight to Zurich for another one tomorrow.

"No problem, Mr. Winter, we have a room for you of course, and I will personally take care of your flight arrangements. Leave it up to me. When you return from your meeting, we will have a new room, and the ticket, waiting for you."

Paul thanked him, took his briefcase and walked out of the hotel; this time much happier and eager to get his hands on that signed letter and take it back to his bank the very next day; bringing the deal of the year.

When Paul arrived at the bank's head office, he found the main entrance closed. An armed guard in a blue uniform and military style cap stood by the door. When he approached the guard, he asked, "Mr. Winter? Please follow me."

They walked to the left side of the building, in front of a heavy, unmarked metal door. The guard took out a key and opened the door, and they then rode up to the top floor in a lift that was used for deliveries and staff. Novotny's private secretary, an elegant woman in her mid-forties, dressed in a stylish grey business suit, greeted Paul.

"Mr. Winter. Welcome back. Please follow me."

He followed the woman through a long hall fitted with a thick blue carpet. Then they reached a double wood panelled door. She opened it and led the way into the bank's stylish, large board room. The CEO, Novotny, the CFO, and the full board of directors were sitting around a large oval table. When Paul entered the room, Novotny walked up to him and shook his hand.

"Welcome, Mr. Winter. Let me introduce Dr. Cerny, Chaiman of the board." Dr. Cerny was in his seventies, dressed in a smart dark grey business suit. He had thin white hair and wore dark-coloured spectacles.

"I am very pleased to meet you, Mr. Winter. I believe you already met our CFO." He then went on to introduce the other directors.

Introductions done, they all sat down and got down to business. Novotny again, now in the presence of Paul, outlined the terms of the US$150 million loan agreement. It was a formality, all present knew the terms by heart. Novotny then signed the letter, followed by Dr. Cerny and the CFO. Paul signed last, AVP Paul Winter, on behalf of his bank. What a moment. He could hardly conceal his emotions, but he just managed and thanked them all for their trust. He went on to inform them that he would be back in his office tomorrow, and the complete loan agreement would be dispatched, by special courier, by Tuesday of next week for their signatures and return despatch. Upon receipt, the funds would be available within ten business days.

The board applauded, with Novotny announcing that a cocktail reception had been arranged to celebrate the agreed transaction and asked them to please follow him to the adjoining dining room, a spacious room richly decorated with flower bouquets. Waiters in immaculate white aprons served ice cold Dom Perignon Champagne, canapes of caviar, smoked salmon, and a variety of cold cuts were offered.

The Finance Minister of the Czech Republic was present, and so was the Director of the Central Bank, together with his colleagues. While Novotny was busy doing the introductions, with Paul shaking lots of hands and collecting their business cards, and handing out his, he could not help but do a quick calculation, just to reassure himself.

At 2.25% spread over Libor, the London Interbank offered rate, his bank would net a clean and whopping US$3.75 million profit per year, in five years totalling a staggering US$18.75 million, plus 0.5% payout fee every time they drew on the facility, plus a one off 0.25% management fee. So his bank would easily make US$ 20 Million plus, out of this loan transaction.

Pushing these wonderful, marvellous thoughts aside, he was concentrating again on making small talk with the high calibre executives present. Small talk, and mostly not so small, detailing possible future transactions, and, when asked his view on the western economies, and the US.

After a good hour, the reception was coming to an end, and with everybody having left, Novotny took Paul by the arm and asked whether he fancied a nightcap in one of Prague's many bars; friendly company included – not all of them, necessarily, of male gender. Paul politely declined, justifying an early flight the next morning; but the truth was he did not want to. After the massive deal they had all just signed, going out with Novotny and maybe talking too much and jeopardising it all. No, he would abstain from this one, although he was in the mood to celebrate a bit longer.

Novotny, apparently, took this decline badly, and was visibly disappointed, but he said, "OK, maybe next time you're in Prague. Our driver will get you back to your hotel. Have a good flight to Zurich, and we'll talk when you're back at your desk."

Paul made sure the signed letter was indeed in his briefcase, shook hands with Novotny, and rode down with Alec, the driver, who had waited outside the room by the lift door.

The streets were quieter now, and shortly afterwards they reached the hotel. When he stepped up to the reception desk, the main concierge greeted him.

"Good evening, Mr. Winter, Sir. Here is the key to suite number 347, your luggage is already in your accommodation. And here's the Ticket for your flight tomorrow, at 10:55 a.m. Lufthansa, I am afraid, Swissair is fully booked for tomorrow. I hope you find this acceptable and convenient." With that, he handed the ticket to Paul, wishing him a good night and pleasant rest.

Paul thanked him for his efficiency and then took the lift to the third floor. Room number 347 was not as spacious as his suite before, but it looked comfortable enough for just one night. He undressed and took a long, hot shower. He then put on the hotel's bathrobe, sat down in the one chair and fixed himself a gin and tonic. With his thoughts beginning to wander again, from the bank to Soph, and Tin, Schultz and Imbach, to all of his colleagues. He could not help or explain, but his thoughts went out to Novak, with him being a Czech, lying in his cold grey grave at the bottom of the lake.

He stood up abruptly and brushed these gloomy thoughts aside. He dialled Soph's number, and she answered after a good eight rings, half asleep but happy to hear his voice. He gave her a quick rundown of the deal, and Soph seemed happy and said she knew he had it in him. She would prepare dinner tomorrow night at his place, with a dessert. She stressed the word dessert, and he immediately realised what she meant by this. They then said goodbye and hung up. His cock had begun to react under the bathrobe, and he was not sure if it was because of the prospect of fame and money, or because he was just eager to fuck Soph

186

tomorrow. He went to bed, sleeping the sleep of the victorious, but not before having opened his briefcase and checking and making sure the trophy was safe and sound inside.

Next day, landing at Zurich Airport on time in the mid-afternoon, he went straight to his flat, unpacked, and called the office. Karen answered and asked how he was. He said he was just fine, and tomorrow he would bring the croissants and sweet pastries he knew everybody liked.

Karen said, "Great, look forward to it." Realising immediately that Paul would bring in a big fish indeed. She immediately informed Meier, the Head of Department, Schultz and Imbach; and also the CEO.

She knew her Paulie and was already happy for him even without knowing any details, or, as a matter of fact, anything at all. The fact he had mentioned sweet pastries that everybody liked was reason enough for her to put everybody on alert.

Next morning, looking sharp and efficient, Paul stepped into the office and sat down at his desk. To his surprise, Schultz was already there talking on the phone, and so were Imbach, Meier and Karen. Even Rosen, who was always in London, had appeared out of nowhere. When Schultz ended his call, Paul asked his colleagues to please gather round his desk. When they were all standing close and leaning over his shoulder, he slowly took out the precious letter and put it on his desk for all of them to see. It was Imbach who reacted first.

"Holy cow. You mean bastard, Paul. You are the man!" Shouting the words and slapping him on his shoulder.

Schultz shook his hand and said. "Congratulations. Well done indeed. I knew you had it in you." He looked Paul in the eyes with pride, admiration, and something else Paul could not read.

Karen kissed him, Meier shook his hand, and Rosen, too, shook his hand. Schultz took the letter and said he had a meeting with the CEO right now, and asked Paul to be on standby, together with Imbach. With that, he left the department immediately, with Paul starting to read the papers, waiting to be summoned, while Imbach was busy making endless calls and smoking non-stop.

After one hour, his phone rang. It was Miss Gautschi, the CEO's personal assistant, inviting him and Imbach to please come up to the board room straight away, if they could. Paul could and called out to Sepp, and together they rode up to the sixth floor. Entering the conference room, he first shook hands with CEO Tobler, and then with Jack Fraser Junior, the son of the Chairman of the Board and major shareholder of the Canadian mother company. Then was the turn of Dr. Seeliger, Chairman of the Board of the Swiss subsidiary, and four more members.

When all were sitting in their chairs around the table again, Schultz stood up and outlined, in grosso modo, the terms of the deal, not without mentioning that this transaction was done under his supervision and guidance. Nobody applauded, but nobody cried either. Then it was Paul's turn. He stood up, right in front of the men, like he had been standing so many times in front of complete strangers in his endless and countless meetings abroad. He explained the terms in detail, getting down to the nitty gritty, mentioning the tough negotiations, the late call from Novotny and good prospects for further deals in the future, and went on to say that, in his estimate, the bank would net a clean US$20 million, plus additional profit. He then sat down, and Fraser Junior stood up and started to applaud, shouting Paul's name out loud. The more contained Swiss directors had no choice but to do the same. After a round of handshaking and congratulations, Paul was dismissed. Schultz and Imbach hung on.

Now at his desk again, he started to make calls, mostly to colleagues and friends in the bank. Lastly, he called Tin to give him the news and inviting him for lunch, but to no avail; Tin's phone remained unanswered. Paul concentrated on other matters now and started checking customer files and accounts on the computer. Shortly before noon, it was time for a break, his internal telephone rang. This time it was Fraser's assistant inviting him for lunch with the Chairman and Fraser in the board room.

When he entered, Fraser was on the phone, but Dr. Seeliger approached him and greeted him again. No Schultz in sight this time, only Fraser, Seeliger and himself. The waiter started bringing in the appetisers, white wine, water, and when Fraser had ended his call, the three sat down, having lunch, and discussing recent geopolitical events and happenings, keeping the tone light and pleasant. After lunch, over coffee, Fraser announced that Paul had a great career ahead of him at the bank. He hinted at a substantial pay rise at the end of the year; he personally would be looking after it. He then presented Paul with a dark blue company tie, with the Canadian mother company's logo stamped on it, and thanked him again for his efforts and achievements. Seeliger did the same, in a sour, more contained tone. Paul left the board room, leaving the two men alone, and went down to his desk, a very happy young man of 27 indeed.

Later in the afternoon, Schultz presented him with a pair of golden cufflinks from Cartier, a personal gift as he called it. Paul thanked him, shaking hands. An hour later he left the bank, walking home, and on the way bought two bottles of his favourite Montepulciano to toast with his lover later tonight.

CHAPTER 15

The next weeks flew by. Paul was still the man of the year and enjoyed all the attention. The $150 million loan transaction was an immediate success, and Imbach had arranged for a few friendly banks to participate in the structure. In total, he had allocated and sold US$40 million to them, but as a matter of fact, he could have sold over $100 million, so strong was the interest to participate. With its attractive terms, the bank kept the bulk of it on its own books. It was structured this way to draw attention from the national and international press. The part he sold brought additional profits for the bank, them included, the total now exceeding US$21 million.

After CSSR, Paul went on another business trip, this time to Hungary, beautiful Budapest, with its ancient, elegant buildings and churches dating back to the Austrian-Hungarian Empire. He almost managed to close another substantial deal, but at the last minute the board of the Hungarian Exim Bank put it on hold for further review. It did not damage his reputation. When he returned to Zurich, further meetings were scheduled for next spring.

By now it was early autumn, and one morning Paul opened his mailbox at the flat and found a letter from the Army, requesting him to report next Monday, 7 a.m. at the Rapperswil logistic centre, to start his four weeks annual repetition course. Shit, October meant cold weather, the battalion would undoubtedly spend their yearly course up in the Prätigau Mountains, some 2,000 metres above sea level. It would be bitterly cold, and normally at this time of year snow would set in. But what the hell, look at it from the positive side; get away from the job, spend time with his army buddies, especially his old pal Moretti, exercise himself, run like crazy and, on arrival, wait for nothing.

He would enjoy the delicious food the army kitchen had to offer, do some shooting, driving, breathing the pure mountain air, and get fit, do nothing much, and worry still less.

On the eve of reporting to the barracks, he packed his rucksack, made sure he got the 48 rounds of ammunition sealed in two tin cans, knife, gas mask with filter, fighting overalls, camouflage overalls, A & B suit, two pairs of boots, helmet, extra food, and a flat man containing a good single malt, the SIG pistol, and the SIG 57 assault rifle, compass, maps, log book, diary and charts.

Soph was unavailable to drive him to Rapperswil, being at work, so he boarded the 5 :15 a.m. train out of Zurich Hauptbahnhof, heading for Rapperswil. He arrived shortly after 6 a.m. and walked to the Army logistics and assembly place, having coffee and breakfast on the way; it would take time until the field kitchen was up and running. The next week passed quickly as he had predicted, high up in the mountains, cut off from the world and the pressure. First weekend home he spent with Soph, and they made good use of the just shy of 48 hours leave.

The next morning he took his car up to the small mountain village where they were stationed, and he stopped by at Moretti's place to give him a lift; he was good company and they chatted away. The time flew by, and on the last Saturday morning, discharge day, he took his army documents and, together with Moretti, drove back to Zurich as fast as the Alfa would go. They were free until next year, when it would commence all over again.

It was early spring by now, and Paul was about to embark on another business trip, this time to the GDR, the German Democratic Republic, with the GDR being the last of the Soviet satellite countries to be visited, and also the biggest and strongest economically speaking, or so the available statistics and country data showed.

Schultz called it his prize number 1, and had intended to visit the country himself, but a few weeks earlier had desisted in doing so alleging urgent commitments elsewhere. So it was up to him to make it all happen. Karen, as always, prepared the itinerary. The meetings would all take place in and around Berlin, banks as usual, but also a fair number of industrial and manufacturing: companies. This was East Germany alright, but more structured and organised than the other places he had visited. When Karen asked for his passport to organise the entry visa, it took longer than usual to get it back; almost ten days, but eventually it arrived, fully stamped and authorised.

Because of the many meetings, the trip would take five full days, and Paul already had mixed feelings about it. On the one hand he was keen and eager to get to know the GDR, and hopefully strike a deal; on the other hand, he was worried about what he might find there.

Too late now, all set. He changed 500 Francs into Ostmark, and the same amount into dollars; the rest he would pay by credit card. His briefcase was full of brochures on his bank and the services they offered. He would take these brochures along, together with all the other customary material he needed for such an extended business trip. He said goodbye to his colleagues. They all wished him the best and lots of luck. Arriving at his flat that evening, he put the brochures into his suitcase, too many of them and too heavy to carry in the briefcase that was already packed and full with other material; Paul liked to travel light, but this time there was no option. He called Soph to say goodbye, promising to be back soon and swearing eternal love. He then called Tin to inform him about his trip and promised to have lunch on his return. Paul felt anxious and restless, for no obvious reason. He had made similar trips on many occasions, and it always went OK; with a few setbacks, alright, and awkward, if not dangerous, situations, but he had always come out of it clean. It would turn out to be the same, he assured himself, pouring a large scotch to soothe the nerves.

Next morning early, at 7:20, he queued at the Swissair check-in desk, as was customary. A good two and a half hours later he landed, on time, at Berlin's Tempelhof Airport, went through immigration, exited the huge Airport complex, and hailed a cab; destination: Checkpoint Charlie in the American Sector. Beyond that point, it was the wild east, with consequences as yet unknown to Paul.

When the cab pulled over in front of Checkpoint Charlie, the driver said no taxi could continue from this point on. "You've got to walk. And take care, man, these eastern bastards can't be trusted."

"That's reassuring," Paul thought to himself while paying the driver. He took his two cases from the taxi's boot, put on his overcoat, and started walking towards a sergeant in a blue uniform. He had a white helmet on his head and held a rifle in front of him.

"Step over here, man, passport ready," the guard announced.

When it was his turn, he showed the passport to the checkpoint chief, a captain, who examined it carefully, asked the purpose of the visit, stamped it, and gestured towards a long passageway with a tall metal fence on either side.

"You walk over that way to the East German checkpoint, just over there. Don't stop on the way, just keep walking."

With that, he handed back the passport and waved him off. Paul started walking and, after a 100 metres, halfway along the passageway, he read a sign saying, "You're now leaving the American sector".

Paul kept on walking until he arrived at the other end, approaching a low lying, cement built post with two soldiers in grey GDR uniforms holding what looked like assault rifles of a large calibre. It was 4 p.m. by now, and the weak sun was about to set on the western horizon, with the temperature dropping already. There were two elderly men in front of him, waiting for their turn. After a good 20 minutes, the officer in charge asked Paul to step forward, examining him from head to toe, and at the same time scrutinising his passport.

"Winter, come over here and follow me," gesturing to a door at the side. He followed the man, who seemed to be a sergeant, and they entered a small room with a desk in the middle, one chair in front, and three steel cabinets fixed on the wall. The room reeked of both stale soup and vomit. Paul stood in front of the desk, briefcase and suitcase on either side, raincoat still on, waiting. After 15 minutes, a mean-looking lieutenant entered, followed by two corporals, both heavily armed, in full battle gear, with their helmets on. The lieutenant, holding his passport, sat down at the desk, not asking Paul to sit as well, but letting him stand in front of him. The officer in charge had short-cut brown hair, and a scar that went from his left ear to his thin lips. He was skinny and looked like he enjoyed inflicting pain on his victims.

Looking at Paul in a dirty, sadistic way, he asked, "What is the purpose of your visit to the GDR? How long do you intend to stay? Are you employed by an American company? Have you ever been in touch with the BKA, the Bundes Kriminal Amt of west Germany?"

While the man kept on asking his questions, Paul became very uneasy and worried, but he kept his calm and answered the man's questions in a professional, precise tone, not showing any fear or weakness. When he had finished with his explanations, the GDR officer asked him to hand over his briefcase and suitcase.

One of the guards put them on the desk in front of the lieutenant. He started to examine the contents, first the briefcase, went through everything, carefully and meticulously, not missing anything. Having finished this examination, which lasted a good ten minutes, he concentrated now on the suitcase, examining every piece of clothing, opening the toilet bag, squeezing out the toothpaste and emptying it.

When he came to the brochures, them being at the bottom of the case, he let out a sarcastic, "What have we got here? Propaganda material of a western bank, with the intent, no doubt, to distribute this filth here in our country, which is, of course, totally against the law."

Paul now started to get really worried, for nobody at the bank had told him that it was illegal to bring information on the bank's services to the GDR, but then none of the poor sods had known either. Or did Schultz know, being himself German? No. That made no sense. They just did not know.

The officer in charge now told the corporal next to him to gather this infromation material immediately, keeping a copy for the lieutenant. The contents of his suitcase were strewn all over the floor.

"Take off all your clothes, now," he ordered.

"You want me to do what? Take off my clothes?"

"You heard me, and get on with it. I don't have the whole afternoon."

Paul had no choice and started undressing. "Go on, and take off your socks, too."

By now it was dark outside, and the room was lit by two powerful fluorescent tubes that threw their hospital-like light on Paul.

He was now fully naked, standing in front of the three men. They looked at him for a while, ordered him to turn around, flex his knees three times, and cough. It was humiliating and frightening at the same time.

"OK, Winter. You can dress now and clean up your mess, hear! You may go."

With that said, he handed back the passport and walked out of the room, looking back at Paul, and smiling slightly while doing so. Paul dressed as quickly as he could, put his belongings into the case, the papers strewn on the desk back into the briefcase, coat on, passport put away into the inner side of his suit jacket and walked out of that ghastly place. When he stepped out of the door in the back of the building, there was nothing but a large empty field; no lights, no lamp post, nothing. Just pitch black. A corporal was standing by the wall, smoking.

"Where can I get a cab here?" he asked the man.

"No cabs here. Just walk in that direction," he said, indicating the way with his hand. "Get going before Vogel changes his mind." He stubbed out his cigarette and entered the post again.

Paul started walking, first over the field, a good 15 minutes, and then down a small street. That one at least was lit, every 100 metres or so, by a weak lamp. There were no buildings on either side, only horses that looked very thin, minding their own business. The suitcase began to wear on him. He was upset, frustrated, tired, thirsty, hungry and afraid. But at the same time glad that he had escaped the East German henchman.

After another 20 minutes, he finally reached a square with houses beginning to appear. They had weak lights shining out from their windows. Paul kept on walking, getting more and more hungry now, and swearing at Vogel and his henchmen. After yet another four kilometres, he arrived at a crossroads with large fully lit buildings on either side. He walked towards them and, in the distance, spotted a taxi rank. The driver regarded him suspiciously, dirty shoes, sweating face, coming out of nowhere. But when Paul indicated the Berliner Hof, a 5-star hotel in the city centre, he opened the door, put the cases into the boot and off they drove. The Taxi was a Trabant, an East German make with a weak two tact motor and heavy exhaust fumes. But it got them to the Berliner Hof.

He paid the driver and stepped into the sumptuous foyer. What a relief. He approached the reception desk, gave his name, and was in no mood for chatter or small talk. He was handed the key, rode up to the seventh floor, opened the door and fell exhausted onto the large double bed. After a moment, about to doze off, he stood up, smoked a cigarette, and composed himself.

"I am Paul Winter, Vice President, man for all seasons and weather. I make it happen against all odds, lover and lady's man. Rich and powerful. I will make it happen here again in this god-forsaken Germany, no matter the cost, and to hell with Vogel." He had managed to insult him and make him look weak, but only for a moment. "Poor bastard, enjoy your Ostmarks and Trabants, and have a good life." Or whatever that meant in this corner of the world.

Paul rode down in the lift, walked past the reception desk, and went straight to the bar. It was 9 p.m. by now, and a good crowd had gathered around the large bar made of mahogany wood. Paul sat down, ordered a gin and tonic, he was in dire need of a drink, and started observing the patrons; five men in business suits and ties, three women wearing short skirts and low-cut blouses, lots of makeup, red lips and rather weird hairdos, with the hair standing high up on their heads. There was a man standing out of the crowd, short haircut, military style, dark blond, a black suit with white shirt and dark blue tie, smoking and talking to one of the barmen. Other than him, it was the usual gathering of travellers, or business or salesmen, and the usual women, selling something as well. The only thing they probably got, it struck him. When he ordered his second G&T, the military type man slowly approached him and sat down on the empty seat next to Paul.

"Good evening. Let me introduce myself. My name is Werner Kowalski." Having said that, he lit a cigarette and ordered a scotch on the rocks. "Pleased to meet you, Paul Winter.` ` I have never seen you in the Berliner Hof before; passing through or on business?"

He made small talk, chatting away, trying to make Paul feel at ease. But Paul was not at ease at all, feeling rather uncomfortable in the presence of this man. KowalskI continued, talking, mostly about the weather, the unfortunately slow economy, travel plans, and so forth. Paul responded half-heartedly, not paying much attention, until Kowalski suggested leaving the bar and sitting in the foyer so as not to be disturbed, as he put it. Paul reluctantly agreed, and they both sat down. After a brief moment, Kowalski took out a manila envelope from his suit jacket. It had no name or address on it, and he placed it in front of Paul on the table.

"This envelope contains a letter, or proposal, to be more precise. It also contains 5,000 westmarks. The cash is yours if you accept this envelope, read its letter, and give me an answer by eight o'clock tomorrow morning. You will have your breakfast at this time, and if the *Neue Frankfurter Zeitung* is on your table with its front page open, it means yes, you have accepted our proposal. If the newspaper is folded and closed, it means the contrary. Either way, the money is yours."

Paul looked at him hard and long, but he could not read Kowalski, who sat relaxed in his chair smoking another cigarette, looking at Paul. His mind raced. What could that letter mean? He came to no conclusion. The only way to find out was to accept the envelope and read the letter; by doing so, getting 5,000 marks. Paul lit a cigarette, still not answering. After a good two minutes, he reached over the table, took the envelope, folded it, and put it into his jacket pocket.

"Very well, Mr. Winter. I am pleased you have accepted to read it. Let me just inform you that if you intend to copy it, photograph it, or xerox it, it will be to no avail. The letter has been written with a self-destructing ink, it will be unreadable and its writing will disappear from the paper within 15 minutes of opening the envelope. It is written with a special type of ink that is unreproducible in any sort of manner. This precaution, of course, is for your and our safety and protection. I will leave you now. You must undoubtedly be tired from your, shall we say, challenging journey. Goodnight Mr. Winter. I will see you tomorrow morning at breakfast."

With that, Kowalski stood up and left Paul sitting there alone, now deep in thought. Kowalski was military alright, and he had known about his encounter with Vogel at the checkpoint earlier today. That made Kowalski STASI, Staats Sicherheits Dienst, the notorious branch of East Germany's state police known for its torture and brutal methods. The STASI was also known for dozens of disappearances in the last few years.

Too late now, Paul had accepted, so he might as well read the letter and grab the cash. He stood up, walked up to the bar, wanting to settle his bill, but was informed that it had been taken care of already.

It was after midnight by now. Paul said thank you to the bartender, gave him a good tip, and retired to his room. He had not eaten all day since the light lunch during the flight, so he called room service and ordered a steak with fries. He then took a shower, and afterwards, unpacked. He put everything in order, ready for tomorrow.

After the late dinner, he sat in the chair and carefully opened the envelope. It contained a letter written on a typewriter in a greyish ink. Underneath, in a smaller envelope, he counted 5,000 West German marks, all in 100 marks notes. He then started reading the letter. He had another 13 minutes or so before it would become unreadable.

The letter did not contain more than five lines, but what it said, in so few words, was dynamite. It instructed Paul to assassinate the West German Finance Minister, Lothar Weidling; the mission had to be accomplished by April 25, in three weeks' time. A down payment of DM 500,000 would be made available within 24 hours of acceptance, the balance of a further DM 500.000, being paid on completion. Bank account and details to be forwarded on acceptance with further details to follow, not least the exact itinerary and timetable of Weidling's travel arrangements during the next three weeks. There was no signature and no name. Only today's date.

Paul's hands were shaking. He stood up and went to the toilet, relieving himself. He then poured a scotch, lit a cigarette and started thinking. One million DM for one well-executed shot. It was challenging and frightening at the same time. He had to call Tin, but not from Berlin, and certainly not from the hotel. The mission wasn't impossible, but it all depended on the venue and timing. A plan began to form in his head. The finance minister must have a busy travel schedule, staying in many different hotels in many different places. This was where Paul would have to strike. Tin had to be in on this venture; no way he could pull this one off alone. How much he would give Tin for participating in this crazy undertaking he had yet to decide. But it would have to be enough to make him take this big risk.

One million was a hefty price, and Paul calculated that, less overheads and Tin's share, he could net a clean DM 800,000. With that kind of money, and the other amount he already had, he could retire, or semi-retire, somewhere of his choice, definitely a warmer climate with much more friendly people.

Strangely, Paul was quite cool and relaxed now, and besides the enormous task ahead of him, he did not panic. He read the letter one more time and then flushed it down the toilet. He went to sleep, a good night's sleep; no nightmares or bother of any kind.

Next morning, showered, shaved, and smartly dressed, he fetched the *Neue Frankfurter Zeitung,* sat down at the table, having breakfast, with the paper with its front page wide open, showing today's headline. A few moments later, Kowalski entered the room and slowly walked over, stopped behind Paul, looking at the open paper, and then walked on, nodding to Paul in an affirmative gesture.

Today's meetings had gone alright, two manufacturing companies and two banks. All on time and satisfactory. By now, after visiting all these countries and conducting business, he had become more detached, but still acted strictly professionally; but the thrill had gone, partly because of the big success last year in CSSR and partly because of Kowalski's letter and its implications. He could not deviate his thoughts from the letter. One million DM was a very big amount. If it all went well, it was his ticket to freedom and independence. It all had to be planned extremely well, with no traces that could lead back to him. But this time again, there would be a corpse, and it was not a nobody, but West Germany's Finance Minister, the repercussions, attention and determination of the German Police would be relentless. It was becoming clear now that he would have to disappear from Switzerland, Europe, or better, from the Earth, for at least five years. Goodbye to Tin, his friends, Soph and the bank. He would have to start from scratch, a total stranger in a strange place; but a very rich one at that.

When he arrived back at the hotel, he saw Kowalski sitting in one of the lounge chairs, alone, smoking. He waved at him discreetly, made a gesture that he would be right back, and went up to his room. He entered, sat down, and wrote on a small piece of paper that he had taken from the hotel's stationery, his bank account details, which he folded and put into his suit jacket. He quickly consulted his itinerary for tomorrow, and satisfied, took the lift and rode down to meet Kowalski.

When he entered the foyer, Kowalski was standing near the hotel entrance. He walked over to him, said hello, and Kowalski suggested a walk. The two men walked down the road away from the hotel, and after 15 minutes, entered a park full of people, alone, or with their dogs, or sitting on one of the many park benches. It was still pleasantly warm, with the sun sinking low, and birds singing, dogs running wild, tongues lolling and ears flapping. A pleasant sight, contrasting starkly with the business at hand between him and the German. The two walked around until they found a bench, and both sat down.

"Have you got the bank information?" Werner asked him in a business-like tone of voice. Paul handed him the folded piece of paper, which Kowalski did not open or look at, but put straight into his pocket. "By 3 p.m. tomorrow you may consult your bank. The funds will be there by then. I suggest we meet tomorrow at 6 p.m., at this very bench again, agreed? Any questions so far? No? Good, tomorrow I will brief you on how to get Weidling's movements on a weekly basis, right there in Zurich. You may not take notes, this information is so vital it can only be in your head. Tomorrow will be our last meeting. See you then."

With that, Kowalski stood up and walked away. Tomorrow would be the last meeting. The sooner this was over the better. Kowalski was a very dangerous man. He felt uncomfortable and threatened in his presence.

He watched Kowalski slowly disappearing behind a large tree and wondered whether any of his colleagues had been following them, protecting their master. He could not tell. These bastards were professionals. He smoked a cigarette and thought hard. Werner would reveal the methods and ways to get Weidling's movements. This was essential and vital, and the fact that he would get this information in his hometown, and all these preparations and setups only showed and proved how professional and determined these people were.

It also reduced the risk greatly for Paul in preparing the assault. Without this intel., no way. Tomorrow he would consult his bank and get confirmation of being half a million richer. If negative, he would abort the mission and fly back as quickly as he could, or so he hoped. Too late for Kowalski now, too. If he wanted this done, he had to come up with the funds.

Paul stood up and walked slowly back to the hotel. Shortly before he arrived, he spotted a cafe with tables on the pavement. He sat down and ordered a pint of local beer; it was nice and cold and helped him to relax and ease his tensions and worries a little; if that was at all possible under the circumstances.

Having paid the waiter, he rose and looked and searched around, trying to spot any of Kowalski's crew, but could see none. This night he would stay in at the hotel, having his dinner in the dining room, and, afterwards, go to his room and get to bed early. Next day he had to be strong and very alert.

Next morning, after a string of now more and more boring business meetings, he walked down a busy road in the city centre. When he spotted a public phone booth, he inserted the required amount of ost pfennigs and marks and called his bank.

After identifying himself and passing the codes, he was given his balance, and confirmation given by a dull office clerk, that his account had just received a remittance for half a million Deutsche Marks.

He said, "thank you," and hung up. The call had not taken more than 90 seconds, but time enough to change his entire life. Satisfied, but at the same time becoming increasingly worried at the implications of this money transfer, Paul walked back to the hotel, but he stopped first at the cafe near the hotel to have his customary pint. There were still two hours to go before meeting Kowalski. Time enough to take a shower, freshen up, and walk to the all-determining meeting.

He entered the park and spotted Werner sitting on that very bench where they had agreed to meet, smoking and looking carelessly around, and watching Paul approach the bench. He said hello without shaking hands.

"Everything satisfactory?" Werner asked in a low voice.

Paul nodded and said "Yes."

"Good. Now, with this matter resolved, let me explain the Zurich arrangements. I want you to listen carefully and do not take any notes. All this stays in your head only. After this meeting we will not see each other again. There will be no further contact." He then explained the operational details of providing the intel on Weidling's every move, which Paul needed to accomplish his task. Kowalski spoke slowly, precisely, and in a low voice,

Paul listened and nodded at Kowalski; from time to time asking a question. After 30 minutes, the briefing was over and Kowalski stood up, this time shaking Paul's hand and saying goodbye. He did not wish him any luck, just walked off, hopefully never to be seen again, he wished.

The two remaining days flew by quickly. Paul even succeeded in closing another deal, this time with the Deutsche Aussenhandelsbank, their foreign commerce bank. A letter of intent had been signed by the Director and Paul, for the amount of US$50 million. That was something indeed, with attractive terms for his bank, but not as attractive as the CSSR deal. Nevertheless, it was a good deal, and Paul felt great about it, he had something to show on his return to Zurich, and would undoubtedly be hailed again as the man that made it all happen.

After the last meeting in Berlin, he walked to his favourite cafe, sat down outside, and had his pint, and then another one. While he drank, people were coming and going. His thoughts wandered to Soph. He meant to call her, wanting to hear her voice and the promises she would undoubtedly make, making him feel good, and wanted. He missed her and needed her company badly, but did not dare to call her from Berlin, not even from a public phone. With Kowalski and his Stasi, no doubt all international calls, and local ones as well, would be monitored and, for that reason, Soph would have to wait.

He was anxious to get back to Zurich as quickly as possible, meeting Tin the very next day and explaining the plan, which depended entirely on Weidling's movements and the accuracy of Kowalski's, intel. Tin would be keen to join in, no doubt there. He liked the action, more so still the money, always being short of cash, burning it fast with his numerous tarts and friends he kept changing, like Paul changed his socks.

Thinking and plotting, Paul was not in the mood to go back to the Berliner Hof yet, it was a nice, warm afternoon, so he decided to enjoy the weather and walk, trying to find a shop to buy a present for Soph, and later, have dinner somewhere, changing the venue. After walking around for a good half an hour, he found a gift shop and bought an elegant gold plated lighter. He paid cash and had it wrapped in blue and white gift paper. He wrote a note for Soph on a small card the sales attendant fixed to the box. Perfect, Soph was going to love it. This done, he kept on walking until he found a venue that looked inviting. He entered and sat at one of the small, empty tables, ordering trout with a salad and a bottle of Riesling. After coffee he headed back to the hotel, and he saw many people still walking the streets. He watched out for Kowalski and his sidekicks, but could not spot any of them, he noted gladly.

Entering the hotel and walking past reception, he entered the bar. He watched the guests, the usual crowd, but somehow he did not feel like sitting down and joining them. He instead took his key and went up to the room. He packed, organised his briefcase and notes, put the signed letter in a plastic folder, for extra protection, and went through his annotations and reports. Satisfied, he took a shower. Afterwards, in his bathrobe, he sat in the one chair on the balcony overlooking the streets and the square below.

He poured himself a scotch, lit a cigarette, and contemplated the view of the Berlin night. What a trip this East Berlin had turned out to be. Exciting, frustrating at first, and very dangerous indeed. It was a life-changer, and nothing Paul had known until now would ever be the same again. He was about to embark on the most dangerous journey of his young life so far, with outcomes and consequences totally unknown.

CHAPTER 16

Next day, arriving at the Airport, in mid-afternoon, he hailed a cab and headed straight to the flat. There had been no problem in leaving East Berlin; Kowalski, Paul was convinced, had made sure of that. First thing he did was call Tin, who answered the call straight away.

"Listen. I have something very important to tell you, but not over the phone. Let's meet tomorrow after work, say 6:15 p.m. at the Bauschanze. Agreed? OK, see you."

He had not given Tin any time or chance to ask any questions. That bombshell would come tomorrow, personally. He then called Soph, saying he had just arrived, and could she come over right now.

"Sure, I've missed you. Be there in 40 minutes." She hung up.

When she arrived, looking gorgeous in a light yellow summer dress, white shoes, her blonde hair smelling of perfume, they embraced and went straight down to business, hungry and impatient, eager to satisfy one another's bottled up needs the way they both liked most.

After showering together, they sat down on the balcony, sipping cold white wine, smoking and looking out at the lake in the distance.

"I've got a present for you," he announced with a grin on his face, putting the small box in her hand.

She opened it carefully, first reading the note and blushing. When the golden lighter was in her hand, she tried it and lit a cigarette. She then kissed him fully on the lips, tongue probing, and finally said, "Paulie my dear, what a lovely gift. You must not do that, but thank you so much. It will remind me of you every time I use it, and it will lighten up my fire for you even more."

Then they embraced and sat in silence for a while, looking at each other from time to time, holding hands and enjoying the view. Paul realised then that he would have to let go of her in the very near future, as a matter of fact in the next three weeks. This thought brought sadness and melancholy. He liked her a lot, loved her a lot. The weeks in Spain together had been fantastic, she was an intelligent, down to earth, honest girl, with an endless appetite for fucking, sucking, and whatever else came to her mind. He was sad, but there was no option. After the Weidling hit, there was no way Paul could stay, at least not for long. He had to disappear for a long time, and there was no room for Soph in this. He turned his face, watching her, and suggested they go out and grab a bite to eat. Soph was game, as she normally was.

Next morning, sitting at his desk, he presented his new deal to Schultz and Imbach. They both liked it a lot, congratulating him on his success. It was not as substantial as the Czech deal, but still would net the bank a clean US$1.5 million a year, or 7.5 million in five years, during its duration. Schultz took the letter and left them, undoubtedly running up to the CEO and showing it off to him.

This time Paul was not invited to attend any meeting in the board room on the top floor, nor was he invited for lunch by the top brass. Paul did not mind, he had much more urgent matters to attend to.

The GWZ, Gas Werk Zurich (or Gas works), was an industrial plant down in Schlieren. It consisted of more than 20 large tanks, each one more than 50 metres high. City council had given small patches of land around this site to amateur gardeners to grow fruit, vegetables and cereals during war time; helping to supply the local community. On these patches of land, the leaseholders had built tiny houses, more like shacks, to keep their tools and everything else they needed. The basis of the construction was made of cement, with the rest of it built with wood, comprising one room, a small kitchen, a bathroom and a small porch.

Kowalski's operational set up was for Paul to, every night for the next two weeks, drive down one of the narrow service roads and look for house number 173. If there was a pot of red begonias standing on the windowsill, there were documents to be retrieved from inside the dumpster located at the small U-turn at the end of the road. No flowers meant to come back the next night. The documents were stacked inside the dumpster, on the left internal side.

Paul knew the GWZ; he had been there once on a school excursion. Tomorrow night, for the first time, he would pass by number 173, checking the window. Paul could not concentrate on his work at the office. He was done with the bank. He would hand in his resignation letter once the hit was done. Depending on Kowalki's intel, he would call in sick to concentrate on organising the assassination of the finance minister. It all depended on Weidling's movements, and the accuracy and timeframe of Kowalski's reports.

He was sitting at a table away from the crowds, smoking a cigarette and waiting for Tin. When he arrived, he was looking tired in a crumpled suit that had seen better days.

"Hi, Tin. How are you? Everything OK at work, and with the ladies? You look a bit worn out. What happened." Paul offered him a cigarette as he sat down.

"I am OK, thanks; but that bitch, Alice, you don't know her, is pissing me off, demanding money for an abortion. I am not sure

I am the father, though. That slut's fucking around anyway. But she threatens that if I don't pay her SFr. 10,000 by month end, she will sue me, saying that if it came to that, it would cost at least double."

"Shit man, that sounds like big time trouble. But what happened to the money from the Cartier job?" Paul asked in a low voice.

"Spent it all."

"On what, for Christ's sake? Hundreds of thousands of Francs within one year! How the hell is this possible?"

"Wine, women and song; and a bit of blow, not necessarily in that order," Tin replied with a faked smile; sipping on his beer that had just arrived.

"I want you to listen very carefully now, and don't interrupt. Ask your questions when I am finished."

Paul laid out the plan in as much detail as he could provide at this point in time, which was not much of a plan at all. He did not leave out any detail. The trip to East Berlin, the encounter with Vogel at Checkpoint Charlie, and Kowalski. Paul did not reveal how much he was being paid, no need to trouble and bother Tin with that.

He did, however, say, "You will get a total of Fr. 180,000; Fr. 50,000 within the next two weeks, with the rest on completion. All expenses on me. How does that sound? Enough money to send Alice back into the hole she crept out from?"

Tin, for a long moment, said nothing at all, just sitting there staring out into the distance. Then he suddenly stood up and embraced Paul. "You made my day again, thank you, I am in 100%, whatever it takes, I am your man. You can count on me. When do we start? For me, the sooner the better. I am getting restless with all this business with Alice. To hell with these whores!"

Paul said, "Tomorrow night. Come by my place at 1 a.m. Dress in something black and bring a torch. We are going to pay a visit to the old GWZ, see whether there are any flowers for us."

Next night, Tin arrived on time, dressed in black jeans and a dark blue T-shirt. Paul was expecting him, already dressed all in black too, and ready to go.

"Let's move, we'll take the Alfa. There will be little traffic at this time of night." They drove north, sticking strictly to the speed limit, and after 25 minutes reached Schlieren, with the large tanks visible in the dark night ahead of them; about one kilometre still to go. There were no other cars in sight, no dog walkers or anything of that sort either. Paul cut the car's lights, leaving the small front position lights on as they slowly entered the narrow road. All these tiny houses stood there in the pitch black and utter silence. These were only used, if at all, during daytime or on weekends. When they reached 173, Tin pointed the torch light at the window, but there was no flowerpot there.

"Shit, nothing," Paul murmured as he swung the Alfa round the U-turn slowly, seeing the garbage dumpster standing there. "Let's get out of here. We will try tomorrow night again, same time." He drove back to Tin's car that was parked near his flat and said goodbye. The following night, same time, they repeated the journey, and this time, passing 173, there was a pot of begonias standing on the windowsill, greeting them.

"Here we go," said Paul. He drove up to the garbage dumpster, keeping the engine running, and stepped out of the car. "Give me the torch," he said, bending over the dumpster now, looking inside and reaching out. There it was, attached to the left inner side, fixed with some black sticky tape. Paul took it off carefully, stuffed it into his jacket, got back in the car and slowly drove down the quiet alley.

The two of them, Paul sitting at the dining table, curtains drawn; Tin standing and looking over Paul's shoulder; read the message at the same time. It was written in a greyish typewriter colour Paul recognised it immediately.

Here were Weidling's exact movements for the next four days; accommodation, timetables, meeting – including all names of people attending – exact location venues, whom he was to see after the meetings and where, and even the content and topics of it all. It was a very precise report, down to the last detail, but, unfortunately, his agenda and duties were all in different cities in Germany, and all gatherings were always behind closed doors, inside buildings, conference halls, and the like, to which Paul had no access.

All this was of no use and presented no opportunity at all to attack him. He had to get Weidling somewhere in a public place, preferably a hotel, or similar, with the target being outside, even better. He looked at Tin and commented, "We know his every move, but it's not good. This week does not present any opportunity for us. Let's concentrate, in the meantime, on the tools we need. Please come by tomorrow at 6 p.m. and we will visit an old friend of mine, Freddy. I have an idea he might have just what we need."

After saying goodbye, and Tin gone, Paul sat down on one of the summer chairs on the balcony, sipping a Huerlimann. He did have some ideas, and they quickly became clearer to him. He was plotting. All he needed was the right place to take Weidling out, the right distance, time, and escape route. He was becoming more confident that the right opportunity would present itself in due course soon. He still had two full weeks to carry it out. Time enough, he hoped. He would use that time to organise and prepare.

Next day at 7:30 p.m., they stepped inside the Olga Bar, at Longstreet (or Langstrasse), the infamous amusement and red-light district. The place smelled of beer, sweat and cheap perfume. Paul spotted Freddy sitting at the bar, a large beer in front of him and a cigarette in his mouth. From a distance, in the dimly lit bar, he looked OK, with his long brown hair and a golden earring in his left ear. But closing in, and staring at his face, one could see the bad teeth and unhealthy skin. Freddy was an old army buddy. They had spent their first training weeks together at the Chur barracks. In the fifth week Freddy was discharged from military service for stealing money from his captain. During his Sunday guard duty, with all personnel being on leave and only him and a few other guards on duty, he had gotten into the captain's private bedroom and stole Fr. 50 that he found in a drawer.

Unfortunately, he was seen coming out of the room by another guard. The captain returned Sunday night, discovered the theft, went to the Military Police, and filed a report of theft of Fr. 50. An enquiry followed and Freddy confessed. He was now doing four weeks per year in a state asylum for the elderly, cleaning their toilets and accommodation.

That was old Freddy, alright. Paul introduced Tin as they shook hands. "How is it going you old bastard?" Paul said, ordering three beers from the waiter, a Chinese-looking woman in her fifties.

Freddy said, "OK, slow and steady here and there, depending from where the wind blows." He smiled at Paul and Tin, opening his mouth, showing a front tooth missing. Freddy might look like a low life bum, but he was connected. He was close friends with the boss of the Hells Angels' Zurich Chapter, and who needed to know, knew.

He was also Paul's occasional blow provider, and more rarely, drinking buddy. "Tin's been with me for a long time. You can trust him, no secrets here." Having said that, he handed Freddy a piece of paper containing the specifics of the long range, heavy calibre assault rifle, together with details of the silencer and high-powered night vision telescope. Freddy looked at the paper, reading with slightly shaking hands.

"Are you going on a safari shooting elephants in the dark?" Freddy asked.

"Something like that. See what you can do, and fast, need it by Thursday," Paul said.

"I'll see to it. The silencer will cost you 2k extra," Freddy said.

"The cash is covered, no problem. Don't worry about that. Meet you tomorrow, same place, same time, OK?" Paul asked.

"Yes, OK. I will get this hammer for you. I'll let you know the total price tomorrow, but bring Fr. 5,000 cash as a down payment. Agreed?" Freddy asked.

Paul paid for the three beers, waved goodbye, and they stepped out. "Let's eat something and talk this arrangement and Freddy over," Tin said.

"Good idea. Let's go to Rioja's down the street," Paul suggested.

Next evening, they met Freddy again, at the same place, Olga Bar. He was sitting in the same chair, wearing the same clothes, with the usual large beer in front of him.

"How's it going?" Paul said, sitting down next to him.

Apart from two old whores that looked like they were going to die any minute, but still managed an encouraging smile directed at Paul and Tin that went unanswered, the place was quiet.

"You got the goodies? What's the price?"

Freddy looked at him, not smiling this time. "This Polish motherfucker is a hell of a blower, a hammer, army grade, fitted with a German night sight telescope, the best, and a Polish manufactured silencer. It will slow down the muzzle speed somewhat, but will still do the job nicely at a range up to 400 metres tops. What do you say? And here's the price."

With that, he took a large gulp of his beer and handed Paul a piece of paper. Looking at the five-digit figure in silence, lighting a cigarette, and turning his head to face Freddy.

"For this price I want immediate delivery. I want this hammer tonight. How many rounds of ammo are included?"

"Thirty," Freddy replied. "Should be enough to wipe out an entire herd of elephants, or whatever else you are aiming at. I don't want to know. You got that kind of cash on you?"

Paul replied, "Yes." Handing him the 5,000 Francs under the bar, out of sight of prying eyes and keen whores. "The rest I got hidden in my car."

Freddy said, "OK, great. Let's meet tonight at 1 a.m. in front of the kiosk at Limmatplatz." With that, he took the envelope full of cash and stood up. "Bring your car, and make sure the boot is empty. This beauty is heavy and big." He walked out of the bar, waving at the two women who were looking desperately at him.

When he was gone, Tin said, "Is this OK and clean? I mean, 5k and nothing but a promise to meet. I don't know, sounds fishy to me. Why don't we follow this guy, see what he's up to. If it's no good, we take the 5,000 off him. What do you say?"

"We will stick to the plan, and he will make the delivery. The 5k is no good to him. If he does not deliver, he knows we will hunt him down and hurt him pretty good. Hells Angels or not, he will be there and deliver; 100%. Another 7k and fuck off. My guess is he's clearing a neat 1,000 for himself. That is a lot of money, considering where Freddy comes from. Buys him a lot of company. Don't worry, he will stick to it and see the deal through."

Sitting in the Alfa, smoking and watching the kiosk at the now deserted square. It was 1.10 a.m. and no Freddy in sight; just a few drunks and junkies staggering by. At 1:25 a.m., Paul became more and more nervous. Was Freddy setting him up? Was he running with the 5k? But at that very instant he saw him coming out from behind the kiosk, alone, smoking. He stood still now, searching for Paul, with Paul now flashing his headlights, and Freddy walked slowly over to the car, no police in sight. Tin opened his door and bent forward to let the guy squeeze in behind him on the small seat.

"Nice car you got yourself here, old Paulie." He reeked of beer and cigarette smoke, and something else a bit sweeter. "Head north to Oerlikon, behind the Hallenstadium. There is a large parking space area. Should be empty now, that's where we make delivery. My associate is waiting there as we speak. You got the remaining cash?"

"All here and shut the fuck up and sit tight." Paul looked back at Freddy, stone-faced, and then at Tin. During the short ride north, not a word was spoken.

When Paul pulled in at the parking space behind the stadium, he saw a battered, dark-coloured delivery van with Basel plates, away from the lights of the parking lot. No other cars or living souls were around. "Well chosen, old Freddy," Paul thought. He slowly approached the van, all lights out now, and turned the car so the boot faced the double rear doors of the van, and stopped, leaving the engine running.

He turned back to Freddy. "Let's do this fast and clean. I don't want to hang around here one minute more than is absolutely necessary. Step out, Freddy, I'll come with you. Tin here will stay back by the car. He has a SIG pistol in his pocket, and I know him for being rather trigger-happy when he smells a rat."

The three got out of the car, Tin hanging back, Freddy in front, with Paul right behind. The bag man was a big, heavy, ugly looking man in his forties with brownish hair, wearing an old black leather jacket and a sports hat on his head, not saying a word. When he saw Freddy, he waved to him, opening the rear doors. He gestured to approach the van while he opened the lid of a large wooden box, showing its contents under the beam of a torch he held in his right hand.

There it lay, shimmering black and oily in the torch's light. "Go check, it's all there," he said in an accent Paul could not identify. Some German or Polish maybe. Yes, he must be Polish alright.

Paul began to check the heavy weapon, carefully taking his time, it was all there, the ammo, 30 rounds as agreed, the silencer, long and black, the Zeiss night vision telescope, and the weapon itself, assault rifle, Polish made PAR, 10.2 mm, a beauty, she would do the task.

The Pole said something he could not understand, but took it for him wanting to get the cash. But before paying, he fitted the silencer on the rifle, checking its position, as well as the night vision telescope fitting perfectly, and for good measure, put a slug in the chamber, checking that was perfect too. He handed the envelope to the bag man with Freddy standing close by, watching the Pole do the count. He nodded his head, saying OK. Paul gestured for Tin to bring the bag, together with its heavy grey, bed cover. The parts went into the bag, together with the ammo, the weapon he wrapped into the blanket. Paul lifted it all and carried it to the boot, putting everything in there.

"OK, fellows, we are all set. Freddy, you better take a cab or something. I don't want to put you in any danger."

Freddy began to protest, but Paul had already entered the car and driven off with Tin at his side, watching the Pole and Freddy standing by the van, staring at them while they drove off. Paul switched on the headlights, rolled down the window, lit a cigarette, Tin doing the same, and headed back to his place; making sure to put their seatbelts on and sticking to the speed limit. Neither of them saying a word.

When he pulled up in front of his flat, the streets were totally empty, no lights on in any of the windows in the buildings around. It was 2:40 a.m. by now, with all law-abiding citizens fast asleep. He took out the blanket with the heavy weapon inside, while Tin took the bag. They entered quickly and quietly, trying not to make the slightest noise. Opening the door, he immediately stored the rifle and the bag in his wardrobe beneath some clothing he kept there. They both sat down at the dining table. Paul grabbed two cans of beer, and they drank in silence still.

"That went well. We now got the tools. What is missing is the right spot to work out the plan for the attack."

Monday night, Paul was driving once again to Schlieren and the gas works. He was smoking a cigarette, thinking of Soph. They had spent the weekend together, doing, as always, what they both liked most. On Sunday he had taken her on an excursion to Uetliberg, Zurich's, mountain, or Hill. They had taken the cable car up to the top and walked the ridge all the way to Leimbach, a good three-hour walk, where they took a bus back to the cable car terminal, where he had parked his car. It was a lovely excursion, and they had enjoyed the fresh air and the walk.

Soph made plans for their future together, keen to travel again, this time to Italy and without her parents; just her and him. Paul said little, only that he first had to check how things were working out at the bank, and he could not commit himself yet to any travel arrangements.

"You and your bloody bank. Don't you have any time for me?" she responded. "Don't you want me around any more. Got tired of me?"

Paul remembered her saying these words in a serious tone. He had responded. "Yes, of course I want you, and to be together with you."

He felt bad about it. He somehow knew this was their last Sunday together for a very long time, if not forever. Paul did not want to spoil their day, but he had to tell her the truth in the next few days, that he would be gone. He had to tell her personally. Writing a letter was out of the question, after all they had together. It would be hell for him, but perhaps worse for her; with no return date, and therefore no hope.

One thing was sure and clear now. Right after the hit, he had to disappear into thin air, far away and out of reach of the dangerous Kowalski, who had made it very clear that if he failed in any way, they would know how to find him and make him pay. A clear threat. Paul realised, thinking back to the Berlin meetings, that Kowalski had the power and means to do just that. He was afraid of what would happen if he failed, but he was also worried about the consequences of his succeeding. He had to get out of Kowalski's reach and power. Whatever it cost, there was no other way.

Driving down the now familiar small alley leading to house number 173 and looking at its window, there it was, the flowerpot of red begonias sitting on the sill. He stopped the car in front of the garbage dumpster, bent over it, and retrieved the envelope. He then put it under his seat and drove off. Reaching his flat at 1:50 a.m., he entered, sat down and opened the envelope straight away. He began to read the report, slowly and carefully. The whole week was again packed with meetings, Munich, Bonn, Berlin and other venues until Thursday, presiding a G8 members meeting, and then... Bingo, a conference with local politicians in the southern town of Konstanz, a stone's throw away from the Swiss border. Weidling was scheduled to arrive there by 9 a.m. Friday morning, and leaving the hotel the next Monday morning, early. Well, if his plan worked out, Weidling would never leave the place, at least not walking, but rather in a bag.

That must be it, the hotel in Konstanz, his one and only and best chance to earn the rest, another half a million Deutsche Marks; and with it, sail into the sunset. He knew Konstanz fairly well, had been there before, both on school excursions and privately. The town lay at the very border with Switzerland, but more importantly was bathed with the waters of lake Bodensee, the large lake, where in its midst lay the border between Germany and Switzerland, a zig zag line, difficult to monitor 24/7. The perfect surroundings for escape and vanishing. But more intriguing and important, there was the island of Mainau, situated just in front of the town of Konstanz, at some spots, a mere 300 metres from the mainland. This was the very opportunity he had been waiting for, and he was quite sure the only one that would present itself. He had to take this one, or fail.

Paul opened a can of beer and smoked a cigarette. He was excited and sharp as a nail. When it came to organising, nobody would be able to beat him. In the army, amongst other tasks, he had been made a sniper, chosen for his excellent high scores in long range shooting competitions. He had to take Weidling out with one masterly kill shot. He had this one shot only, max two, until the bodyguards would react and drag their boss to safety. Yes, this had to be his master shot. One bullet only, he knew he was able to deliver this.

During the last few days he had made himself familiar with the PAR rifle, training and aiming in the night on his balcony. He was setting his score on innocent boaters on the lake, a distance between 300 and 400 metres; the distance he had calculated he had to master to shoot down his target. He was convinced he could have taken out some proud hobby captains and friends boating on the lake in the distance from his very balcony. He now became more excited. He had to call Tin, wake him up, poor bastard. This could not wait. They had to move early tomorrow morning, not a minute to waste now. He called him, with Tin taking his call on the fourth ring.

"Listen, I've got a plan. We have to move quickly, come by this morning, no later than 7 a.m. and bring clothes for a week; all dark colours. Also, bring your SIG pistol and ammo and call in sick first thing in the morning. You won't be back before next week."

He hung up without a further word, went to the bathroom, and took a shower. He was as sharp as a knife, his brain working overtime, unable to slow down. The hot water pouring down on his face relaxed him a bit. Stepping out of the shower cubicle, he dried himself, put on fresh underwear, grabbed another can and sat down in the chair on the balcony, enjoying the cool breeze, coming up from the lake. He had to get some sleep. The next days would be some of the most demanding ones, so far, in his life.

CHAPTER 17

The doorbell rang at 6.50 a.m. Paul quickly let Tin in and they sat at the small kitchen table, drinking coffee Paul had just made and eating a not too fresh piece of bread with butter and marmalade. Tin looked relaxed and sharp, eager for action. He too had been waiting impatiently for this moment during the last two weeks. He had already been paid Fr. 50,000, so he had reason to smile; even more so when the job at hand had been completed, with him getting another Fr. 130,000.

"That kind of money will put me right," Tin thought, sipping his coffee and smoking one of his cigarillos. He looked at Paul and had to admit that he admired his friend. At first, when he heard about this new plan and enterprise, he felt it was crazy, impossible to carry out and see it through; much too risky and complicated, depending on too many imponderables they could not control. But as the time passed on, and reflecting on the two assaults they had done together before, he slowly became convinced that Paul could pull this one off too, making it happen again. His friend was a maker, a doer, and standup guy. But still, he had no clue how, but he trusted him with his life, and was committed 100%. He would stand by his side, assisting him to carry out this very dangerous hit, and thereafter keep his mouth shut for as long as he lived. He was deeply indebted to Paul, in more ways than one, not only for the money he had made but also because the man had saved his life. This very fact he would never, ever forget. Besides, he needed the fresh cash desperately.

"We will drive to the region of Lake Bodensee," said Paul. He pulled out a map, unfolded it, and put it on the table. He pointed at the isle of Mainau. "That is where we will strike. I will shoot him from there, right across the water to the hotel the poor sod will stay at. The distance at this tip of the island to the mainland is not more than 300 metres; perfect shooting range for the blower I have at my disposal. Our customer will stay at the Hotel Egli just facing the isle of Mainau, where we will be hidden out of sight. We have got a window of three nights to take him out. Time enough, I hope, for a good opportunity presenting itself. All it takes is for him to have his dinner on the large terrace of the hotel, enjoying the view, the dinner and the fresh spring night air. I'll be waiting for him, lying low and hidden at the most eastern tip of the island, facing right across to the hotel, and looking at his face through my telescope while he enjoys his lobster dinner; his last one as far as I am concerned."

Lighting a cigarette, he looked at Tin. "What do you say, possible or not?"

"I think you got yourself a hell of a plan. What do we need? How do we escape?"

"First things first. I want you to go up to Kesswil and buy one of them black rubber Zodiac boats, seating four. I also want you to get a 60 horsepower Johnson engine, or Evinrude, or similar, painted black. The motor has to be black, and it has to be new. You will pay for everything in cash. Here is Fr. 15,000; that should be sufficient, and also get one of those trailers to carry the boat. You will go fishing. Speaking of fishing, also get two fishing rods, just for appearance's sake." He sipped his coffee and then continued. "After the purchases, you drive to Göttingen, check into the , zum Hecht stay there until I call. If they ask, you will stay for two nights, pay cash in advance. Don't venture out too much, don't walk around. Have your meals in the hotel. I will get in touch, at the latest the day after tomorrow. We cannot be seen together, not before, and not after. I will be staying at the small town of Altnau, a few kilometres south of your place, but before checking in, I will pay a visit to the lovely island of Mainau and its famous rose gardens. Expect my call around 6 p.m. and stay low. You are a fisherman trying to catch a big one, and otherwise enjoying the lovely surroundings. Any questions? No? Good. Make sure you get all that stuff. Without it there will be no action. Mission failed."

"Relax, I will get the boat and the engine. I've got the whole day to do that. The boat will be there with the engine's tank full to the brim."

"OK, right. The blower is already in the boot; I put it there last night. I will see you, latest, the day after tomorrow, as planned. By then I will have worked on the plan in more detail, and will explain it to you, and your vital role in it. Have a safe drive."

They shook hands and Tin left. Paul cleaned the kitchen, checked his bag, clothes, extra pair of boots, binoculars, cash, knife – all there. It was Wednesday morning. He locked the door, walked to his car, put the bag next to him on the passenger seat, and drove off. First telephone booth, he made a call to the bank, calling in sick. No need to let them worry about him during his absence, that could very well prove to be eternal.

When the old woman at reception in the hotel asked him how long he would stay, he said two nights and paid cash in advance. He said he was there to fish, and otherwise would not want to be disturbed. The old woman nodded, handing him the key. The rifle would have to stay in the boot of the car until he went out to the island, not ideal, but in this neck of the woods people minded their own business, happy not to be bothered with anything. He had his lunch near the hotel, and afterwards walked towards the main road, catching the bus to Konstanz at a nearby bus stop; he had to wait a good 20 minutes until it arrived. He climbed in, paid the fare, and sat down. There were few people, mostly elderly, who did not even glance at him and his silly fisherman hat he had bought earlier for extra disguise, together with the dark Ray-Ban shades; nobody would ever be able to give It a description of that man sitting in the last row of the bus. He was just another passenger looking out of the window, enjoying the view. Twenty minutes later the bus came to a halt at the bus terminal.

Everybody disembarked and walked slowly down the road towards a big German flag, swaying gently in the low wind. This was the customs building, but nobody cared to stop anyone or check any documents, the mass of old and mostly retired folks just walked through without a bother, to spend the day at the Isle of Mainau, or do some shopping in Konstanz, or else having lunch. Paul mixed in with the crowd, heading for the bridge connecting the mainland with the island; now walking over it. The bridge was just wide enough to let a car pass for emergency purposes, but otherwise was strictly used for walking only. On the other side was the large reception area, with tourist information, and stalls to pay the entry fee. Paul queued, paid his ticket, and then separated from the crowd, having first bought a map of the island.

He kept on walking, alone now, keeping the hat and sunglasses on, consulting the map from time to time; otherwise enjoying the immaculate rose gardens, the rhododendrons, the tulip fields in full bloom, and observing the thousands of tourists doing just the same. But Paul was not interested in the sights. He was heading for the northern tip of the island, looking out for a good shooting position, camouflaged and out of sight. When he arrived at the utmost point of the island, he noticed that the area was fenced off. The flower beds had given way to grassland, with a few trees scattered around, standing tall; and a hut that looked without recent use, half abandoned. The hut must contain machinery and tools for maintenance purposes. Nobody was in sight, and nobody would venture up here, for there was nothing to be seen or admired; it was all fenced off.

He carefully slipped underneath the metal fence to the other side, and headed slowly towards the waterline, with Konstanz

225

clearly in sight now – even without binoculars – across the water some 400 metres away. Paul took the binoculars out of his jacket, adjusted the sight, and started scanning the shoreline on the other side, searching for the hotel Weidling was supposed to stay at the day after tomorrow. After a while of searching, he spotted it, lying right there in plain sight, a bit further north from his current position, its large terrace with the brightly coloured umbrellas clearly visible in the distance. He walked through the grass for some 60 metres, trying to find a straight line between him and the hotel. He had to act fast, he could not be seen up here. After another four minutes searching around, he found the ideal spot, slightly hidden out of sight by undergrowth, trees and small bushes, both from the island and from across the water. The spot was about 20 metres from the water; Paul marking it with a dry branch, ramming the stick into the soft ground; clearly visible if one knew where to look for it, approaching on the water by boat. He tried to memorise the water line in front of the hideout. He spotted a large, black, pointed stone sticking partly out of the water, in a straight line to the hideout. Paul hoped he could identify this stone in the dark, approaching by boat. Behind the hideout spot, some 30 metres to the left, a tall oak tree was standing alone, giving further bearings. The tree would definitely help him find the spot.

He again slipped underneath the fence, passed by the hut, walking slowly now, and soon found himself amidst the crowd of old folks, mostly in groups of two to four, talking to each other and taking endless pictures of the flower beds and landscape. He had identified his shooting position and was sure he could find it again. The rest of the island was of no interest to him. He passed through the entry/exit gates and walked over the bridge, passing now the customs house; still nobody interested in anything. Back on Swiss soil, he entered a cafe on the lake side with a beautiful view of the lake. He sat down and ordered a pint of local beer, smoking a cigarette and contemplating the view. After a while, he paid, left the cafe, and walked over to a public telephone and calling Tin at the hotel.

When the call was transferred to Tin's room. He just said, "Tomorrow, 8 a.m. Be ready, we'll go fishing."

He then took the same bus back to his hotel, went to his room, and stayed there until the next morning. After breakfast, he took another bus, this time to the village where Tin was staying. He found the hotel in no time and waited outside, some 20 metres to the left of the entrance, smoking. A few moments later, he spotted Tin stepping out of the hotel. He gestured to him from the distance for him to bring his car round. He then walked down the road slowly, away from the hotel. When Tin, in his Corolla, slowed down next to him, he quickly entered the car and said, "Drive south to Uttwil. We will start testing the Zodiac there."

Uttwil has a small public harbour where the hobby fisherman can put their fishing boats into the water to start another day of fishing. It was low key, only small boats and local folks, fishermen, or just spare time captains, keen to enjoy a sunny spring day on the lake.

They lowered the small boat into the water, Paul stepping into it now, while Tin backed up the trailer and parked the car. He then stepped into the boat too.

"Welcome on board," said Paul. "Let's get this beauty steaming."

With that, he pulled the cord hard, trying to kick the engine into life, but no sound came out of the black Johnson. "Turn the valve to get the gasoline flowing. No gas, no power," said Tin.

Doing just that, on the next pull, the engine came to life. They headed straight out to get familiar with the lake and its surroundings. They had to know the shoreline inside out; all the landmarks for identification. They had to know by heart where they were going in the pitch black night if they wanted to escape unnoticed, and as quickly as possible after the hit. Paul had to find a place to ditch the Zodiac, out of sight, for at least 24 hours, but near enough to make it back to land and to the cars quickly. They would stab holes into its rubber hull to sink it. The weapon, engine, and the rest of the gear would all be dumped into the lake, sinking to the bottom, never to be found. The trailer would just stay there at the small port. He had seen lots of trailers sitting there in the parking area, probably for weeks or months, waiting to be used again someday by their owners. Besides, the trailer had no plates, hence identification was difficult, with them all being the same size and mark.

Steering the boat towards the middle of the big lake for a better overall view, and getting their general bearings, testing the engine, he explained the procedures of ditching all the material to Tin, and also mentioned his idea about the hiding (i.e., sinking) of the boat. Tin came up with the idea to get some heavy stones to hold the rubber hull beneath the surface after it had been scuppered, keeping it invisible for as long as possible. Agreed, good idea.

After 20 minutes, they thought they had finally reached what Paul figured was the middle of the lake, judging by the distance, looking both south and north. He consulted the compass, reading the bearings, noting down their current position. They had driven straight out, so they were still just north of Uttwil, where they had departed from. OK, he checked the position again, turning the boat, and heading west now. With the borderline between the two countries invisible in the water, Paul could not determine whether they were in Switzerland or Germany, but it did not really matter. There were no police patrol boats in sight, and there would hopefully be none around during the night either. The Police, normally, kept their patrol boats anchored at their stations, and only ventured out when they received a distress signal, from some hobby captain unable to find his way home, or in a storm rescue operation.

Still heading west, Tin gestured to a small dot in the water, growing by the minute. That must be the island of Mainau coming slowly into sight. Another seven minutes and they could now clearly see it in plain sight ahead of them. Paul noted the cruising time and position again. They had been going at full speed, using all the power the Johnson was able to deliver. He slowed down now and killed the engine. The Zodiac swung gently in the water, while Paul took out the binoculars and Tin the two fishing rods, throwing one of the lines into the water, pretending to try to catch something. Paul scanned the island with his binoculars. It was a bright, sunny day, and he could clearly make out the flower beds and the green lawns, with the tourists walking about the island.

After some ten minutes, he started the engine again and slowly approached the island. When they finally reached its northern tip, he swung the Zodiac around and headed south, trying to make out the ambush site. At first he was lost, could not identify anything, searching hard for a familiar landmark but finding none. He headed a bit further in towards the island for a better view and told Tin what to look out for. After another few minutes' searching, he could see the oak tree, and then was able to identify the black rock in the water.

"There it is. See that rock in the water with the tall oak tree some 30 metres behind it? That's our site. That is exactly where we land tomorrow night. So try to memorise it. It will be pitch dark when we arrive here tomorrow."

Tin took the binoculars and stared long and hard, scanning the site, memorising its landmarks. "OK, OK, I believe I got it. I will find it again tomorrow night."

With that, Paul turned the Zodiac around and headed back the same route they had come, first putting the chronometer on his Breitling to work. He wanted to know how many minutes, exactly, it would take them to get back to the harbour at Uttwil. Having reached a safe distance from the island, he opened the throttle of the Johnson to the max again, with the Johnson delivering its 60 horsepower in a low constant humming, not really making any loud noise at all. The waves were splashing water into their faces and wetting the boat. Still no police in sight, only a big pleasure cruiser in the distance. Paul constantly checked his compass while Tin was steering the boat now.

Having reached the exact position, Paul yelled, "Turn her around. South now." Tin did just that and the Zodiac leaned dangerously low to its inner side, water almost gushing in while Tin brought her around. After another six minutes, they reached the harbour.

"Kill the engine and let the boat drift towards the harbour. See that tall willow tree standing there, to the right, with its branches hanging into the water? That's where we will ditch her, right there under the willow, together with everything else," Paul said.

From the ambush site to the harbour of Utwil, the ride had taken exactly 22 minutes; 22 vital minutes to escape without any hitches, plus an estimated 6 minutes to ditch the boat. This running time was short enough so that no police would be able to react in time; the bodyguards would still be trying to figure out what had happened, with the police about to arrive at the hotel. The chaos that would ensue after Weidling's collapse would give them the precious, and necessary, time they needed. Twenty-eight minutes was all they got, and then running to their cars and speeding off, southbound on the Swiss highway and back to Zurich. The hunt for the killers would initially be done by the German police force alone, since, Weidling would be shot on German soil; and being their finance minister. But without any doubt, they would soon ask the Swiss police force to join in the hunt, but this all would still take time, and by then they would be safely back in Zurich, so he hoped.

Approaching the willow, Paul asked Tin to measure the water's depth at this point with the fishing line. Tin came up with about eight metres depth; enough to ditch the boat and make it disappear for a few days. The engine and gas canister he would dump before, in deeper water, along with the rifle, ammo, and everything else already gone to the bottom, in a depth of over 100 metres in the middle of the lake.

They lifted the boat out of the water and carried it to the trailer, heaving it on and covering it with the thick, black, heavy plastic cover that came with the purchase. Both having examined it, and being satisfied, they walked to Tin's car and drove off. It was mid-afternoon and still nobody was in sight at the small harbour and the car park. Paul guessed the boat owners would arrive early in the day, get their tackle ready and head out on the lake, taking advantage of the early hour, and spending the whole day on the water. In any case, he had decided to take the boat out tomorrow just at nightfall; by then, the hobby captains would have all gone for the day; or so he hoped.

After a 30-minute drive, they reached Münsterlingen where Paul, together with his brother-in-arms, intended to have lunch; far away from their hotels. When they arrived at the village, he spotted a place down at the shoreline called Die Angel. A plate in front of the place announced, "Warm kitchen throughout the day".

They parked the car as far away from the entrance as possible, Paul putting on his hat and shades, while Tin put on a basketball cap and dark glasses. They sat down at one of the tables facing the lake, with their backs to the service door. The hotel's summer terrace was large, with a few elderly folks enjoying their beers and coffees. No one paid attention to the two new arrivals with their hats and sunglasses. The waiter, a bald man in his sixties wearing thick spectacles, brought the menu. They ordered two pints of beer, made a toast, and began studying the menu. Both ordered today's menu number 3, waiting for the food, not talking, smoking, drinking their beers and watching the few boats on the lake. Both knew, without saying it, that this was their last social gathering for a long time to come.

They, though, still had lots of time together; tomorrow, and perhaps another two days, lying in ambush, plotting and making plans for the future – depending on Weidling's movements at the hotel, it could take them up to three nights until an opportunity presented itself to take him out. And then, they knew, all hell would break loose. So they concentrated on the food and talked about women and fishing, two of their favourite topics. They also talked about the trips they had made together, keeping their voices down so nobody could overhear them.

After more than three hours, night had fallen, and they settled the bill. They first drove back to Paul's hotel, stopping the car a good 200 metres away from it, and then Tin drove on to his hotel. Everything was in place, ready and set up. They would meet at Uttwil harbour at 7:30 p.m. the next day, and then embark on their most dangerous journey so far.

CHAPTER 18

Early next day, Paul had his breakfast in the hotel's dining room, he was the only diner, the other guests of the hotel must have had already gone out, or the hotel was empty. Having finished, he smoked a cigarette, putting his thoughts together. Most importantly, the weather was fine; it was a brisk, sunny spring day with temperatures in the low twenties. The weather forecast informed that it would stay this way until late afternoon, when some local thunderstorms might emerge. Well, possible thunderstorms was not ideal, but they would have to wait and see. If there was rain, Weidling would not sit outside on the terrace having dinner and getting soaked. He would stay inside the hotel, out of reach of Paul's rifle.

He left the hotel and walked to the car park. The Alfa was sitting there at the far end with its boot facing the wall. He approached the car, checking for anybody in sight, but there was no one. He then slowly opened the boot, and there she was, the Polish Hammer, lying there untouched in the blanket, just the way he had left her there. Reassured, he closed the boot, locked the car, and went back to the hotel. The same old lady was standing at the reception desk, reading some local paper. He asked her to prepare the bill and told her he was checking out today, around 5 p.m.; he asked if there was a problem with checking out late? She said there wasn't and handed him the bill. Business was slow, so he could stay until five, no problem. Paul thanked her, paid in cash, and gave her a good tip.

"Going fishing Mr. ...?"

"Schmid. Yes, wish me luck."

"Good luck to you, Mr. Schmid, and Petri Heil. Leave your key on the desk should I not be around when you go."

"OK, thank you, will do." He turned and went up to his room on the second floor. He made sure the door was firmly locked and then spread the map out on the bed. He studied it, memorising every turn, town and village they had to pass until they reached the highway leading them to Zurich. It was all set up, no mistakes to be made.

He then went through his belongings and packed his bag; going through every item slowly and carefully. He checked the black and green hunting knife with its spring blade, opening and closing it a few times, and put it in the bag. He then prepared the clothes he would be wearing: a dark blue T-shirt, a thick grey flannel shirt, the dark sweater, the black jeans, the black boots, and finally the black cap. All there. He spread everything out on the bed, ready for use tonight. He then checked the torch-light, switched it on and off; all OK, together with the red multi-purpose army knife; OK too. Lastly, he checked the cash and counted it. Fr. 4,000, in 50 and 100 notes, OK too. He took Fr. 500 and put it into his wallet. The rest went back into the bottom of the bag. He checked his driving licences, car registration documents and bank cards. All there.

He put the wallet back into his back pocket, opened the window and looked out, trying to soothe his nerves. Appreciating the view of the big lake, shimmering in the distance, but he was too anxious and restless, unable to calm down. He had to get out of this room. Stepping out and closing the door, he went down, using the staircase, past reception; nobody, good, so he kept the key, and at the front of the hotel he turned right, walking down the road to the local Konsum. Supermarket.He intended to buy provisions for up to three nights and days. He had asked Tin to do the same, telling him no beers and no spirits; they had to stay focused and sharp.

He bought tinned sardines and tuna, two loaves of bread, a good piece of vacuum-packed dried meat, and a chunk of cheese, also vacuum-packed. He also bought six bottles of still water, 1.5 litres each, that should do it. He had no intentions of having leisurely picnics, he just needed enough calories to keep him going for as long as this might take. He went to the till, paid, and put all the groceries into two large brownish plastic bags. Instead of heading back to the hotel he went in the other direction, trying to find a place to have lunch. After some 500 metres he spotted a small restaurant that seemed to be already open for lunch. Before entering, he put on his fisherman hat and the sunglasses. He sat at a table far away from the buffet, starting to read the menu, when a sour-looking waitress in her fifties approached him.

He ordered menu number 2 and a glass of Sprite, not looking into her eyes. He ate his meal in silence, lost in his thoughts, not wanting to hang on too long there. Done, he put a 10 and a 20 Franc note on the table and left the premises as quickly as he could, carrying his grocery bags under his arm. Walking away from that dreadful place, he saw a bench, sat down and lit a cigarette, looking around, not seeing anything or anybody. It seems this place is pretty quiet, with not much going on. He headed back to the hotel, still no one at the reception, and went up to his room. He checked his watch; it read 1:30 p.m.; time for a shower and a nap. He laid down on the bed with heavy thoughts going through his mind and soon fell asleep.

He woke up to the sound of the garbage collector truck emptying the hotel's bins into its holding space. It was 4:30 p.m., perfect, still time enough to go through the bag again, just to make sure. He showered again and put on his mission clothes. The sweater, together with the bag, he took under his arm; it was too hot to wear the sweater, but he would need it during the nights out on the island. He carefully walked down the stairs, left the key where the old lady had indicated, and went to his car. Opening it, he put the bag beside him on the passenger seat, started the engine and rolled slowly out of the car park, turning right, and entered the main road with his hat on and the window rolled down. Sticking to the speed limit, he looked just like any other tourist, enjoying the ride and the scenery of Lake Bodensee, had it not been for the contents of his car boot.

Driving in the direction of the small harbour, he reached it just before nightfall, as he had planned, the sun sinking low now, barely visible any more on the western horizon. In a few minutes it would be dark. He rolled into the harbour's car park and parked the car as near as possible to the shoreline, front facing the exit for a quick escape. He found a good spot and killed the engine, sitting low in the seat, smoking and waiting for Tin to arrive. He saw two guys walking to their cars, but they did not see him, sitting low behind the wheel. The two cars left, and now the parking area was empty, with no movement again. The sun had disappeared behind the horizon and a steady breeze came in from the lake, cooling down the air.

The temperature began to drop rapidly now, so he put on his sweater and waited, but still no sign of Tin. Damn it, he was already ten minutes late. Had something happened? Was he held up, or worse? Drumming with his fingers on the steering wheel and smoking, trying to keep calm, he heard the sound of a car engine growing louder and, looking out of the window, saw Tin's Corolla entering the area. He stepped out and gestured, showing an empty parking space two spaces away from his. Tin saw it and parked.

"Hi there. You nearly gave me a heart attack being late," Paul said.

"Sorry, it took longer to drive down here than I thought. Are you OK?" Tin replied.

"Yeah, I'm fine. Let's do this."

236

They lifted the Zodiac off the trailer and carried it to the water, letting it sink in gently, tying its rope to a pole. They both then took out their bags and put them into the boat. Tin stayed in the boat while Paul brought the heavy weapon, laying it down. Then went back to his car and closed and locked it, quickly returning to the boat and getting into it.

"OK, start the engine and turn her around, no position lights. And put on your cap," Paul said.

The Johnson came to life on the first pull and they headed out, no other boat in sight, and nobody at the car park either. Their direction was strictly north and steady. Paul did not stop checking the compass, and when they reached their position in the middle of the lake, the shores barely visible now, he ordered Tin to turn her around again, heading west. The engine was humming low, barely making any noise. The only noise came from the waves hitting the hull.

Paul scanned the water with his binoculars, he saw a large vessel to the north, but it was not a police patrol boat, but a German excursion boat, cruising the lake from stop to stop. To the south he made out a smaller boat heading to the shoreline, away from them. Other than that, nothing, no movement at all. Tin held the course steady, and after a few more minutes they could make out the features of the small island in the distance. Closing in now, Paul directed Tin to head for the northern tip turning point there to start heading south, getting closer to the ambush site.

Slowing down the engine, they began to get closer to the spot, with Paul making it out first, having spotted the tree that served as a marker for him. Moments later they made out the black rock in the water, just in front of their position, and steered towards it, engine out now, drifting towards dry land. On reaching the exact position, Tin lifted the motor out of the water and they pulled the Zodiac onto the grass; securing it with a rope tied to a stone. They took their bags out, together with the boat's plastic cover. They intended to use it as a makeshift tent. Lastly, Paul took the weapon and laid it down in front of him, fixing its metal legs onto it.

"Tin, go up there and under the fence. Check whether we've got any company." Tin slipped away cautiously, making no sound at all, and after ten metres, he was barely visible any more in the dark night, wearing his dark clothes and cap.

Paul lay down behind the rifle, fixing the telescope and silencer. He put the full magazine into the slot and adjusted the night vision. The hotel came into full sight, clearly visible, with the large terrace and the tables scattered around it under the big umbrellas. He could even make out the colour of the flowers in their tiny vases on the tables, but not Weidling. He had memorised the photo Kowalski had given him back in Berlin. The photo showed a man in his early fifties, blond hair with a receding hairline, wearing dark-rimmed spectacles. The image had burnt itself into his brain. He would identify the man even if he was disguised as his own mother.

Training his eyes on the telescope and scanning the hotel terrace, he heard and noticed Tin slipping down beside him. At that moment, a fine rain started to fall. "Damn it," he thought, "exactly as the weather forecast had predicted."

The rain started to fall harder now. There was no way Weidling would enjoy his dinner on the terrace, getting soaking wet. Shit, he folded the two metal legs, putting the rifle down on its side, and covered it with the heavy blanket it had been wrapped in before.

"Get the cover from the Zodiac," he said to Tin over the noise of the hard rain now. "We will have to improvise a sort of tent for cover."

With four thick branches, they managed to improvise a makeshift tent, and both slipped under it. "Hope this bloody rain doesn't last," Paul said, but there was no sign of it easing anytime soon with the sky a grey dark mass of clouds. Checking the terrace with the binoculars, he could see the waiters had hurriedly cleared the tables and folded the umbrellas; no outside dining tonight. Paul would have to wait and pray for fair weather. After three hours, the rain began to ease, but the lights in front of the hotel had been cut. All was dark there now. It was 12:40 a.m. and both men tried to find a sleeping position and said goodnight.

Next morning, Paul woke up with a sore back and stiff legs. The sun had come up over the eastern horizon, and the temperature began to rise. According to yesterday's forecast, the next 48 hours should be fair and sunny with temperatures around 22°C, and low easterly winds. Tin was lying next to him in a foetal position, snoring. Paul stood up, smoking a cigarette and scanning their surroundings; listening hard to see whether he could hear anything. There was nothing, total silence, no dogs, no people, no motors running.

It was almost 7 a.m. now, soon the hordes of tourists would begin to invade the island, taking their pictures, enjoying the scenery, and getting close, but not too close, to their improvised hideout. By the afternoon, it would be all over, with the island closing for the night. It was a sunny, clear and warm spring morning, and the birds knew it. Paul's thoughts wandered back to Berlin, and Kowalski, and their first meeting at the hotel bar on the very night he had arrived, after his dreadful journey from Checkpoint Charlie. Why Kowalski had picked him out was a big mystery still. Paul could not figure it out. There was no way Kowalski could make the connection between the Cartier heist and him – two years ago now – or the Urdorf job on the Migros van. No way. No, Kowalski had chosen Paul because of his extensive travelling to eastern bloc countries, his age and profession, and position at the bank. Undoubtedly, he knew a lot about

Paul, and had taken his chances on him; a shot in the dark. Had he refused to accept the envelope, no harm done, and had he refused to do the job, no harm done either. Paul could not prove anything, much less link Kowalski to the job. No, the master spy had taken his chances, and so far it had worked out just right for him; miserable shithead that he was. What remained, though, was carrying it out successfully, and this he could not control, but fact was, Kowalski was down DM 500,000, and this made him continue to be very interested in Paul indeed.

Paul brushed away these unpleasant troubling thoughts and started instead to concentrate on his target, Weidling. He had learned about the minister's every move in the past two weeks. No doubt, he was a very powerful man, an efficient finance minister, shrewd politician, and manager of the economics of Europe's most powerful nation by far. Kowalski and his STASI superiors must have their own good reasons for wanting to take him out. Paul did not care about their motives; he was here to do a job, and that was exactly what he was going to do, hopefully tonight.

After having finished his second cigarette, Tin started to come to life, a somewhat baffled expression on his face, trying, no doubt, to figure out where he was and why. After a short moment, he appeared to come to grips with his surroundings and muttered a low hello to Paul.

"I am starving. What about you?" Paul asked.

With this, he unzipped his backpack and took out the loaf of bread, together with cheese and ham. Last, he grabbed the bottle of water and both men sat down outside the tent on the damp grass, having their breakfast; on the lovely island of Mainau, Germany.

"No hot coffee. Pity we can't make a fire," Paul said. That would be way too risky and attract unwanted attention. They ate their bread in silence. When they had both finished, Paul stored everything in his backpack, while Tin lit his first cigarillo of the day, staring out at the water and watching the seagulls in their rapid flight, and the ducks and white swans swimming close to the shore, looking for food, and minding their business. Now and then they could see a trout jumping out of the water, trying to catch a distracted fly.

"What will you do when this job is all over?" Tin asked, looking at Paul's face blowing smoke.

"I will disappear, vanish into thin air," Paul responded.

"Where to?" Tin asked.

"South America, I guess. Brazil. But keep this strictly to yourself. Nobody must know about this, not even Soph. So keep your mouth shut, you know nothing. After some months, three maybe, when things have cooled down, I will get in touch, see whether you can come down and pay me a visit, relax and check out the ladies," said Paul.

"Sounds great. I will stay put, keep a low profile, continue my present job, try to help my mother, who is becoming increasingly ill, and otherwise mind my own business. See some girls if I feel like it, but I would very much like to come down and visit you, see what's going on. If I like it, maybe hang on for a while in the warmer climate, with friendly people," said Tin.

"That's the spirit, old sport. Continue your routine. Nothing has happened, and you know nothing. Stick to it and everything will work out just fine. Let's go over the plan of action for today. But before that, check out the surroundings. Be careful, we don't want any birdwatchers sneaking up on us," said Paul.

When Tin came back after ten minutes or so, he reported that there was not a living soul in the area, but the island must have opened for visitors by now since he could hear far away chattering from his position at the fence. No one was in sight for a good 300 metres. Dogs were not permitted on the island, so the chance of them being discovered at their ambush site was very remote; but they had to stay vigilant and careful. They then went over today's course of action, down to the last smallest detail.

The boat had to be ready before Paul took the kill shot. All traces of them had to be erased. The smallest crumbs of bread and cigarette butts had to be collected and put into a plastic bag they would take along with them. Paul would begin training his aim shortly after nightfall. Tin was to check the engine, run it and warm the Zodiac up ready for take off within five seconds after the shot. Other than that, they could not organise or prepare much. It was basically the long wait. Every full hour, Paul aimed the rifle at the hotel, while Tin did the same with the binoculars, scanning the area for any movement, but there was none to be seen, other than some guests having their lunch; with no Weidling in sight.

Around noon, they had their light lunch; bread with tinned tuna, and water. They both took a nap, and by 5 p.m. got down to business, preparing for action. Tin had stored all their belongings in the boat, which he had turned, facing the open lake now. They had both changed into their black clothes, caps on. They both had blackened their faces with charcoal Tin had brought along in a small bag. They cleared the ambush site of all and any possible traces. It was Tin's job to collect the empty shell, or shells after firing, and take them along to dispose of in the water, later, together with the equipment. They checked their car keys, apartment keys, all there and put back into their trouser pockets. After that, they both lay down, monitoring the hotel terrace again with the respective devices, waiting to do the job they had come to do. Every 40 minutes, Tin walked to the fence to check on any activity there.

The Terrace had slowly begun to fill up during the afternoon, folks enjoying the warm weather, their drinks, and each other's company. Sometimes Paul thought he could hear laughter coming across the water from the hotel, but then reminded himself that this was highly unlikely, the sound having to cross a distance of about 350 metres over open water. His mind must have played tricks on him. He asked Tin whether he was hearing anything coming over from the hotel, and Tin said no, nothing, only the birds making any sounds.

By nightfall, the terrace was almost fully occupied, only two tables remaining empty, but still no Weidling and party to be seen. One of the two remaining tables had a "Reserved" sign put on it.

"Can you see the sign on that table?" Paul asked.

"Yes, I can see it," Tin responded. "Must be for our boy."

And then it all happened at once. Weidling appeared on the terrace, arm-in-arm with a tall blonde woman, followed closely by two sporty looking men in dark suits. Weidling and the lady sat down at the reserved table, while the two bodyguards sat at the other free table, just to the left of their boss.

"Do you see him? Have you made out the guy?" asked Tin.

The binoculars had no night vision, so it must be much harder for Tin to make him out, or identify anything on the terrace out there in the distance.

Paul nodded and said, "Yes. I got Weidling. He is sitting in the middle chair, staring right out to the water in our direction, with the lady sitting to his right. The two security men are sitting to his left, close by, at the next table," said Paul. "Affirmative, that's it, that's him alright, be ready any moment now."

Weidling lit a cigar, saying something into the woman's ear. He then turned his face, looking straight out to the water, puffing on his cigar, when Paul pulled the trigger. It was a kill shot, right between the eyes. The impact of the heavy calibre bullet was so hard it knocked Weidling over, together with his chair; he fell backward in one swift movement. Paul still watched his face, blood pouring out of the entry wound on his head. Nobody heard the shot, other than Paul and Tin. The Silencer had seen to that.

Weidling was lying dead on the floor with a pool of blood forming around his head. The two bodyguards drew their pistols, one bending over his boss, the other aiming at nothing, trying to figure out what had just happened, and from where the shot had come.

Paul rose, collecting the rifle and carrying it now, with Tin already in the boat, motor running, and jumped into the Zodiac. They drove off at full speed. The time that had passed since the shot was no more than 20 seconds. In the boat, they heard nothing other than the engine and the water and waves splashing around them. Paul lay low in the boat, down on its floor, with Tin doing much the same, steering them away from the island, speeding off as fast as the engine would go; first north, and then east. Already having passed the northern tip of the island, cruising now in the middle of the lake in the pitch dark, the depth of the surrounding water must be about 140 metres.

"Slow her down and give me the shell," Paul said, taking it and putting it together with the rest of the ammunition, and threw, first the rifle and then all the rest into the dark water. It would sink to the bottom fast, all the stuff dumped. He shouted, "Drive, full speed, give it all there is," while putting a heavy stone into the garbage bag for extra weight, throwing it overboard, too. The boat was empty now except for the two backpacks and rudders, the fuel canister, and the motor itself.

Paul checked his watch and compass, exactly 16 minutes had passed since the shot, and they were already approaching the position where they had to turn south, to the harbour. Black night, black water, no boat or similar to be seen, other than some vaguely shimmering lights on either side of the Lake.

"Now, turn her around 90 degrees and head south, full speed."

Tin did exactly as ordered, with the shoreline on the Swiss side becoming more and more visible. When they both saw the small harbour with the big willow tree, Paul shouted, "Cut the engine." But Tin had already done so.

While their small boat slowly glided towards the shore, distance now about 30 metres, Tin unbolted the motor from its base and let it slide into the dark water. It sank and disappeared immediately. Paul did the same with the red gas canister, followed by the rudders. The boat was empty now, ready to be ditched. When they reached the spot, some ten metres in front of that tree, they took out their knives and started punching holes into the rubber hull of the Zodiac. It was hard work, but after a short while the compressed air started hissing out of the rubber body, and the Zodiac began to sink, pulled down by some heavy stones.

They quietly swam to the shore, cleaned their black faces, and, other than being soaking wet, they both looked presentable. They ran to their cars with nobody in sight. Paul took a towel out of the Alfa's boot and dried himself, and then changed into dry clothes: jeans, T-shirt, dry shoes and socks. Hurrying and slipping behind the wheel, he drove off and out of the car park.

The last thing he saw of his friend was him sitting behind the wheel, having changed too. They had agreed that Paul would exit first, with Tin following after exactly three minutes. Paul was already driving on the Cantonal Road, checking his watch. Exactly 26 minutes had passed since Weidling fell dead. Driving further south, he heard the sirens of ambulances and police cars, far away in the distance, faintly; fading away rapidly. Shortly after, he entered the Motorway and drove south west, towards Zurich and safety, with Tin some three minutes behind him, doing just the same.

He opened the glove compartment and took out a fresh pack of Marlboros. He lit one and reflected on what he had just done, the hunt that was about to unfold, while speeding down the highway towards safety. The investigation, and hunt, would first be conducted by the German police, the BKA, and affiliated services, but, in due course they would ask their Swiss counterparts to join in. But all this procedure would take time. They did not know where the shot came from, had no leads whatsoever, no witnesses, nobody in the hotel, or elsewhere, had seen anything or could help with information. There was no information, just a dead body.

For the time being, the police were completely in the dark. That would give Paul and Tin the precious time they needed to disappear and go undercover. In the next 24 hours, they would not get to any conclusions, let alone leads. Paul speculated that it would take them at least 72 hours to identify the very spot where the shot had been fired from, but then what? It would not bring them any closer to beginning to solve the case. On the other hand, the BKA, the Swiss Criminal Police, and Interpol would soon join and organise a task force, but still, all this would take time, and by then Paul would have long gone.

Ninety minutes later, Paul opened the door to his flat and stepped in. First thing, even before taking a shower, he opened a can of beer, lit a cigarette, and sat down on the couch. Having turned on the TV, he immediately tuned in to ARD, the first German TV channel, and was promptly informed by a special bulletin, that the German Finance Minister, Lothar Weidling, had been shot to death earlier tonight at a local hotel in Konstanz. Weidling's body had been flown to the University Hospital in Karlsruhe to undergo autopsy. The report went on to inform that the minister had been shot with a single high calibre bullet, and further investigations were already underway, giving it top priority, and that the Swiss Special Police had joined the investigation, together with the special German Criminal Police, BKA, and special Anti-Terrorist Unit. The next report would be broadcast at 6 a.m. Any information should be directed to a toll-free number at the BKA shown on the screen, or any local police station. A Nationwide red Alert, level 1, had been issued. End of briefing.

After another beer and more cigarettes, Paul took his shower and went to bed. He fell asleep immediately, with his last thought being he would be half a million Deutsche Marks richer by the next morning.

CHAPTER 19

First thing the next morning, he turned on the TV. The spokes-woman was informing that the police continued searching the surroundings of the hotel, with no conclusive findings or results at this moment. Police forces on both sides of the lake and border continued the search for the killers, both on land and water. So far, though, to no avail. Roadblocks had been erected within a radius of 40 kilometres on both sides of the border, and a massive task force had been organised and was working at full speed. The Anti-Terrorist Unit had performed house searches in Munich, Bonn Karlsruhe, Dortmund, Hamburg and Berlin.

A member of the Baader-Meinhof Gang, the notorious terrorist group, had been arrested and was currently being interrogated in Munich, further leads were being followed, with any arrests imminent. Swiss Criminal Police and the Terrorist Special Unit had joined the task force, which was led by Chief Inspector Karl Bauer of the BKA. Family members of Weidling had been brought to an undisclosed location to guarantee their safety. The Chancellor had expressed his deep concern and demanded immediate results regarding the vile assassination of his finance minister. He was quoted as having demanded that no stone be left unturned until the killers were arrested and brought to justice. A further bulletin would be broadcast at noon today. The breaking news programme ended, showing telephone numbers, with a hotline number at the BKA. Any information leading to the arrest of the suspects would be rewarded with DM 100,000.

He turned off the TV set, having heard enough. The concentrated efforts of hunting down terrorist cells in Germany was good news, leading the investigation into a dead end and wasting precious time and manpower. What he did not like was the reward of DM 100,000 being offered. That was bad news. For that kind of money, almost anybody was bound to talk, even those not knowing much, or nothing. He only had 72 hours to vanish. He would call Soph and invite her for lunch at the Zurich Horn, down by the lake. It was a nice place, usually crowded, even more so on a sunny Sunday afternoon. He did not want her to come to his flat and give her the bad news there. She was bound to become upset and emotional. In a crowded place, she would have to react more composed... so he hoped.

After the call, he took out his Samsonite suitcase and started packing. For carry on, he took the dark brown leather sports bag, packing it as well. Having completed this packing task, he prepared himself a strong black coffee and called Tin. He answered immediately.

"Have you seen the latest news on ARD?" Paul asked straight away.

"I've just watched it. They're going after terrorists. Let them do that," Tin said.

"Yeah, but there is a price tag of DM 100,000 involved."

"I know, but still, they got shit!"

"You are probably right. I want you to meet me tomorrow noon at Antinori, at Paradeplatz, for a debriefing and lunch. And bring a bag or similar, you will need one." Having said that, Paul hung up on his buddy. He then went through his personal belongings, passport, watch, cufflinks, driver's licence and ID. The files on his business trips and personal annotations ,together with all the photos of Soph and him ,went into a black garbage bag, not before shredding it all into small pieces. After that, he went through his address and telephone contacts, searching for a name he vaguely remembered, but the name would not come back to him yet. What was it again? Imbach had mentioned it some months ago, a diamond trader or dealer, somewhere in...? Where was it again? He had a watch repair shop as a front. What the hell was his name! Rosy, Ruti, something with leaves, and then it struck him; Jakob Rosenblatt, that was it, that was his name. He searched the agenda and found it. An address in Aussersihl, a less known suburb of Zurich. He thought he knew the street, and the address, too. Tomorrow, he would pay Jakob a visit, making him a business proposal the greedy old diamond dealer could not refuse.

He wrote a letter to the real estate agency, advising the cancellation of his lease, stating he was well aware of the two months' rent penalty for rescinding the contract. He attached his cheque, rounding the figure up. He sealed the envelope, and today he would post it in the nearest post drop box. The next letter was a two liner, addressed to Helmut Schultz, his boss, with a cc to personnel, informing of his immediate resignation from the services of the bank – no reason given, no need for that. He put this letter in an envelope too and left it on the dining table.

"What else?" he thought. "Tin's money." He opened the old shoe box, his stash, and separated Fr. 130,000, all in Fr. 100 notes. The cash was not too bulky. He took another bigger envelope and stuffed it all in ,sealed it ,and put it on the table, next to the others. "What else?" he thought; that was pretty much it. He checked his watch, 11 a.m. already, he had to hurry to his meeting with Soph, breaking the bad news and saying goodbye. Shit, this would not be easy. But damn it, he had other plans now. Last, before taking a shower, he made a mental note to call his bank and check on Kowalski having met his end of the bargain and ordering the cash he needed, same day, after lunch, being pretty sure that the money had been transferred, and was all there in the account.

Smoking, putting on a blue pair of Chinos, together with a light beige, short-sleeved summer shirt, black Gucci leather sneakers and his Ray-Bans, he locked the door, envelopes in hand, and walked to the car. On the way to Zurich Horn, he stopped briefly to mail the envelope,and arrived punctually, at 12:30 p.m. at the agreed venue, spotting an empty table and sitting down, searching for Soph; but could not see her.

He ordered a draft beer, smoking, overlooking the Lake. After some 15 minutes, Soph arrived. He gestured to her, stood up and kissed her lightly, and she sat down.

"Hi, sunshine, what can I get you? Look at the lake, isn't it beautiful?"

He was trying to keep everything light, but Soph didn't buy it. She knew her Paul, and asking her to meet in a restaurant rather than at his flat was unusual. Normally he could not wait to get down to business, her business, but not today.

"I'll have a glass of Rose," Soph said, while lighting one of her Marlboros with the gold lighter Paul had given her a few weeks ago. When her drink arrived, they made a toast and then Soph bent over, whispering into Paul's ear. "What is it? Normally you can't wait to fuck me. Are you sick? Or what's the matter with you? I'd rather hear it straight away if it is what I think it is. You can spare yourself the lunch expenditure."

Paul looked into her eyes. That was Soph, alright. Head up high, not showing despair or weakness. Good, it was better that way.

"Soph, you know I love you and I am desperate to be with you. Enjoying you, us, together, and everything, but," now look-ing out into the distance, "something has come up. I've given up the job, I will have to travel and I don't know when I will be back. That is all I can say now. Don't press me on the motive; it won't help. I cannot tell you anything and I cannot promise any-thing either, not even when I will be in touch again. It's good-bye, Soph." Having said all this, he turned his face, looking at her and waiting for a reaction.

Soph took her time. When she finally faced him, she only said, "I am sad and disappointed. I had plans for us, big plans, but now they are all gone, destroyed. Somehow I knew it. I know you and I felt this moment would come sooner or later. You have two sides, Paul, one very dedicated, honest, and straightforward, and the other one, a dark one, one I cannot even begin to imagine, and I don't want to. You do what you have to do. Just make sure your dark side does not get the better of you." With that, she stubbed out the cigarette, took a sip of her drink, kissed him lightly on his right cheek, stood up, and was gone.

Paul sat in his chair for a long time, not moving. That was Soph alright, to the bone. My God, what a strong young woman. He felt like shit. Had she yelled out and cried it would have been much easier. But no, she stood her ground and accepted it with her head held high. It would take a long time for him to forget her, but then again, what the hell, he had no choice. What he had done, and was about to do, there was simply no place for Soph in it.

He lit a cigarette and waved to the waiter to bring the menu. He was hungry, nervous, and anxious; the next 48 hours would be crucial. He ordered lunch and another beer, finished it all without any enthusiasm, paid, and drove home. He needed some quiet, bringing his thoughts and emotions under control. He spent the rest of the afternoon and night at his flat, watching the news and making plans for the next days. When he finally got tired and bored, he went to bed, but not without checking, for the last time, the German news. Same thing, no new developments, still chasing after terrorists.

Next morning, Paul dressed in a light grey suit, white shirt with a dark blue tie, black leather shoes, his briefcase, containing Tin's cash, and the letter He made sure he got the car keys, locked the door, and stepped out into the bright, sunny morning. It was 8:10 a.m. and he decided to ignore the car, walked past it, and entered the first telephone booth he saw, calling the bank.

When the call completed, he heard the same dull voice of the clerk. After identifying himself, and having provided the passwords and codes, he was informed that a remittance of DM 500,000 had been credited to his account today.

When he asked for the current balance, the clerk informed him, without hesitating, "Fr. 1.435 million. Is there anything else I can do for you today?"

"As a matter of fact, there is, yes," Paul replied. "Please have Fr. 1 million in cash ready for me today. I'll pick it up shortly after lunch, at around 2 p.m., and make sure to get it in large bills only. OK?"

"Yes, Sir, Mr. Winter. The cash will be ready for you by the requested time. Please ask for Mr. Weiss, our head cashier, and let me inform you that we will charge a cash payout fee of…"

Paul cut into the clerk's lecturing monologue. "That's alright, just make sure it is all ready today." He hung up on this lame servant.

He then took a tram to his now former employer and went up to the first floor. Passing the doorman and entering the department, which was empty except for Karen standing at the coffee machine, and Meier sitting at his desk, reading the papers.

"Hi there, stranger," Karen said, kissing him on his cheek. "How are you? All recovered from the flu?"

"Yes, thank you. I'm fine. Is Schultz here?"

"Helmut is on a business trip to Germany, won't be back until next week. Rosen is in London and Imbach should arrive any minute now."

"OK." Having heard this he went do his desk, sat down and cleared the contents of his drawers, emptying them of any personal belongings. While doing so, Imbach stepped in, greeting Paul warmly. "Sepp, can I have a word with you, but first I need to talk to Meier."

"Sure," Sepp said. "I'll be right here. Is everything OK with you?"

"Everything's fine. Just give me a minute." With that, he approached Meier's desk, who looked up from his papers and gestured for him to sit in one of the chairs in front of his desk.

"Mr Meier. I have prepared a letter. I'd like you to read it, please."

Meier took the letter and read it carefully, taking his time. "Are you sure about this, young Paul? You have a great career and future ahead of you at this bank, and in my department."

"Yes, I am sure," Paul responded. He shook Meier's hand and thanked him for his support. Meier looked somewhat baffled and astonished. Paul then went to Imbach's desk and asked him to join him in the conference room. "Won't take long," he said.

Sepp saw the serious expression on his face and stood up immediately, following him. They both sat down and Paul informed him of his resignation from the bank, decision taken, no way back. Sepp nodded. Paul took a document out of his briefcase, signed it, and handed it over to Sepp.

"This is my power of attorney in your favour. Can you look after my account and investments while I am absent?"

"Sure, leave it to me. I will treat your affairs as if they were my own. Anyway, can I convince you to stay?"

"My decision is taken. I will stay in touch, and greetings to everyone, especially Helmut." With that, he shook Sepp's hand and left the bank; for good this time.

With still two hours to go before midday, he decided to have a coffee at a nearby cafe, near the River Limmat. But before he entered, he bought the local newspaper, *the NZZ*, and a pack of cigarettes. He then sat down at one of the outside tables overlooking the Limmat and looked out to the river. Everybody was running up and down, busy with something, minding their own business, not paying attention to anyone or anything. The waitress, a pretty, young, dark-haired woman with a ponytail, brought him his coffee without him having uttered a word.

"Thank you. What a beautiful morning." With that, he lit his cigarette and started reading the paper. He had to turn to page eight to find anything on the latest developments of the Weidling assassination. *The NZZ* was not inclined to render to screaming manchettes or trivialities. The paper left this to its more aggressive competitors. The paper was, however, very thorough in analysing in detail, local or international stories and news, and reported on the demise of Germany's Finance Minister, that the German police, in straight collaboration with the Swiss Criminal police force, had yesterday discovered the ambush site on the island of Mainau, from where Weidling was shot. Paul had to control the shaking of his hand to avoid spilling his coffee when he read this latest piece of information. Less than 60 hours had passed and they had already found the site of the attack. That was very disturbing news. The paper then went on to say that further promising leads were being followed by the international joint task force, and the Domestic Affairs Minister was scheduled to hold a press conference at 4 p.m. today.

Paul stubbed out his cigarette, finished the coffee, left a generous tip and left the cafe. He walked to Bahnhofstrasse, more specifically to the Kuoni Travel Agency. Arriving there, he entered and walked straight up to one of the attendants, who sat idle at his desk, pretending to be busy.

"What can I do for you this morning, Sir?" motioning for Paul to please sit down.

"Could you please let me know the availability of the Swissair non-stop flight to Sao Paulo tonight? Business class, one way only, if you please," Paul said.

The clerk, somewhat astonished, looked at him but regained control over his facial expression, and started to click away on his computer system. After a short while, he confirmed, "Swissair flight number 2458, leaving Zurich at 11:30 p.m., Boeing 747, non-stop to Sao Paulo; scheduled to arrive there at 8:10 a.m., local time. Business class seat available too. Would that arrangement suit you, Sir? And are you quite sure it is a one-way ticket only?"

"Yes, I am sure, thank you. That's just fine. Go ahead and book it, please."

"Can I see your passport or ID, and what will be the form of payment, please?"

"Cash," Paul responded, handing over his ID.

"Marvellous," he said, passing Paul an information sheet and the price. "Please direct yourself to the till over there. Your ticket will be issued in a minute."

Paul walked over to the till, with nobody queuing, and paid for the ticket in large bills, smiling at the attendant. Receipt in hand, he went back to the clerk's desk, who handed him his ticket. "Have a nice flight, Sir, and enjoy your stay in Brazil."

Paul thanked him and left the agency. There were no travel restrictions, no search warrant from Interpol, they had no confirmed suspects or names, so everything was still cool, but Paul felt the increasing heat running down his spine. He felt he had to disappear, and quickly. Ticket safely put away in the inner pocket of his suit coat, he slowly strolled down Bahnhofstrasse. When he passed by Cartier, he could not help but look into the window display. Business as usual, the best Cartier had to offer was laid out in the vitrines. Rich ladies were checking out the goodies inside the shop. Paul smiled to himself and began to walk, at a leisurely pace, towards Antinori, just off Paradeplatz.

When he entered the venue, Giorgio, the Maitre d', greeted him warmly. "Mr. Winter, welcome. Is the young lady not accompanying you today?"

"No, Giorgio. I am here to meet an old friend, not of the female gender, I am afraid. Oh, there he is, right over there at the corner table."

"Very well, Sir. Enjoy your lunch. What can I bring you to start with? A G&T perhaps?"

"No, Giorgio, not today. Bring us a bottle of chilled champagne, Mumm s , if you have it, and two glasses."

"Very well, Sir." With that, Giorgio disappeared behind the counter.

"Hi there, Tin," Paul said, greeting his friend while they shook hands. Tin looked smart, business-like in a blue double-breasted suit and white shirt. "You look fresh, you old bugger." Paul grinned.

"And so do you," Tin responded.

"I ordered a bottle of champagne for good times' sake. Do you mind?" Paul said, grinning at Tin.

"Great idea. And by the way, the farewell lunch is on me. No arguments."

"OK. Thanks, Tin." They both sat down. When the champagne arrived, they made a toast to their friendship; and may it last forever.

"I'll drink to that," Tin said as they clinked their glasses.

Paul, leaning over close to Tin's ear, whispered, "They found the site."

"That quick?" said Tin. "Shit."

"Yes, did not waste any time, dangerous. I will disappear tonight, direct flight to Sao Paulo, and you will have to lie low, as always. And again, no flashing cash around, no big buys, just the routine. I will call you in a couple of days to see how things are going. Once I am established down there, in a couple of months, two at the earliest, you can come down for a spell and check out the ladies. I hear they are fantastic."

With this subject out of the way, he reached into his inner pocket and took out the fat, brownish envelope, putting it right in front of Tin on the table. "Here's your cut. Don't open it, don't count it, it's all there. Put it away."

Tin grabbed the envelope and put it straight away. They drank the champagne, smoking, quiet for a while and looking at each other.

"Thanks, Paul. For everything. You helped me a lot; I will never forget that. Is there anything you want done during your exile?"

"As a matter of fact, there is." Paul handed him his car keys. "Here are the keys to the Alfa Romeo, together with the car registration documents." Paul handed all this over to Tin. "I want you to sell the car, should fetch between 22 to 25k. Here's the bank details where you deposit the cash." Paul passed Tin a folded piece of paper. "The car is parked in front of the flat. It must go within the next three days. I suggest you do the same with yours. Go to a big place, like the one down at Badenerstrasse, in Schlieren. They won't remember a thing, selling dozens of cars a day."

"Sure thing, you can rely on me. Consider it done. When we speak next time the money will be in your account," said Tin.

"Cheers, great. OK, now let's see what is good today." They both studied the menu. "I will go for the sea bass carpaccio, followed by a filetto de manzo with rucolla and baked potatoes, and to wash it down, a bottle of 78 Brunello de Montalcino. How about you?" said Paul.

"Excellent choice. I'll join you. Keeps it simple," said Tin.

When the plates arrived with the tasty food, they both dug in like there was no tomorrow. If there was a tomorrow, it would never ever be the same again, both realised.

In the midst of the second course, Paul ordered another bottle of the same wine. "To old times. Cheers, I'll drink to that."

After a fresh fruit salad and two brandies to go with them, Tin settled the bill, and the two left Antinori, and it would be a long time before they returned.

At Paradeplatz, they hugged each other and finally said goodbye. Paul would walk to his bank to collect the one million cash, and after that, take a taxi to Aussersihl, while Tin would walk back to his workplace. They looked at each other one last time, and then went their separate ways. When he was sitting in the taxi looking out of the window, Paul's mind wandered back to Tin. He thought he had seen a small tear behind Tin's gold-rimmed glasses. But he could not be sure.

Half an hour later, the cab pulled over at Jakob Rosenblatt's watch shop. He was not too familiar with Aussersihl, but remembered the large avenue cutting the working-class neighbourhood into half. He entered the shop and the movement of the door triggered the sound of a small bell hanging from the door frame.

"How can I help you?" a sourly looking woman in her sixties addressed Paul.

"I would like to talk to Herr Rosenblatt, please."

"Just a moment," the woman replied, disappearing behind a thick brown curtain.

After a short while, a tiny man in his early seventies appeared in front of him. The little hair that was left was grey. He wore thick glasses and was dressed in a dark grey apron and black trousers that looked like they had seen better days. His brown shoes were old and worn out, and he smelled of garlic.

"What can I do for you, Sir?" Rosenblatt addressed Paul, offering his hand, that had black, dirty fingernails.

"An acquaintance in common has given me your name. No need for further questions. I have a business request involving a substantial amount of money."

Having said this, he briefly laid the two ,fat dark yellow envelopes on the table, long enough for Rosenblatt to cast an eye over them before ,putting them back into his jacket pockets. The two envelopes contained one million Francs in cash.

"Will you follow me, please Sir, and Esther put the 'We are closed' sign in the door."

With that he brushed another curtain aside, leading first into a chamber full of watch repair tools, and then out of this room, down the hall, and finally opening a steel door that let to yet another room. The steel door was camouflaged by a heavy tapestry hanging down in front of it, concealing the entrance. When Rosenblatt entered the room, he gestured for Paul to sit down in one of the chairs, while he sat behind a large desk.

He then lit a powerful table light, illuminating the desk and the space, and said, "By the bulk of the envelopes, I would say they contain roughly 0.9 million. Am I correct?"

"I have exactly Fr. 1 million, all in 100 Franc notes on me. I want to buy flawless, assorted, first class diamonds, ranging from 1.5 carats to 4 carats. And I want to take them with me now."

"To provide diamonds worth one million, I need at least two hours."

"You've got one hour. I will be back in exactly 60 minutes to conclude this transaction, and don't make me wait, Rosenblatt, I am in a hurry. You want the cash, you deliver the stones."

"OK, OK, one hour."

With that, Paul looked into the eyes of the old Jew, hard, and said, "And throw in a gold lighter to sweeten the deal."

Leaving the old man sitting at his desk and exiting the shop the way he had entered; he then walked down the dirty, dusty road, and found a cafe. Ordering a coffee and a bottle of water, he sat down to read the papers, but was unable to concentrate. After 50 minutes, he went out again, searching for a kiosk. When he spotted one, he selected a pack of cigarettes and two packs of condoms containing three rubbers each. He paid, putting it all into his coat, and walked back to the watch shop.

He knocked on the door, and Esther, probably his wife, opened it immediately, trying to manage a smile this time, showing bad brown teeth. She led the way and closed the steel door behind him. Rosenblatt was sitting at his desk, a balance, magnifying glasses, a special type of heavy, steel-rimmed spectacles lying in front of him, together with a small wax paper envelope, in an off-white colour. Paul sat down while Rosenblatt carefully unfolded the small container. When it was fully open, it revealed some 30 stones, varying in size and colour, glittering under the strong light. Paul stared at them closely, amazed and intrigued that this tiny heap of diamonds was worth one million.

"As requested, the smallest stone being of 1.5 carats, with the largest, a beauty, being the size of 4.2 carats; this one, over here." He took a small pair of tweezers, holding the stone under the light. "Have a look for yourself at this flawless, beautifully-cut stone, cut, I may add, to perfection. This one alone is worth 100,000 Francs."

Paul examined the stone as well as he could, holding it under the magnifying glass and studying it closely. He took his time, looking for inlets or flaws, the colour being a whitish light blue, shimmering and sparkling.

Taking it back, Rosenblatt selected another five stones for examination. Paul looked at the small pile and chose one, randomly examining again the best he could. Imbach had told him that Rosenblatt was one of the best diamond experts and appraisers, not only in Switzerland, but in the whole of Europe.

Putting the stone back with the others, he looked at the old man. "Where's the gold lighter?" Jakob responded by putting a nice, square-shaped Ronson lighter in front of him. It was not the Cartier he remembered so well, but it would do.

"Do we have a deal?" the diamond expert enquired.

"Yes, we do," Paul said, laying the banknotes on the table. "Go ahead and count it. It's all there."

Jakob slowly began to count the cash, making nice, even piles of 50,000 each, now and then examining a bill more closely, holding it under the light; the whole procedure dragging on forever.

Finally, he nodded. "All OK," he said, folding and closing the small envelope in front of Paul, and handing it to him. Paul took it immediately.

"Nice doing business with you, Mr ...?"

"No names needed," Paul replied, exiting the chamber and noticing a muscular young man in his twenties wearing a black suit, standing by the door. The old man's muscle, in case things turned sour. He passed by the muscle and exited the shop as quickly as he could. The old dealer had no interest at all in denouncing Paul, the stranger. It was a cash business and completely illegal, but he knew the old man represented no threat.

He hurried down the avenue and hailed the first cab that came in sight. He asked to be taken to Bellevue Square, not giving an exact address. He'd rather walk the last few kilometres to his flat. Arriving home, he sat down at the table, opening the envelope carefully and stared at the stones again, sparkling beautifully, even in this dimly lit dining room. He took out two condoms, folding one into the other. The package read, "Long John, for extra pleasure and safety". Good, he then trickled the diamonds carefully into the double condom. Finishing, he made a strong double knot at the end of it and added yet another one to the two already used. They had to be more than watertight in the place he intended to stuff them. Hidden away from prying eyes, police, dogs, metal detectors, and the like.

That evening, around 9 p.m., Paul arrived at Zurich Airport and waited in the business class line to be attended to. He handed his passport, Samsonite suitcase and ticket reservation to the attendant. Moments later, he was given the boarding pass and went straight to the gate indicated. An hour later he boarded the aircraft, sitting down in seat no 7A on the upper deck. The friendly stewardess, a business-like woman in her mid-forties, greeted and welcomed him warmly, and asked whether he would like a drink while they waited for take-off. He ordered a gin and tonic and began to relax in his comfortable seat. When the drink arrived, together with a bowl of mixed nuts, he began taking stock. He had left Fr. 600,000 with Imbach, for him to continue trading and investing on his behalf, a further Fr. 25,000 would come from the sale of the car, and he was sitting on Fr. 1 million in diamonds, literally.

The Captain of the Boeing introduced himself, informing that the weather forecast was good, and they would land at Guarulhos International Airport on time, at 8:05 a.m. local time. Paul started to smile. Not bad for a 28-year-old ambitious young man. Free as a bird and sailing into the sunset.

At 9 a.m. next morning, he was sitting in a white Sao Paulo cab, disappearing into thin air.

THE END

HERZ FÜR AUTOREN A HEART FOR AUTHORS À L'ÉCOUTE DES AUTEURS MIA ΚΑΡΔΙΑ ΓΙΑ ΣΥΓΓΡ
HJÄRTA FÖR FÖRFATTARE UN CORAZÓN POR LOS AUTORES YAZARLARIMIZA GÖNÜL VERELIM SZ
CUORE PER AUTORI ET HJERTE FOR FORFATTERE EEN HART VOOR SCHRIJVERS TEMOS OS AUTO
ZÖINKÉRT SERCE DLA AUTORÓW EIN HERZ FÜR AUTOREN A HEART FOR AUTHORS À L'ÉCOU
AÇÃO ВСЕЙ ДУШОЙ К АВТОРАМ ETT HJÄRTA FÖR FÖRFATTARE Á LA ESCUCHA DE LOS AUTO
ΜΙΑ ΚΑΡΔΙΑ ΓΙΑ ΣΥΓΓΡΑΦΕΙΣ UN CUORE PER AUTORI ET HJERTE FOR FORFATTERE EEN
 ZÖINKÉRT SERCE DLA AUTORÓW EIN HERZ FÜ
AÇÃO ВСЕЙ ДУШОЙ К АВТОРАМ ETT HJÄRTA FÖ

The author

Peter Schneider is a man of diverse interests. His love for the outdoors, fine dining and writing is complemented by his skills in analysing situations and people.

Born and raised in Zurich, Switzerland, Peter's upbringing provided him with a strong foundation of structure and organisation that has carried him through his remarkable journey.

After working in international finance in Switzerland, Peter sought new horizons and moved to Brazil, where he met and married his wife. With the arrival of their two children, the couple sought to strike a balance between their Swiss roots and their newfound Brazilian connections.

They divide their time between Switzerland and Brazil, nurturing a multicultural environment and providing their children with the best of both worlds. Peter Schneider's life is a testament to the power of embracing one's passions, following a path less travelled, and weaving together the tapestry of diverse experiences.